ROUGH MESA

**Center Point
Large Print**

**This Large Print Book carries the
Seal of Approval of N.A.V.H.**

ROUGH MESA

BENNETT FOSTER

CENTER POINT PUBLISHING
THORNDIKE, MAINE

This Center Point Large Print edition
is published in the year 2004 by arrangement with
Golden West Literary Agency.

The text of this Large Print edition is unabridged. In other
aspects, this book may vary from the original edition. Printed in
Thailand. Set in 16-point Times New Roman type.

ISBN 1-58547-454-1

Library of Congress Cataloging-in-Publication Data

Foster, Bennett.
   Rough mesa / Bennett Foster.--Center Point large print ed.
     p. cm.
   ISBN 1-58547-454-1 (lib. bdg. : alk. paper)
   1. Large type books. I. Title.

PS3511.O6812R68 2004
813'.54--dc22

                                      2004000964

ROUGH MESA

CONTENTS

CHAPTER I
GOOD GRASS AND A FIGHT

THERE WERE THREE MEN ON THE LEATHER CHAIRS AND the sofa that occupied the center of the hotel lobby and, of these, two were plainly traveling salesmen. The third, lank, gaunt, with the look of the perpetual humorist about his eyes and mouth, regaled the others with drawling sentences.

"Nobody wanted them Butlers," the tall man related. "Nobody wanted any part of 'em. They owned Ojo Negro an' they aimed to run it. They stole cattle, they run Chinks, they done whatever there was money in doin' an' that wasn't honest. They kind of had a little country all to their ownse'ves, you might say." He puffed with relish on his cigarette, recrossed his sprawling, booted feet and grinned at his audience. "Then they went an' killed a deputy sheriff an' so a Ranger come down on 'em."

One traveling man, brown checked suit wrinkled from its night on the train, heavy gold-plated watch chain dangling as he leaned forward, supplied the necessary question. "What did the Ranger do?"

"Do?" The tall man bent his knees and his boot heels clicked on the floor as he sat up. "Why, he cleaned 'em out, that's what he done. He went into Ojo Negro an' scouted around a little an' then he went to arrest the Butlers. Natchully they wasn't in favor of it. So when the smoke cleared away the Ranger brung 'em out in a wagon. He was leakin' pretty bad his own se'f, but the

9

Butler boys was plumb drained dry."

The commercial tourist in the checked suit produced a cigar. "You were there, I suppose?" he said skeptically. "You can vouch for all this?"

"Huh-huh." One of the recounter's long brown hands slid up and settled the battered Stetson a little further back on his head. "I wasn't there, but the yarn's true just the same. You see, I'm workin' for the Ranger. His name's Lin McCord an' that's him comin' down the stairs."

Seated just beyond the trio of men, Eleanor Patrick turned her head until her gaze encompassed the stairway. A man was descending, a tall man whose breadth was lost in his height and whose height masked his breadth. He moved smoothly as though even in so commonplace a task as walking down a flight of stairs his muscles reserved some power; and his square-cut, rugged face contained a pair of the bluest eyes that Eleanor Patrick had ever seen. The blue eyes traveled around the lobby, met the girl's and passed on. The descent of the stairs complete, the newcomer walked across to the little group beside the sofa. There the tall storyteller hoisted himself to his feet.

"You about ready to eat, Lin?" the storyteller asked.

"All ready, Windy," Lin McCord answered.

The traveling men were staring at Lin McCord, some amazement in their eyes, as though they were startled to find the hero of the tale they had just heard so ordinary a person. Windy lifted one finger to the curled brim of his hat. "I'll see you, gents," he announced, and moved toward the door beside his companion. Eleanor Patrick,

10

rising from her chair, took three swift steps and spoke. "Mr. McCord?"

Lin McCord stopped. Beside the door his companion halted, and McCord raised his hand, removing his hat from his head. "Yes, ma'am. My name's McCord."

"I'm Eleanor Patrick," the girl said nervously. "I . . . I wanted to talk with you."

Windy had returned to McCord's side and he too lifted his hat. Lin McCord, looking from the girl to his companion, gravely made introduction. "Windy, this is Miss Patrick. Windy Tillitson, Miss Patrick. What is there that I could do for you?" His voice held a soft burr, a deceptive accent that, approaching an "R," almost elided it. He was looking down at the girl as he asked the question.

Eleanor Patrick's brown eyes were very earnest. Her face, too broad for beauty, the mouth too wide and generous, the cheekbones a little high, endorsed the earnestness of her eyes. "I understand that you are looking for pastureland," she said. "Is that true?"

Lin McCord nodded gravely. "I'm lookin' for pasture," he agreed. "I heard that there was some good grass in this country. So far, I've found that the grass around Junction is leased. Did you have somethin' in mind, ma'am?"

Eleanor Patrick took a deep breath as though about to plunge into cold water. "I have twelve thousand acres of mesaland," she said. "It's been logged a little but there is no slash or down timber on it. I want to lease it to you." There, the thing was out, the plunge taken; the decision, so carefully reached, put into words!

"Whereabouts is it, ma'am?" Lin McCord asked. "Around Junction?"

"No." The girl shook her head. "It's west of here about sixty miles. It's west of Adelphi."

One of Windy's big knuckles cracked sharply as he snapped his fingers, and a frown came over Lin McCord's face. "We were in that Adelphi country yesterday, ma'am," Lin said. "We talked to Mr. Melcomb of the Hoysen Lumber Company there, an' he showed us some country. We wasn't interested. It's all littered with slash an' down timber where they've cut overripe trees."

"But you didn't see my country," the girl said bravely. "I heard that you were in Adelphi yesterday. That's why I'm here. I want you to look at Rough Mesa."

"Suppose we sit down an' talk a little?" Lin suggested, turning toward an unoccupied chair. "You say your country has been logged?"

"There has been a little timber cut," the girl answered, sinking into the chair. "Not a great deal. There isn't any slash and there isn't any down timber. We piled and burned the slash and we didn't cut the overripe trees."

Lin and Windy exchanged glances. "How far out from Adelphi?" Lin asked.

"Fifteen miles west." The answer was definite.

"An' the grass is good?"

"It's . . ." The girl held her hand above the floor, measuring the height of the grass. "You can wade through it," she concluded defiantly.

"I've got to ask questions," Lin explained, heeding the touch of defiance in Eleanor Patrick's voice. "I've

12

got to get some idea of the country. How is it watered, ma'am?"

"There's a creek that runs across the mesa and comes down Pinál Canyon," Eleanor answered. "There are springs too, and there is one little lake. I—"

"An' what price do you ask for it?" Lin asked, interrupting.

Again Eleanor Patrick took a deep breath. "Ten cents an acre," she announced. "And I'd like to have all the money right away."

Again the exchange of glances flashed between Lin and Windy. Lin, lowering his eyes, waited a perceptible moment and then asked another question. "When could we see this country?"

"Tomorrow!" The girl's voice was eager. "Any time. I want—"

"Suppose," Lin said, "that we go up there tomorrow? Could we get out to the place?"

"There's a train out of here early in the morning," Eleanor answered steadily, as though repeating some speech that had been rehearsed again and again in her mind. "I left my buggy in Adelphi. We can go up on the train tomorrow and I'll take you to Rough Mesa. You can—"

"We'd like to look it over, Miss Patrick," Lin said. "If it suits, we can do business. What time does the train leave in the mornin'?"

"At six o'clock." The girl got up. "You'll go?" she asked, uncertainty in her voice. "You'll . . . ?"

"We'll be at the depot at five-thirty," Lin answered. "I'd like to see your country."

13

For a brief moment Eleanor Patrick hesitated. Then "I'll be at the depot," she announced and, moving past Lin, walked toward the stairs.

Lin followed the girl with his eyes. Eleanor Patrick climbed the stairs, stopped on the landing and looked back. She paused a moment, smiled hesitantly and then went on. When she was out of sight Lin McCord still stood rooted to the lobby floor.

"It's just grass you want," Windy drawled, breaking the silence. "Just grass, Lin. Come on! Ain't we goin' to eat?"

"She's in trouble," Lin said slowly. "She wants to lease that pasture pretty bad, Windy."

"An' that makes you money," Windy Tillitson said heartily. "If what she says is true, yo're gettin' it cheap. Most of these jaspers are askin' twelve an' a half cents an acre, an' nothin' on it but old pine boughs. Come on, Lin. Let's eat." Windy's big fingers closed on Lin McCord's arm and under their pressure Lin moved toward the door.

Outside the lobby of the Barclay House the two men tramped along the wooden sidewalk. Junction was dimly lit by lamps that stood on the corners of the unpaved streets. The stores were closed and only the lights of the saloons and restaurants came to aid the street lamps. Halfway down the block they entered a restaurant and seated themselves at a table. While they waited for their orders to be brought Lin absently drew lines across the oilcloth table covering with his finger and, with a napkin, Windy methodically polished the knife, fork and spoon that lay before him.

"Good-lookin' gal," Windy suggested, surveying the dark streaks left on the napkin by the fork. "She'd be mighty good-lookin' if she wasn't so skinny. Why didn't you ask her to eat with us, Lin?"

Under the tan the warm color flooded Lin's cheeks. In his thirty years Lin McCord had done many things and met many people, and in all those thirty years he had never overcome his shyness in the presence of women. Windy, noting his companion's flush, widened on his idea.

"Now if you'd asked her, she might of had a friend," Windy suggested. "One that was a little thicker. I never went for these thin gals much myse'f. You an' her an' me an' her friend, we could of rolled around an' saw the bright lights. We could of—"

"Shut up, Windy!" Lin commanded.

Windy Tillitson concealed his amusement behind the long mask of his face. "There you go," he complained. "Always breakin' up my parties. Why, Lin—"

"Shut up, I said!" Lin snapped.

The restaurant door opened to admit a small, gray-mustached man. For a moment the newcomer stood within the door, holding his broad-brimmed hat in his hands, and then he turned toward the counter, boot heels thumping as he walked. Windy craned his long neck to look at the small man's feet and, audible in his surprise, made comment. "Boots, sure as I'm a foot high!"

The newcomer turned quickly, a frown on his ruddy face and a glitter in his gray eyes. The sudden movement caused his coat to swing wide and the light

15

flashed from a shield pinned on his vest. Then with quick steps the man moved toward the table, came halfway and stopped. He had seen the Stetsons, personal property of Windy and Lin McCord, hanging on the wall. There was no mistaking those wide-brimmed, tall-crowned hats. They said, "Cowman." The angry gleam in the small man's eyes receded and the frown wrinkles left his forehead.

"You boys just come in?" he drawled.

Lin rose slowly to his feet. "Been here a day, Sheriff," he said. "My name's McCord. This long drink of water is Windy Tillitson. Boots are kind of a scarcity around here an' Windy couldn't help noticing yours."

The officer advanced to the table and held out his hand. "I'm Sam Rideout," he said as he took Lin's proffered hand. "You up on business, McCord?"

"Lookin' for grass," Lin answered. "Sit down, Sheriff. We just ordered."

Rideout seated himself. "Coffee an' pie," he said to the waitress who came to take his order. "Lookin' for grass, huh? Whereabouts you from, McCord?"

"Duffyville," Lin answered. "That's down in . . ."

"Texas," the officer finished, and laughed softly. "I come from Constantine myself. Tell me, do you know Dave Nickerson down there?"

"I worked with the Slash Y wagon when I was a kid," Lin answered. "Nickerson's was just east of us. I've known Dave all my life."

"Dave an' me punched cows together." Rideout's voice was warm with friendship. "He stayed around

16

Constantine an' I went hellin' off along the border. How is Dave?"

"Good, the last I heard," Lin answered. "I've been gone from around there quite a while."

The waitress brought food and placed it before the men. The talk drawled on, Rideout making inquiries, Lin and Windy answering them as best they could.

"An' so yo're lookin' for grass up here?" Rideout asked, pushing back his empty plate. "How much do you think you'll need?"

"Ten or twelve thousand acres," Lin answered. "My brother an' me have got three thousand Mexicos bought. We want to run 'em on this high country a season an' then take 'em to town."

"Located any?" The officer drank his coffee.

"I think so," Lin replied. "There's some above Adelphi I'm goin' to look at."

For a long moment Rideout was silent, then: "On the Hoysen holdings?" he asked.

Lin shook his head. "We saw that. This belongs to a girl named Patrick."

All the joviality was gone from Rideout's face. "I don't think you'll like that country," he said slowly. "I don't think it will suit you, McCord."

"Why? Isn't the grass good?"

"Good enough grass, I guess." Rideout toyed with his coffee spoon. "I just . . . Look, McCord, I don't think you'll like that country."

Lin's face was an expressionless mask, and Windy was leaning forward. "You think there's trouble up there?" Windy demanded. "Lin ain't afraid of trouble an' I ain't neither. You don't get gun-shy in the Rangers."

Rideout's face lighted swiftly. "Were you in the Rangers?" he asked, looking steadily at Lin.

"Captain Truett's company," Lin answered. "Windy was too. Why, Sheriff?"

"I served four years with Truett when he was sergeant in B Company," Rideout said. "That kind of makes it look different, McCord."

"Makes what look different?"

The officer leaned back in his chair. His eyes sought Lin's and stayed, staring unblinkingly. "About five years ago," Rideout drawled, "a man named Dan Patrick bought Rough Mesa up above Adelphi. That was the year before I was elected sheriff here. There was one damned thing right after another. You don't *sabe* a lumberjack, McCord, an' neither did I, then. There was fights an' all kinds of trouble. Patrick had a little sawmill an' a camp. He cut some timber. Finally, just before election, there was a big fight. Patrick got crippled. He was damned near killed. His mill shut down an' his camp blowed up. There hasn't been any trouble since I was elected an' there won't be if I can help it. But I wasn't goin' to see any Texas boy go into that country without knowin' what it was all about."

"I just want to run cattle," Lin said slowly. "I want to put weight on a bunch of Mexicos, that's all."

Rideout tapped the spoon on the table top. "I don't think there'll be any trouble," he said, more to himself than to Lin. "It's all quieted down. Well, if I can help you any, let me know. Maybe it would be a good thing for me if you were up there. You could kind of keep an eye on things." The sheriff got up, grinned warmly at Lin, nodded to Windy and walked toward the door. "I'll see you boys around," he said. "So long. Come into the office when you're in town."

When Rideout was gone Windy drank the last of his coffee. Lin, already finished with his meal, tilted his chair back and looked at the ceiling, his lips pursed to make a little soundless whistle.

"You can sure get took care of in this country," Windy drawled.

"Uh-huh," Lin agreed.

Silence for a moment. Then: "Nice of him to give us the low-down," Windy suggested. "You don't reckon there's anythin' *crooked* about that girl, do you, Lin?"

"Not about the girl," Lin said.

"You goin' to look at that country?"

"Tomorrow." Lin was very definite.

"An' lease it if you like it?"

"An' lease it if I like it. I told the sheriff, Windy; All I want to do is run steers. I'm lookin' for grass."

Windy said, "Uh-huh," and, bringing his big knife from his pocket, opened it and carefully sharpened a match to pick his teeth.

"But why did he tell us all that?" Windy queried after a moment. "Why did he say you wouldn't like the country an' then turn around an' tell us there wouldn't be any trouble and that it was all right?"

"I don't know," Lin said quietly. "Maybe we'll find out, Windy."

"Yeah," Windy drawled. "I *know* we'll find out. If the

grass is like that girl said it was, there won't be any keepin' you off that country."

Lin's eyes were quizzical as he looked at his companion. "Why do you think that?" he asked curiously.

"Because the sheriff hinted at a fight," Windy answered succinctly. "Good grass an' a fight, an' there's no stoppin' a McCord. Let's go if yo're done eatin'."

CHAPTER II
THE SKUNK SMELL

LIN AND WINDY TILLITSON WERE ON THE JUNCTION depot platform at five-thirty. Their grips and sacked saddles leaning against the depot wall, the two watched the trainmen making up the little accommodation train, the "Polly," which ran between Junction and Adelphi. The Polly went up the hills in the morning, taking a full five hours to cover the forty-five miles, and returned later in the evening, getting back into Junction about nine o'clock. Before the train was completely made up, Eleanor Patrick, looking cool and fresh as the morning itself, appeared and joined them.

With the switching finished, the three passengers for Adelphi climbed into the single coach—part baggage, part passenger car—and within minutes the Polly creaked out of Junction.

The trip to Adelphi was uneventful enough. Eleanor Patrick was friendly, although not over cordial; Windy carried on the customary monologue that had given him his name, and Lin looked at the country and at the girl,

20

particularly at the girl. Once Eleanor, turning suddenly, surprised him in his long inspection and a flood of rich color mounted to her throat and cheeks. Lin, too, colored and averted his eyes.

When finally Adelphi was reached and the three had disembarked, the girl made a suggestion. "You can leave your grips and saddles here," she said, nodding toward the depot. "I'll meet you here after lunch." It was evident that she did not want their company in town, and Lin and Windy agreed to the suggestion. Still they walked toward the center of the village with the girl between them, down past the mill where saws rumbled and planers screeched, along the length of the lumberyard with its clean smell of pine, and on to where Adephi's few stores, its two saloons and the hotel made the business section. Here Eleanor left them at the hotel, going on down the street and stopping at a small building some distance east of the hotel. Lin and Windy, the latter perennially hungry, went into the hotel dining room and ordered a meal.

As they ate they were conscious that the eyes of the other occupants of the dining room were upon them. There was one long table, seating perhaps ten men, and these, from their talk and the persiflage exchanged with the waitress, must be regular customers. Lin and Windy ate slowly and methodically and were last to leave the dining room. As they filed out through the hotel lobby, stopping at the desk to pay for their meal, a hush fell over the little room and they knew that their entrance had stifled the talk and conjecture as to who they were and what they were doing.

Leaving the hotel, the two cowmen walked back toward the depot and had almost reached it when Eleanor Patrick came along the street driving a bay team hitched to a buckboard. She stopped and waited for the men to join her and, when they had climbed in, drove on to the depot. There, saddles and grips were collected under the jaundiced eye of the depot agent who brightened visibly when Eleanor smiled at him and called him "Pop!"

Leaving the depot, the girl drove south a short distance, following along the tracks. Where the road turned, perhaps a quarter of a mile from town, the right-of-way was bordered by a small and dilapidated stockyards. Lin grunted when he saw the yards, and Windy stood up the better to observe.

"They ain't much yards, Lin," he commented, sitting down again. "There's about half the panels busted in that back fence."

"They'd do," Lin said. "All we need is a chute to get 'em out of the cars."

"An' a crew to hold 'em," Windy added.

"There haven't been any cattle shipped from here for a long time," Eleanor informed. "This used to be quite a shipping point. The old Zozaya Grant is west of us; in fact, this country I'm taking you to is part of the grant. There were a lot of cattle shipped from Adelphi before the Hoysen Company came into the country."

"Now it's lumber," Lin said. "Is your father a lumberman, Miss Patrick?"

The girl glanced at him sharply. "Father was a lumberman," she said after that brief inspection. "He's been

22

hurt and we aren't running the mill. We haven't run it for three years."

The road wound toward the west, twisting along across the level country. Lin, watching the side of the road, saw the litter of slash, down timber, stumps, all the debris of wasteful logging, and grunted his disapproval. "Bad," he commented. "You'd think they'd clean it up. There's fire danger, an' the country isn't good for a thing when it's left like that."

"They're not lumbermen; they're lumber hogs," the girl said bitterly. "All this country is like that: spoiled!"

"You said there wasn't any slash up on the mesa?" Lin asked, looking ahead toward the dark hillside that stood squarely athwart the road, blocking it.

"My father is a lumberman," Eleanor answered. "There isn't any slash."

Windy, who was rolling a quid of tobacco about in his mouth, spat furtively over the wheel. "You kind of wonder what makes men so ornery," he remarked. "Takes just a little while to turn a paradise into a da . . . blame' desert."

Eleanor did not rise to Windy's suggestion but slapped the rumps of the horses briskly with the lines, sending them into a trot.

There was little further conversation. As they neared the battlements of the mesa, the girl, whip in hand, pointed out landmarks and named them. The great canyon into which the road poured itself was Pinál, she said. It was the one thoroughfare to the top of the mesa. There were other canyons, but these were so rough as to be impassable for a road. The mountains beyond this sheer escarpment were the Brutos, and she named the peaks: Baldy, Iron Mountain, Marble Peak, Las Mujeres. Where the road entered Pinál Canyon, a creek wound down, and at the ford the team stopped and drank. Then once more they were moving, traveling, and now the litter and the slash, the skeleton stumps and the gaunt dry trees that, felled, had been unusable for timber, gave way to pines that stood straight and tall, pointing up to the canyon cleft above.

The ascent grew steeper, and once the girl stopped to breathe the team; then, with a final last pull, they were out of the canyon and on top, and the horses trotted in their eagerness to be home. Still they went through pines; and then, rounding a turn, an opening spread before them, a vista of grass and rolling country, and beyond it the dark line of the timber again rising into the hills.

"There's the house," Eleanor announced, pointing with the whip, and, following that line, Lin and Windy could see a little cluster of buildings.

When the buckboard rolled to a stop they were in a little settlement. There was one big, wide-spreading house made of peeled logs, low-lying and friendly, with a veranda all around its front. There were other smaller houses, deserted now; a big barn that was dilapidated and flanked with broken corrals; and beyond house and barn, gaunt and brooding over a pile of slabs and sawdust, was a mill. The buckboard stood in front of the house and a man, gray-haired and blue-eyed, came from the rear and went to the horses.

"You can put up the team, Sandy," Eleanor directed.

"We won't use them this afternoon."

Lin and Windy were already on the ground, Lin waiting to help the girl alight, Windy reaching long arms in for the grips.

"Leave your saddles," Eleanor directed. "They'll be all right in the buckboard." She got down, steadying herself momentarily with one small hand in Lin's broad palm, and then with a smile moved on toward the main building. "We'll go to the house," she said. "Sandy will look after things here."

The two men following her, Eleanor crossed the yard and mounted the porch. At the door the girl stopped. "I'll show you where you can put your things," she said, and led the way across the living room.

"But I thought—" Lin began.

Eleanor stopped and turned. "You thought that we could see the lease this afternoon," she completed, smiling. "I'm sorry, but we can't. I'll take you in the morning. I hope it won't inconvenience you."

"No, ma'am"—Lin's voice was earnest "but we don't like to put you out. We can—"

"You aren't putting me out," the girl assured. "There's plenty of room. I'll show you where you can put your bags." Once more she led the way.

Left alone in the neat, clean room that Eleanor had shown them, Windy sat down on the bed and Lin pulled a chair out from the wall and carefully seated himself.

"Big outfit," Windy commented. "Dead now, though. That mill ain't run for a long time."

"Remember what Rideout said?" Lin asked, and as Windy nodded: "What did you think when you saw it?"

"If it's all like that grassland, it'll be a steer heaven," Windy answered. "Lord, but that was pretty grass! There's enough old grass to run a summer."

"An' spring not hardly here," Lin said softly. "There's still snow back in the canyon."

"But I didn't see much fence," Windy said, playing pessimist. "That barn's in a hell of a shape an' the corrals all broke down. It'll take a year's work to make this anythin'."

"We won't need a barn, an' you know that about three days' work will fix the corrals," Lin answered. "The only thing that bothers me is the fences."

"Wonder if we can smoke in here," Windy said. "I reckon we'd better go outside."

On the porch, with lighted cigarettes, the two looked out across the expanse of grassland toward the hills. The builder of the house had faced it west, apparently with the view in mind. Lin and Windy were silent, drinking in the sheer beauty of the scene.

They stayed on the porch until Eleanor Patrick, dressed now in neat gingham and with a smudge of flour on one rounded arm, came to tell them that supper was ready. Following her into the house, they saw that a table had been set in one end of the long living room and that a man, bent and gray-haired, occupied a chair at the head of the table. Eleanor took her guests to him and introduced him gravely.

"This is Mr. McCord, Father, and Mr. Tillitson." Lin shook a limp hand and looked into lackluster brown eyes. There was no strength, no warmth in Patrick's voice as he said that they were welcome.

"You sit there, Mr. McCord"—Eleanor indicated a chair—"and you there, Mr. Tillitson. Sit down, please, and don't wait for me." She was gone through the door into the kitchen.

During the meal that followed, Lin and Windy tried vainly to interest Patrick in conversation. They attempted various subjects, to no avail. Patrick would say a few words, seem to try to give his guests attention, but always failing. Eleanor, hurrying in and out of the kitchen, talked briefly as she had time, but Patrick was quiet, almost, it seemed to Lin, not at the table at all but wandering away in his mind to some far place. Both Lin and Windy were glad when the meal was finished. Eleanor, standing beside her father, helped him to arise, and then with dragging steps, and with his daughter close beside him, Patrick made his way across the room and through a door.

Lin looked at Windy and shook his head pityingly. Windy, for once, had no comment but fumbled for his tobacco and papers.

"You can smoke here if you like," Eleanor said, coming back into the room. "Put a match to the fire, Mr. McCord. It's chilly."

She went on to the kitchen and Lin, bending, struck a match and applied it to the kindling in the fireplace.

When the girl returned the fire was blazing and Lin and Windy were in chairs on either side of the fireplace. Both men arose, but the girl waved them back into their chairs and seated herself on a hassock in front of the fire.

"My father was crippled," she said without preamble,

"in a fight. His chest was caved in and his back was hurt. For a year we didn't know whether he could live or not."

Lin was intensely silent, and Windy made a little clicking sound with his tongue.

"He takes no interest in anything," the girl continued abruptly. "Nothing. He sits on the porch and looks at the hills." She lifted troubled eyes to Lin. "We've had doctors," she said. "They tell me that he is as well as he will ever be, that there's nothing wrong organically. He just hasn't any interest. He—"

"Mebbe somethin' will come along that will rouse him," Lin said. "Sometimes that happens. Sometimes a man kind of loses his grip an' you've got to get it back for him."

"Like John," Windy said.

"But how?" Eleanor asked.

"I don't know." Lin stared at the fire. "It's like Windy said. My brother John lost his wife. He's got a boy, an' you'd think that the kid would have kept him interested, but he didn't. Nothing stirred him up till I cooked up the idea of running steers this summer. John seems to be interested in that."

Silence fell over the little group, and then the girl said softly: "We all have trouble, haven't we?" and got up from the hassock.

"I guess," Lin agreed.

"I'll get your room ready for the night," Eleanor proffered, moving toward the door. "If there's anything—"

"We're mighty comfortable." Lin was on his feet. "Don't you bother, please. Yo're tired an' want to go to bed, an' me an' Windy had better turn in too."

The girl's smile was bright. "Good night," she said.

The following morning, with Eleanor as guide, Lin and Windy rode the Rough Mesa. They found the good stirrup-high grass lying in open parks and along timberless ridges. They found the water, just as Eleanor had said, and they found that there was a fence— broken in places but perfectly capable of being repaired—bordering along the western side of the lease. "The grant fence," Eleanor said.

When at noon the trio returned to the house, Lin announced himself satisfied. "I want it," he said. "It looks good."

Eleanor's eyes were bright. "Can you . . . ?" She hesitated.

"You said that you wanted all the payment," Lin interrupted the hesitation. "I can give you a deposit of two hundred dollars cash and a draft on the First State Bank in El Paso. You can hold the lease until the draft goes through. Is that all right?"

Eleanor thought that over. "That's all right," she agreed. "We'll have to go to Junction to draw the lease."

"What time does the train leave Adelphi for Junction?" Windy asked practically.

Eleanor gave a little startled exclamation. "At four o'clock," she said. "We'll have to hurry."

"Well, then," said Lin, "let's hurry. I want to get a telegram off to John to start the steers along, an' I've got a lot of things to do."

During the noon hour Lin and Windy got sight of some

of the economy of the Patrick household. Eleanor, changing her clothes for the ride to town, was not in evidence; and a middle-aged native woman waited on the table at which they ate. Patrick, like his daughter, did not attend the meal; and Sandy Donald, reticent and keeping his eyes on his plate, ate with Windy and Lin. Immediately after the meal Eleanor appeared, ready to go, and Lin and Windy collecting their grips and putting their saddles in the back of the buckboard, the three departed.

As they drew away from the house the girl turned the team and, in place of taking the main road, went out through the pines. Within two hundred yards she pulled the team to a stop. Before them was a little clearing, and almost at the further edge, yet still clear of the lesser timber, stood three tall pines. Beneath the pines, with a neat fence about it, was a grave and headstone. For a long moment Eleanor Patrick looked at the pines and at the headstone, then, wordlessly, she turned the team and started back. "I won't lease the timber rights," she said suddenly. "If you're expecting to get them, we're just wasting time. I'll take you to Adelphi and . . ."

"I want grass," Lin said gently. "I'm lookin' for grass, not timber."

The girl turned her head and looked at Lin, searching his face. Apparently satisfied with what she saw there, she smiled faintly. "I'm . . ." she began. "I guess I'm upset. I know that you want grass and not timber, Mr. McCord. That park I showed you just now is no part of the lease."

Lin nodded. "Whatever you say," he agreed. "It's a pretty place."

"My mother loved it," Eleanor Patrick said and, her face straight to the front, drove along.

The trip to Adelphi was marked by a lack of conversation and was uneventful. Windy, sitting on the outside of the seat, whistled tunelessly and earnestly through two gleaming gold teeth. Lin looked at the country, absorbed with his thoughts. Eleanor Patrick drove the team and occasionally made some small comment. But for the most part there was silence.

When she reached Adelphi the girl left the men at the depot and went on into town to dispose of the team. She returned just as Lin and Windy came back from an inspection of the stockyards, and with the Polly made up, the accommodation car coupled now behind flatcars piled with lumber, the three began the journey to Junction.

It was a little after nine o'clock when they reached Junction. Lin carried his own and Eleanor's grip to the hotel, Windy swaggering along beside him. The saddles had been left in the baggage room at the depot. At the hotel, after registering, the girl went to her room and the two men went out to the restaurant. When they came back they took their grips and went upstairs.

With a lamp lit and his boots off, Windy sat down on the bed and leaned back, hauling up his feet to a comfortable position. Lin sat at the table writing, the lamplight casting his shadow big and black against the further wall.

"Sure looks good," Windy commented. "It sure does, Lin."

"Uh-huh." Lin did not look up from his writing.

31

"An' cheap," Windy went on. "That kind of grass is worth fifteen cents anyhow. Yo're gettin' it for ten."

"I'm trying to write a letter," Lin announced irritably.

"Oh," Windy grunted. Lin's pen scratched on in the silence that followed. Windy fished for tobacco and papers.

There was a knock, sharp and imperative, on the door. Lin got up to answer. Windy had also risen and, crossing to the table, bent down to light his cigarette over the lamp chimney. Windy's back was toward the door. He heard Lin say: "Come in, Mr. Melcomb." Windy puffed his cigarette alight and turned.

The man who had come in was big. As tall as Windy, he overtopped Lin by at least three inches. His face was big, as were his shoulders and hands. The suit he wore was well cut but carelessly kept. There were ashes on the vest and the man's boots were dusty. Coupled with all his bigness, with his well-cut clothes, with his ease, there was a certain shiftiness, a sort of air about the man that belied size and hearty voice and appearance. When Windy looked at Melcomb's face he caught that impression. It was nothing definite, nothing that could be put into words, and yet the thing was there.

"Have a chair," Lin said hospitably. "I'm glad to see you."

Melcomb sat down and crossed his legs, one big thigh swelling his trousers' leg tight. His hat, a derby, was pushed back on his head, exposing rusty hair that was liberally sprinkled with gray. Despite the gray hair Melcomb was not old; barely forty, Windy surmised.

"I saw your name on the register and thought I'd

come up a minute," the big man said, hearty bluffness in his voice. "Are you still looking for pasture, McCord?"

Lin sat down on the edge of the bed. Windy, thus displaced, squatted on his heels beside the dresser, looking up through the smoke that trailed from his cigarette. "Not exactly," Lin answered Melcomb's question. "I guess I've found a pasture."

"So?" Melcomb's eyebrows lifted to make bushy tents above his eyes. "Whereabouts?"

"Up above Adelphi," Lin answered. "On Rough Mesa."

Melcomb pursed his lips and shook his head. "That would be Patrick's place," he said. Lin nodded.

"Signed the lease yet?"

"No."

Melcomb looked steadily at Lin. "I wouldn't do it," he said slowly. "I don't think you'll like that country, McCord."

"It looked mighty good," Lin said quietly.

"Oh, it's a good country." Melcomb's gesture bestowed a sort of benign benediction upon Rough Mesa. "The thing is that we'll be loggin' in there this fall."

"So?" It was Lin's turn to lift his eyebrows.

Melcomb nodded. "I figure to put a camp up there in early August," he said.

"I plan on having a camp up there in a week," Lin commented gently.

Melcomb produced a cigar from a vest pocket, looked at it critically and held it out. "Smoke?"

"I don't use 'em." Lin made no move toward the cigar. Melcomb bit off the end of it, put it in his mouth and struck a match.

"I believe I can make you a better deal," he announced around the cigar. "I'll lease you what you want of that lower country at five cents an acre."

"You come down in price." Lin watched the big man steadily. "When I talked to you last, it was twelve and a half cents."

"Well"—Melcomb puffed out smoke—"I've been thinking."

"So have I." Lin rocked back on the bed. "That country you've got is covered with slash an' down timber. I don't believe I'd be interested."

There was silence for a moment while Melcomb smoked. "You're going to lease Rough Mesa, then," he said.

"Tomorrow," Lin agreed.

Melcomb took the cigar from his mouth and stared at it. "We've been havin' a little trouble getting that tract," he said slowly. "I might put you in the way of a piece of money, McCord."

"So?"

Melcomb nodded. "That girl has caused some trouble," he said. "She wants that timber."

"It's good timber." Lin's eyes did not leave the big man's face.

"Tell you what I'll do." Melcomb leaned forward. "You take that lease. Get the timber rights. I'll pay you what you paid for it after you're through usin' it this fall."

"I'll talk to Miss Patrick about it," Lin said.

"She won't let you have it at all then." Melcomb's voice held a little contempt. "Don't you see that? We've offered to buy the timber and she won't sell. This way you get your pasture and we get what we want. What do you say, McCord?"

Windy had risen from his heels and, nose in the air, was sniffing as might a man who smells something faintly bad. Lin glanced at Melcomb and then over to Windy. "You smell it too?" he asked, a quizzical smile on his lips.

"That skunk smell?" Windy answered. "It's gettin' stronger every minute."

Melcomb flushed, the slow red suffusing his cheeks. "I didn't come here to be insulted," he snapped. "I've offered you a legitimate business proposition—"

"Of double-crossing a girl," Lin said softly. "I've turned it down. Don't look under the bed, Windy. The skunk ain't there."

Melcomb was on his feet now, glaring at Lin. "You young pup!" he snapped. "I've broken better men than you. I'll—"

Lin, too, got up. Melcomb towered over him, but oddly, in that little hotel room, Lin seemed the larger. "You can turn your wolf loose on me," Lin invited. "Just any time. Now get out. I thought it was skunk I smelled but it was somethin' worse. Get out!"

Melcomb reached back a big hand, twisted the knob and jerked the door open. "I've told you," he warned.

"An' I told you," Lin retorted.

The door banged shut. Angry steps thumped along the

hall. Windy relaxed gracefully against the bureau. "Oh, mama, but he's mad!" Windy drawled. "An' ain't you mad too!"

CHAPTER III
YOU'LL BE THE FIRST MAN DOWN

LIN, WINDY AND ELEANOR PATRICK MET IN THE LOBBY of the Barclay House and from that meeting point sallied out to attend to the details of leasing Rough Mesa. They went first to the bank where Lin made a deposit, and from there to the office of a lawyer, Walter Yawl, where a contract was drawn. Returning to the bank where Lin's credit had been substantiated by telegraph, the deal was consummated. Lin wrote a check and gave it to Eleanor, and she in turn gave him a copy of the lease, signed by herself, as acting for Dan Patrick, and by Lin. They parted there, Lin to go to the depot to telegraph his brother and Eleanor to do some minor shopping in the town. That evening Lin left for the South, to return in ten days or two weeks with the first trainload of cattle. Windy was left in Junction to assemble a crew to move the steers when they came in, to get an outfit together and to visit the lease and make it ready for the arrival of the steers.

Eleanor Patrick did not leave Junction until the following morning, then she took the Polly to Adelphi, arriving a little before noon.

From the depot Eleanor went to town, passing the lumberyard, the store, the company offices and stopping eventually at a small frame building through the windows of which could be seen a display of hats. Pushing open the door, Eleanor went in. The door closed, accompanied by the tinkle of a bell and, summoned by that sound, a plump woman of perhaps thirty-five made her appearance at the rear door of the millinery shop.

Eleanor sat down in a chair, leaned back and announced: "I've done it, Cora. I've leased Rough Mesa!"

Cora Ferguson plucked pins from her mouth with one hand and carefully put down the hat she held in the other hand. "I'm so glad, dearie," she said when her mouth was free. "I was sayin' to Bessie, just this morning, I said: 'Bessie, do you suppose Eleanor is havin' trouble?' I said: 'You know she's had a hard row to hoe and it would be too bad if she had trouble now.'"

Eleanor Patrick laughed. Cora Ferguson was an inveterate gossip but there was not a kinder heart in all the Brutos country. "No trouble, Cora," she assured. "I've leased the mesa. I haven't a care in the world now except Dad."

Cora's eyes were shrewd. "I'm just as glad as I can be," she said. "I expect there's others that aren't so pleased though."

A frown wrinkled Eleanor Patrick's wide forehead and she looked questioningly at Cora.

"I mean Otis Melcomb," Cora amplified.

The frown remained. Cora picked up the hat again and, selecting a pin, fastened a wisp of veil to the brim. "Mr. Melcomb drove up the canyon pretty regularly last fall," she suggested archly.

It was fatal to make a confidante of Cora, and Eleanor knew it. Cora could not and would not recognize a secret. Still, it is sometimes necessary to talk to someone.

"He came to see me," Eleanor admitted, bitterness in her voice.

"We all thought so, dearie," Cora prompted. "He's a good catch. What with the company and all, he's worth a lot of money."

Eleanor shuddered. "He sits and stares at you," she said, not talking so much to Cora as to herself. "He stares at you until you feel as though you haven't on any clothes. I hate him!"

Cora opened her mouth to speak and then wisely refrained from voicing her thoughts.

"He kept calling me 'Little Girl,'" Eleanor said, venom fairly dripping from the title. "He thought that I'd marry him."

Cora's eyebrows lifted and she leaned forward eagerly. "Did he ask you to?" she questioned.

Eleanor nodded, not looking at Cora but staring at a hat on a stand. "He said he thought it would make a fitting match," she reported. "As though I'd marry him! I found out what he wanted."

"What did he want, dearie?" Cora prompted.

"Rough Mesa," Eleanor said slowly. "Sandy was in town and he heard something that was said in the saloon. Otis Melcomb bragged that he would marry me and get the mesa. He'll never get the mesa, not as long as I live."

"Talking about it has made you all upset," Cora sympathized.

"I'll keep the mesa and I'll keep my home." Eleanor Patrick's voice was fierce. "Cora, are all men like that? Are all men beasts? Do they always want something? Isn't there any real love in the world?"

"Men are just men, dearie," Cora said wisely. "I've had dealin's with 'em, dearie. I tell you: you try on some hats. When a woman's upset there's nothing like tryin' on a nice hat to make her feel better. We'll try some on. I've got some pretty things, if I do say so myself." Rising, she placed the hat she was trimming on a table and bustled over to a showcase.

"Now here's one . . ." she began.

Eleanor Patrick laughed. "I believe you'd think of trying on hats at a funeral," she said. "All right, Cora. I'll try some on."

At the end of ten days Lin McCord returned to Junction. He came riding in a caboose at the end of a long string of cattle cars. Fifteen hundred motley, long-horned Chihuahua steers rode ahead of Lin, and in the car next the caboose there were twenty-eight head of horses. Windy was at the yards when the cattle came in, and when Lin climbed down from the steps of the caboose Windy was waiting for him.

"Everything all right?" Lin asked, releasing Windy's hand. "Did you get a crew?"

"I got five men," Windy answered. "They ain't exactly what you'd call cowpunchers, but I guess they'll have to do. One of 'em's a cook. Who'd you bring with you, Lin?"

"Sacatone," Lin answered. "John an' Bobby an' Carl

will be along with the next trainload. Did you . . . ? Here's Sacatone now."

A small man, weathered and hard as a pine knot, climbed down from the caboose steps and shambled up to shake hands with Windy. Sacatone Thomas was part Comanche; his black eyes and high cheekbones showed his breeding. Face utterly expressionless, he released Windy's hand and looked around the Junction yards. "This the place?" he asked.

"Fifty miles more to Adelphi, Sacatone," Lin said. "Windy's got a crew and a cook."

Sacatone grunted and limped stiffly along the side of the caboose toward the horsecar. "Talks just as much as he ever did, don't he?" Windy commented.

Lin laughed. "Just about," he agreed. "How about the lease? Have you been up there?"

Windy nodded. "I took a man up an' we worked on the corrals," he said. "I've got some hay for the horses at the Adelphi yards. I think I've got everything lined up, Lin."

A trainman, a lantern still dangling from his arm although the dawn was breaking, came down the side of the train and stopped when he reached Lin and Windy. "Got to switch here," he said. "We can't put a mainline engine on that branch. It'll be about half an hour."

"Let's go to town an' eat breakfast," Windy suggested. "I've got the boys I hired over at the depot."

"Let's go eat, Sacatone," Lin called, and followed Windy toward the station.

The yardmaster at Junction had been optimistic. It was a full hour after Lin's arrival before the cattle train

40

rolled slowly out on the Adelphi branch. In the caboose, besides the conductor and the rear brakeman, were Lin McCord, Windy, Sacatone Thomas and five others. Bedrolls and saddles filled the caboose until it was difficult to move about. Lin sat on one of the long seats and looked at the crew Windy had hired on. There was Abel Lewis, big and grizzled; Roy Nixon, Tom Perry, Shorty Morgan with a head red as fire, and Cal McBride who was the cook. Of the men, only Shorty Morgan bore that ineffable something that stamps a man as a rider. The others, although they owned bedrolls and saddles, although they wore boots, did not size up as cowboys.

"Best I could do," Windy commented under his breath.

"They're all right," Lin returned.

The engine made heavy weather of the trip. There was a heavy load behind the engine, and on the hill below Adelphi it was necessary to take the train up in two sections. It was one o'clock and later before Adelphi was reached.

"I want to get the horses right out," Lin told the conductor. "If I can get that car spotted, we'll unload and feed them. We're goin' to have to use 'em right away."

The conductor grunted and complained about a damned yardmaster that would put the horsecar on the back end. Nevertheless the horsecar and caboose were cut off and taken on to the yards.

At the yards the men piled out. Bedrolls and saddles were dragged from the caboose and stacked against the fence and the horsecar spotted at the chutes. The conductor rolled the door back while Lin and Windy placed the chute sides, then, with the bull boards removed, the horses cautiously came down the chute and into a pen.

There was water in the pen, and Windy broke open bales of hay and tossed it across the fence. The horses drank and then fell to eating, and Lin, turning to his crew, addressed them.

"I want to get unloaded and out of here this afternoon," he announced. "I'd like a couple of you boys to stay here an' the rest of you go to town with Windy an' eat. When you come back we'll go. How about it?"

Morgan, Lewis and Sacatone said that they would stay with Lin, and the others, led by Windy, started toward town. Lin turned to the train crew.

"How does that suit you?" he asked.

The arrangement was agreeable with the trainmen. The engineer and the fireman had lunches in their tin grips. One brakeman volunteered to stay, and the conductor and the other brakeman followed Windy toward Adelphi. The engineer spotted the first of the cattle cars and the work of unloading began.

"We'll fill the pens an' hold the rest out on the grass," Lin directed. "By the time the others get back we ought to have four or five cars unloaded."

The work progressed smoothly. There were three pens in the Adelphi stockyards. The horses occupied one of these and would not be disturbed. From the car, spotted at the chute, the bull boards were removed and the first of the Chihuahuas, long head weaving nervously, set foot on the gangway and then came on down. The other steers followed, walking down into the alley. The alley filled, the gate was closed and the engine spotted another car while the steers were shoved into a pen.

"They just kind of do it themselves," Shorty commented to Lin as he climbed up to the loading platform once more. "They sure handle nice."

"Nicest cattle in the world," Lin said heartily. "You never handled any Mexicos before?"

"I come from Montana," Shorty explained. "We don't get 'em up there."

Another car door rolled back, and again Lin and Shorty toiled at the bull boards. The work went on until the pens were filled to overflowing and even the alley was filled.

"We've got the yards full," Lin announced, wiping the sweat from his forehead. "Funny the other boys aren't back yet."

The brakeman had climbed up on the car side and was looking toward town. "Here comes the Brains," he announced. "Runnin', too. Must be trouble."

Lin stepped up beside the brakeman. The conductor, fat and making the best time he could in a sort of rolling run, was coming up toward the yards from the depot. Lin stepped down to the loading platform.

When the conductor, panting and perspiring, reached the yards, every man was on the ground waiting for him. Even the engineer and the fireman had deserted the engine and joined Lin, Shorty, Lewis and Sacatone. The conductor gasped for breath, rolled his eyes and tried to make a statement.

"Fight . . ." he gasped. "They . . ."

"Easy," Lin said. "Get yore breath."

The conductor panted a minute, swallowed and tried again. "There was a fight in town. That tall fellow an' a lumberjack got into it. The whole bunch was arrested."

"How did this happen?" Lin demanded sternly.

The fat railroader, having regained his breath, plunged into his explanation. "We ate in a restaurant," he said needlessly. "That tall man, the one you call Windy, an' one of the others finished first. They went outside an' waited. First thing I knew, there was a fight goin' on outside. The rest of your men piled out an' got into it an' the marshal come along an' arrested the whole bunch."

"The marshal?" Lin questioned.

"Ed Draper," the conductor informed. "Him an' Otis Melcomb an' Melcomb's woods boss, Spike Samms. They waded in on your boys."

A little frown crinkled the corners of Lin's eyes. "Put all the boys in jail?" he asked.

"All of 'em," the conductor reiterated. "You won't have any crew out here to unload your cattle. They were all arrested."

"Melcomb, huh?" Lin said slowly, and turned and walked toward the bedding and the saddles.

"Wait a minute." Sacatone followed Lin. "I'm goin' with you."

Lin stopped. "No, Sacatone," he said. "You boys will stay here. Get somethin' to eat out of the chuck box an' go on an' unload steers. One of you can hold what we've got outside the pens and the others unload. I can handle this."

Sacatone stood hesitant. "I think I ought to go," he growled. "You'll run into trouble . . ."

"There won't be any trouble." Lin's voice was decisive. "You'll stay here." Bending over his grip, he opened it and pulled out a gun belt.

"But . . ." Sacatone began to expostulate.

"Damn it, Sacatone!" Lin latched the belt about his middle and glared at the older man. "I've told you what I wanted done."

Sacatone's dissatisfied scowl remained, but the wiry little man moved off slowly toward Shorty and Lewis. Lin bent down and lifted his saddle.

It took Lin but a few minutes to catch a horse and put on his saddle. The horse pen had an outside gate and, leading his horse through, Lin mounted. Once more he spoke to the men. "I'll be right back," he promised, then the big dun horse he had chosen started for town, feet sending dust puffs flying.

When he reached Adelphi Lin rode down the street looking to right and left, locating the scene of the disturbance. There were three or four men standing in front of a restaurant, but further down the street there was a little crowd and here, Lin surmised, was the center of excitement. He rode up, stopped the dun and, dismounting, let the reins trail.

"Marshal's office?" he asked one of the loafers.

"Yeah." The man Lin had addressed stared at him curiously. Lin nodded and, shoving through the crowd, reached the door of the building and went in.

Windy was sitting on a bench against the wall. Beside him were Nixon, Perry and McBride. The railroad

45

brakeman stood at the further end of the bench, separated from Windy by some little distance. Melcomb's big bulk was ensconced behind a desk. At one side of the desk was a huge black-bearded man, heavy-shouldered and scowling. On the opposite side of the desk was a brown-faced, medium-sized individual with "tough" written in his every action and appearance. Mechanically Lin noted the star on the man's vest, and from the star his eyes traveled to a gun swung from the officer's hip by a belt that was innocent of any holster. Lin had seen just that sort of rigging before. The gun swung from a swivel, and the rig was about the fastest thing in gunplay that existed—that is, if a man knew how to use it.

"Well, gentlemen?" Lin said, stopping just inside the door.

The brown-faced man stared at Lin and said nothing. The black-bearded man glared hostilely. It was Melcomb who spoke. "These men were creating a disturbance," he stated, defiance in his voice. "The marshal brought them in."

Lin looked at the brown-faced man. "What's the charge, Marshal?" he asked.

"Disturbin' the peace." The marshal's eyes were fixed on Lin's face. "I'll tell you somethin' else, mister. It's against the law to carry a gun in Adelphi."

"So?" Lin drawled. He had met many men like this brown-faced officer. The breed was familiar.

"An' I'll take that gun," the marshal stated.

"How bad do you want it?" Lin's eyes were calculating, his voice cool.

"Bad enough, I guess," the marshal said slowly. "Hand it over."

Lin smiled a little, no amusement in the expression. "No," he said mildly; "you'll have to take it."

"Now wait a minute," Melcomb expostulated. "Mr. McCord didn't know the rule, Ed. You—"

"I've explained it to him," the marshal drawled. "You notice I didn't arrest him for carryin' a gun. If he'd known the rule I'd of thrown him in jail."

"Now I'll tell one," Lin said carefully. "I won't hand over my gun and it won't be taken. If there's trouble over this the first man down is you, Melcomb!"

Melcomb's big face turned a dirty gray. "I've nothing to do with this," he began.

"Remember, the first man down is you, Melcomb," Lin said implacably. "How about it? Do you want to go?"

Lin spoke to Melcomb but he kept his eyes on the officer. For the first time the marshal took his eyes from Lin's face and glanced at Otis Melcomb. With a shrug he turned back to Lin.

"All right, keep it," the marshal said; "but don't get the idea I'm afraid of you."

"I'd be the last man to say you were," Lin agreed, soft-voiced. "We've got that settled. What's against my men?"

Again the officer looked at Melcomb, studying the big man carefully. He turned back to Lin. "They were fightin'," he said at length.

"Each other?" Lin asked.

"No." The marshal shook his head.

"Where's the men they fought with?" Lin glanced around the office.

Melcomb found his voice. "Why not drop it, Ed?" he asked. "They were all fighting. Why not let Mr. McCord take his men? They'll leave town and there won't be any·more trouble, I'm sure."

An odd expression stole over the officer's face. He did not glance toward Melcomb. His voice was flat when he spoke. "That suit you, McCord? You seem to be the boss."

"It suits me," Lin said.

"All right, then, take 'em along," the marshal drawled.

"Windy, you an' the boys step outside," Lin ordered. "I'll be with you."

Windy, with the other two beside him, got up from the bench. The brakeman, moving hurriedly, passed by Lin and went out the door. Windy, Nixon, Perry and McBride filed out.

Lin looked at the marshal. "Thanks," he said.

"Don't thank me," the marshal replied.

Lin backed out the door, closing it behind him. The sidewalk was clear now, save for Lin's men. The loiterers had moved along and stood silently watching from beneath a tin awning that stretched out from a store.

"Sacatone's comin' with the horses," Windy said as Lin joined them. Lin looked up the street. Sacatone Thomas was riding toward them, leading a string of saddled horses.

CHAPTER IV
INSURANCE

THE CREW RODE OUT WITH SACATONE IN THE LEAD AND Windy and Lin bringing up the rear. When they reached the yards they found Shorty Morgan and Abel Lewis holding about two hundred head of steers on grass and the stockyards empty of cattle. Immediately they fell to work. The pens were filled and the cars emptied. Steers were moved out from the pens to join the growing herd, and when the last car was vacated Lin gave orders.

"Windy, you take the remuda. McBride, Windy will give you a couple of horses that you can pack. There's a creek crossing about six miles along from here and I want to bed there. Sacatone, you point 'em west along the road. Shorty, you ride point with Sacatone; you know the country. Lewis, you an' Perry ride the swing, an' I'll come along behind 'em. Let's go."

The men moved out toward the herd. Windy, rope in hand, approached the horse pen intending to rope out two pack animals for McBride, who had dragged two packsaddles out from the bedding and dumped them down as Lin spoke. There was yet a good deal of work for McBride and Windy. They had the kitchen to load, the beds to lash on loose horses, all the little details to attend. They fell to work, and out from the yards, their voices lifted and their horses moving back and forth, the men started the cattle.

The Chihuahuas moved along in good fashion. They were tired from their ride in the cars, they had not

49

watered, and they plodded steadily ahead. Up on the point of the herd, Sacatone and little redheaded Shorty Morgan kept direction. Along the flanks, Lewis and Perry watched to see that no animal strayed. Behind them all Lin McCord rode, constantly alert, keeping the drags going, keeping steers from turning back. Now Lewis, now Perry, dropped back to help him. Fifteen hundred big steers were on the march.

It would have been easier with another man, Lin realized. He had taken the hardest job himself. He should have tolled off another man for the drag work; still, there was a sort of savage satisfaction, a kind of release of tension for Lin, in doing it all. He needed that outlet, for he was still angry, still tuned tight as a fiddlestring. The steers had gone a mile and more when Windy came loping up to help.

"McBride's takin' the remuda an' the kitchen," he called, falling in beside Lin. "He's all right; he can handle 'em. See? Yonder he goes."

Windy pointed out through the dust, and Lin could see Cal McBride riding behind the remuda, perhaps two hundred yards off the road and paralleling it.

"He know where we're goin' to bed?" Lin called.

"I told him the creek," Windy answered, and swung off to urge a lagging steer along.

As they rode, their duties slack now that the cattle were strung out, Lin and Windy found time to talk. Windy told about the fight in Adelphi, for once talking without embellishing details. He and Perry had finished eating and had gone out of the restaurant to wait for the others. Standing there, talking together, they had been approached by a man who asked to borrow a match.

"I reached for a match an' Perry got one out an' handed it over," Windy recounted. "That feller took it an' struck it an' it went out. He turned right back an' called Perry a dirty son-of-a-slut. Perry let him have it right between the eyes, an' we went from there. I don't know how many was on us, but there was plenty. Then Melcomb an' them two sheep dogs of his showed up an' they arrested us. That marshal, Ed Draper, is bad, Lin."

"It was framed," Lin stated briefly. "They wanted trouble. They wanted to hang us up."

"Of course," Windy agreed. "You kind of went to the he-coon when you told Melcomb that he'd be the first man down."

"I meant it," Lin countered.

"He knew you meant it." Windy chuckled. "Lord, but he faded when you told him that. Draper wasn't afraid, though."

"No," Lin agreed. "Draper wasn't afraid."

Again Windy turned off to push a steer along. When he came back he was grinning. "Old Sac is sore as a boil," he commented, riding close to Lin. "He wanted to go to town with you when you got us loose."

"I didn't dare take him," Lin explained seriously. "Somebody would of got killed."

"Anyhow"—Windy was still grinning—"you got your crew solid behind you. The brakeman an' some of the boys told the rest what happened in town. That little redheaded Morgan was askin' me if there was a chance to get on steady with you."

Perforce Lin smiled. "There might be for him," he said. "He kind of knows what it's all about. Hi-yo cattle! Git along. Git along there!"

McBride had made camp where Pinál Creek, wandering across the slash-filled country, came close to the road. The crew threw the herd along the creek to water, and while the steers drank, a rope corral was made and change horses caught up. With that done, the cattle were taken off the water and thrown into a park, a cleared space in the stumpage and slash, which would serve for a bedground. Windy, with Lin helping, hobbled some of the horses, those that would stray and others that would follow. The remuda went to the herd, and two riders stayed, loose herding the steers. The rest of the crew rode in to supper.

When they had finished eating and Lewis and Morgan had gone out to relieve Perry and Nixon with the cattle, Lin got up and, moving a short distance from the fire, jerked his head at Windy and Sacatone. Windy came immediately, but Sacatone, still sulky, took his time obeying Lin's summons. Finally, however, he ambled over and squatted down on his boot heels, staring sullenly at the ground. Sacatone had been with the McCords a long time. He was intensely loyal, combative whenever McCord interests were threatened, and a first-class fighting man in any language and with any weapons. Lin he liked—tolerated would be the better phrase—but to John McCord, Lin's older brother, Sacatone gave an undivided devotion.

"What's on your mind, Lin?" Windy asked.

"I want you to be foreman tonight," Lin answered,

making no explanation, simply a statement. "Sacatone and I have got a little business to tend to."

Sacatone glanced up, then got slowly to his feet. His face was expressionless but there was an unmistakable gleam of interest in his black eyes. "We goin' back to town?" he asked.

Lin shook his head. He knew that Sacatone had learned all that had happened in Adelphi and that Sacatone's idea of going back to town would be to ride in shooting and clean up the place. "Not to town," Lin said.

The eagerness dimmed in Sacatone's eyes.

"But we're right here in the open," Lin went on, "and if we had a run in this slash country, it would play hell with the steers and we'd be a week gatherin' them. You and me, Sacatone, are goin' back down the road a ways and spread out. We're kind of goin' to be insurance."

Sacatone grunted, but he was pleased, Lin could tell. He could not have a better man than Sacatone Thomas for the job he had in hand. Sacatone could go without sleep endlessly, could sit patiently and motionless for hours at a time. Sacatone had ears that were as alert as his Comanche forebears and eyes that missed nothing.

"Maybe there won't be anything stirring," Lin went on. "Maybe there will. They tried to hang us up once today. They might try again."

"Melcomb?" Windy asked.

"Who else?" Lin grunted. "He don't like us any, an' it's no trick to stampede a bunch of Mexicos."

Windy nodded. Sacatone glanced at Lin and strolled off to his bed. Lin saw the old man getting a rifle from his bedroll. There was a scabbard on Sacatone's saddle.

"It'll be moonlight after a while," Lin said to Windy. "We'll wait till the moon comes up an' then we'll come in. The boys will stand long guards, but we'll help 'em after moonrise."

He too moved off to where his horse was staked to a stump. Sacatone was already mounted.

When Lin climbed up on his horse Perry and Nixon looked at him curiously but asked no questions. McBride was working at the fire, washing dishes. He also glanced toward the two mounted men but made no comment.

"Windy's running the spread," Lin said casually.

"We'll be back after a while." He turned his horse, joined Sacatone, and the two rode together down the road.

Half a mile below the camp they stopped. Darkness had come and the sky was clear dark steel above them, the stars studding its metal. There was a little clump of trees, small pines that had been too young for the lumberman's ax, near by the road, and Lin pointed toward them. "That's a pretty good place," he suggested.

Sacatone grunted and then spoke slowly. "What makes you think they'd stick to the road?"

"Because," Lin said, "it would be too hard going through the slash. Maybe there's other roads where they hauled logs, but we'll have to chance that. Anyhow, we could hear them going through the slash, an' they won't branch out until they're closer than this place."

Once more Sacatone grunted, but evidently he thought Lin's reasoning sound, for he started his horse toward the clump of pines. Dead branches snapped and crackled under the horses' hoofs. Lin's mount lifted to jump a fallen tree and came down, crashing the brush on the opposite side. "You see, Sacatone?" Lin questioned.

Sacatone did not deign to reply. Reaching the pines, ten yards from the road, the two men stopped and dismounted. The horses were hidden in the shadow of the trees, and Sacatone slipped his rifle from its scabbard and seated himself on a rock. Lin sat down, leaning against a pine trunk. A horse stamped and shook himself and then, all about, there was quiet.

Occasionally Lin shifted position. Sacatone remained motionless as his rock seat. Little noises filled the night insect sounds, the twitter of some sleepy bird, the scurrying sounds of small animals moving. Sometimes the horses shifted with a creak of leather and the dull plop of a hoof coming down. That was all. Time wore on. In the east the edge of a cloud was bathed in silver. The moon was rising.

"Nothin' to it," Lin said. "I guess I was just spooked."

"Shut up," Sacatone said dourly. "There's horses on the road."

Lin was silent; he could hear nothing other than the night noises; then, distinctly, he caught the sound of a rock rolling and sharp clicks as it struck against other rocks. Sacatone was right; there were horses coming along the road. Under Sacatone's thumb the hammer of the Winchester clicked suggestively, and Lin spoke.

"No shooting!" he ordered, low-voiced. "We'll just go out an' meet 'em."

For some reason, that pleased Sacatone and he chuckled.

They could hear the horses plainly now, coming along the road at a steady walk. Lin stood up and reached back for his reins. It was time to move. Sacatone also had risen. Lin led his horse out a step, and Sacatone remained in the shadow of the trees. The horsemen were plain on the road now, two men riding side by side.

"Hello," Lin called cheerfully, and led his horse toward the road.

The unexpected salute precipitated activity on the road. The riders reined in, facing the source of the sound. The moon was rising now, and in its brilliance Lin saw that the horsemen were Ed Draper and the black-bearded man who had sat beside Melcomb.

"How are you, Marshal?" Lin asked affably, advancing toward the riders. "Comin' up to see us?"

Draper bent a little in his saddle and looked down at Lin, who had stopped beside the road. "What you doin' down here?" Draper demanded.

Lin grinned, his teeth flashing white in the moonlight. "We've got a herd up the road a piece," he said. "Big steers. They scare awful easy, an' me an' one of the boys thought we'd ride down here an' make sure nobody come along to scare 'em. It would sure be bad if a man got caught in a stampede in this country."

In the darkness of the pine clump Sacatone rasped: "Whoa, you damned jughead!"

"Havin' trouble with his horse," Lin explained cheerfully. "If you boys are headed up the canyon I'll side you past the herd."

Draper found his voice. "We just rode out to see how you made it," he said, his accent belying every friendly word. "Guess we'll go back to town now."

Sacatone was still in the shadow of the pine clump, his motions making his presence audible. Lin grinned up at the mounted men. "Better come on to camp an' have a cup of coffee," he invited.

"No," Draper drawled. "We'll just shove along back. Glad to see you're lookin' after the steers so careful, McCord."

"It was neighborly of you to come out," Lin replied. "Come see us when we get 'em home. You're always welcome, you an' your friend."

"Thanks." Draper reined his horse around. "Come on, Spike."

Lin stepped back, and Draper and his companion rode back down the road. When they had gone perhaps a hundred feet Draper stopped his horse. "I said this was a damned-fool idea," he called back. "Don't think it was mine, McCord."

Lin made no answer, and Draper started his horse again, loping to catch up with Spike Samms who had not stopped.

When the sounds of their horses had died away Sacatone came riding out from the pines, an unwonted grin creasing his thin face. The whole thing had tickled Sacatone, stirred his sense of humor. His rifle was across his saddlebows and he rode up to Lin and stopped. "Goin' to stay a while longer?" Sacatone asked.

Lin shook his head. "They're all through for the night," he answered.

"I had my sights lined right on that fellow's brisket," Sacatone said regretfully. "I thought maybe he'd try."

"Not him," Lin said. "He's smart. Like he said, this wasn't his idea. Right now he's takin' orders. I hope he don't get to givin' 'em. Let's go home, Sac."

The following morning, before day was well born, the steers moved on. All that morning they marched and well into the afternoon, winding along the road up Pinál Canyon, a mottled snake of cattle. By midafternoon they were almost at the top, and by five o'clock the steers were through the lower fence and the riders were shoving them on out to grass while Windy and McBride hazed the remuda toward the barn and the corrals.

Coming back from the herd, Lin dropped wearily from his saddle and looked up at Eleanor Patrick who stood on the porch. "Well," he announced, "there's half of 'em. What do you think?"

The girl's eyes were alive with interest. "I've never seen so many cows," she said. "I didn't know there could be so many."

"Steers," Lin corrected automatically. "There's lots more where those come from. We bought 'em from Terrazas, an' I guess he's got a hundred thousand anyhow."

Lin's horse swung his head against his rider, a reminder that the day was done, and Lin reached out and scratched a bay cheek.

"I like your horses," Eleanor said.

"Buck's a pretty good pony," Lin answered. "I've got some horses that you could ride if you'd like to go out tomorrow an' look at the cattle. There's Chub an' Light-foot that are all right an' gentle." He made the offer diffidently, not sure of its reception.

The girl laughed. "I was just going to ask you if I couldn't go," she confided. "What time will you start?"

"Will six o'clock be too early?" Lin asked, setting the time an hour later than his usual time of departure.

"You come and have breakfast with us and I'll be ready," the girl agreed, her eyes dancing.

"Hey, Lin," Windy called from the corral. "Can you come down here a minute?"

"I'll be up for breakfast," Lin promised and, smiling, mounted and rode down to answer Windy's call.

So it was that the next morning Lin McCord and Eleanor Patrick rode out across the mesa. The steers, tired, had not drifted far but were in the big park west of the house, grazing on the tall grama. Lin had sent Windy and two men to work on the west fence. The others, under Sacatone's direction, were repairing the gaps in the short fences that blocked the canyons leading to the east. The two, man and woman, rode through the cattle, looking them over, watching big steers, contented and grazing steadily, lift their heads and move sedately away as the riders approached.

The two rode on to the west fence and saw Windy and Lewis, with Shorty Morgan ably assisting, stretch and replace wire that was sagged or down. North of Pinál, as they returned, they visited Sacatone and his crew who were putting up a fence across Loblolly Canyon, the girl naming the sharp break in the mesa rim for Lin. When they left Sacatone it was eleven o'clock, and

Eleanor let Lightfoot gallop; Lin, on big dun Jug, loping along behind and admiring every movement the girl made. When she pulled Lightfoot up to a walk again, Lin reined in beside her.

"You ride mighty good," he said, grinning. "I've a mind to put you on the pay roll for a hand."

The girl's echoing smile was bright. "I love to ride," she said. "Maybe I'll strike you for a job, Mr. McCord."

"Any time," Lin agreed.

He was looking at the girl as he spoke, and she must have read through his eyes something of what was in his mind. She turned her head away quickly.

"Almost noon," she said. "I've Dad's lunch to get. Come on!" Once more Lightfoot lifted into a run.

That afternoon Lin, toiling with Windy at the west fence, straightened and wiped the sweat from his forehead. The others were further along the fence and he and Windy were alone. "Windy," Lin said seriously, "you've known me a long time. What kind of a fellow do you think I am?"

Windy was resetting a post, tamping down dirt. He looked at Lin as though seeing an apparition. "Why, yo're all right, Lin," he said, amazement in his voice. "What's got into you, anyway?"

"Nothin'," Lin answered. "I just got to thinkin'."

A slow smile broke over Windy's long face, exposing his two gold teeth. "I've got to thinkin' that-a-way too," he drawled. "Don't do it, Lin. This of business about two livin' cheap as one is all a damned lie!"

Lin jabbed the posthole digger down into the dirt. "Who said anythin' about gettin' married?" he snapped.

"Can't a man ask a question?"

"Uh-huh," Windy answered. "He can ask a heap of 'em, but the one that gits him is when he asks 'Will you marry me?' That gits the best of 'em."

"Shut up!" Lin growled, and came down vigorously with the posthole digger.

For a week there was activity atop Rough Mesa. Twice during that week Eleanor Patrick rode with Lin when he looked over the cattle. The steers were located now, little bunches staying together, going in to water together. They had spread out, and a ride covered more territory. Three times, after supper, Lin wandered down from the house that was used as a camp and sat on the Patrick porch until dark came, not talking, just content to sit there on the steps, hearing the creak of Eleanor's rocker and her voice as occasionally she addressed some question or comment to him or to her father. Then at the end of the week Windy brought a letter out from Adelphi. John McCord was coming with the second trainload of steers.

CHAPTER V
THE LAME AND THE HALT

LIN AND SACATONE MET JOHN MCCORD IN JUNCTION. Windy, with the rest of the crew, was to come to Adelphi and receive the cattle; but Lin was anxious to see his brother, anxious to know how John was, both mentally and physically. The cattle train arrived about two o'clock in the morning, and Lin was at the depot when the engine's headlight came thrusting through the darkness.

As the train rolled to a stop Lin and Sacatone crunched along the cinders toward the caboose. Momentarily one rear marker was obliterated as a man's body interposed, and then the conductor alighted, lantern on his arm. Immediately following the trainman, John McCord got down. In the light of the trainman's lantern he appeared, an older edition of Lin but with definite differences. John McCord's face was not so rugged as that of his brother; his lips were thinner and drooped a trifle at the corners, and there were lines that spoke of petulance. The face lighted in a smile now as he saw Lin and Sacatone, and with a step he reached the two men and was pumphandling Lin's hand. "How are things at the lease?" John asked.

"Good," Lin said heartily. "We got there, an' the steers are takin' to that grama like a sick kitten to a hot rock. Everything all right with you, John?"

"Fine," John McCord answered. "We came through in good shape. How long will it take us to get to Adelphi?"

"About five hours after we pull out of here," Lin said. "Windy an' the crew will meet us there. Where's Bobby, John?"

"Sleepin'." John grinned broadly. "He was goin' to sit up with me till we got in, but he played his hand out an' went to bed. Carl's with him."

By mutual consent the men climbed up on the caboose platform. Inside the car they saw Carl Yetman, fat, placid and round-faced, sitting beside a sleeping boy. John McCord reached down and touched his son's shoulder.

"Wake up, Bobby," he commanded. "We're here."

Blue eyes blinked sleepily and then Bobby McCord sat up. He looked at Lin and then past Lin to where Sacatone stood waiting. Instantly the blanket that wrapped the boy was kicked aside and Bobby was on his feet. "Sac!" he exclaimed.

"I see yuh got here all right," Sacatone said gruffly. Bobby took two hitching steps, his right leg dragging, and Sacatone's big hands, their tenderness belying the gruffness of his voice, lifted him up.

"I brought the steers through all right too, Sac," Bobby declared. "They're fine. We never had but three get down on us."

"Pretty good cowpuncher you are," Sacatone answered. "Just a pretty fair hand."

Lin and John had stood by, witnessing the little scene. Now Lin turned to Yetman and shook hands. "We've been waitin' for you, Carl," he said. "We've all of us kind of been hungry for your cookin'."

"Yah, you bat you," Yetman grunted. "I fix you up pretty soon."

The conductor thrust his head into the car. "We're goin' to switch now," he announced. "You fellows better get what you want off of here. We're changin' cabooses."

John McCord, Lin and Yetman unloaded beds, saddles, grips and two clanging gunny sacks that contained Yetman's pots and skillets. A switch engine came chuffing through the night to bump the caboose and pull it away, and the men, their belongings carried to the depot and stored there, walked on toward the town, intent on finding a restaurant that was open. Sacatone carried Bobby, holding the boy high on his shoulder, never letting him put foot to the ground.

"I see you've got your horse back, Bobby," John McCord said.

"Quite a walk to town," Sacatone announced, making no move to put the boy down. "Guess you can ride me till you get a horse, huh, Bobby?"

"I can walk all right," Bobby said sturdily. "You can put me down, Sac."

"Plenty walkin' at the lease," Sacatone grunted, and kept the boy on his shoulder.

Reinforced with breakfast, the men returned to the depot. The switchmen were almost finished with the train and, not longer than half an hour after they returned, Lin and John, Bobby, Sacatone and Carl Yetman were loading their belongings on a caboose and climbing up.

At Adelphi Windy was waiting with the crew. He had brought the men down from the ranch, together with horses and a cooking outfit. Yetman immediately supplanted McBride as cook, and McBride, coming over to Lin, complained:

"I thought I was cookin'."

John McCord, standing by Lin, looked at McBride. "Carl's the regular cook," he said shortly. "You can punch cows."

McBride still looked at Lin. Lin had hired him and,

according to McBride's philosophy, was the boss.

Lin nodded. "You help move cattle, Cal," he agreed; and McBride, his face still wearing a scowl, went back to join his companions.

With the spring sun high overhead the crew unloaded steers. At noon Yetman called them gruffly and they went to dinner. Yetman was a cook. With the meager supplies brought down from the lease, and with a few additions from the gunny sacks, he had made a tasty meal from potatoes, salt pork, his sourdough crock and canned corn. The men enjoyed the meal, even McBride, still somewhat disgruntled, looking respectfully at the fat cook.

On into the afternoon the crew worked, the steers coming from the cars to the pens, from the pens to the herd growing on the prairie. It was John McCord who gave the orders, John McCord who, when the last car was clear, placed the men and gave the word to start. Lin was content to have it so. True, it was largely his money that had bought these cattle, true that he had made the lease; but this whole business, this whole idea of leasing land and buying Mexico cattle, had but one real purpose: to interest John McCord once more, to stabilize him and give him something that he could grip. There can be but one boss on a cow outfit. Lin was satisfied that John should be that boss.

A few small boys and a loafer or two had come out from town to see the unloading. Aside from these there was no audience. Adelphi showed no interest. This suited Lin. He had said nothing to John of the difficulties already encountered. He did not want to worry John or sidetrack him. Lin knew his brother thoroughly and he knew John's temper. Given but an opportunity and John McCord could flare into a killing rage.

Under John's orders they strung the cattle out and started with them. Now it was Lin who rode the point, John opposite him, and Sacatone and Windy who had the drag. Yetman, fat and competent, was dealing with the kitchen and the remuda. There was no need to tell Carl Yetman what to do; he was a veteran. Bobby rode with his father, and Shorty Morgan, coming up to Lin as the cattle started, commented on that fact.

"Can the kid make it all right?" Shorty asked.

"John will look after him," Lin answered. "Bobby had infantile paralysis. It's hurt his right leg an' he can't use it good except with that brace, but he'll ride all right."

Shorty nodded and rode away. Lin followed the little man with his eyes. Shorty had the makings of a real one, Lin thought. He fitted in. Already the McCord outfit was Shorty's outfit, the McCord horses were the best horses, the McCord steers the best steers. Shorty had the makings, and Lin intended to keep him on after the rest of the hands were paid off.

They camped that night at the creek, and John McCord placed the guards. Sacatone, coming up to Lin, spoke quietly after the guards had been tolled off. "Think we'd better drop back?" Sacatone asked.

Lin shook his head. "They won't try that again," he said. "They know we're watchin'. Just keep your ears open, Sacatone, an' don't say anything to John. I don't want him riled up."

For an instant Sacatone looked steadily at Lin and then reluctantly he nodded. "All right," he agreed.

Lin was relieved when Sacatone gave consent. The first hump was over. He had been afraid that Sacatone would go to John with the whole story and excite him.

Most of the night Lin stayed awake. John McCord too, like any good trail boss, stood a full night's guard. Three or four times Lin heard John get up, take his horse and go out to the steers. Lin himself made one inspection with his brother. In the morning, early, they went on, pushing the cattle along.

When the lease was reached Lin and John dropped off, leaving the others to throw the cattle out on the grass. With John and Bobby beside him, Lin rode back to the Patrick house and there, dismounting, summoned Eleanor to the porch. When the girl made her appearance introductions were made, and then the brothers and the small boy rode on to the house that was used by the crew.

"I don't know that I like that setup any too well," John McCord said as they rode. "I don't think that it's a good thing to have the owner around a leased outfit. First thing you know, she'll be puttin' her nose in our business."

"I don't think so," Lin answered easily. "The Patricks don't have any place to go and this is home to them. Anyhow, she reserved the house and a place over south when we made the lease."

"What place over south?" John demanded.

"Her mother's buried over there," Lin said. "It's just a patch."

John was silent, his face moody and his eyes blank with retrospection. Lin knew of what his brother thought. John was thinking about another grave back in Duffyville.

"How'd you like the grass, John?" Lin asked, seeking to break through those thoughts.

"It's all right," John said absently.

"You'll pay off the spare hands tomorrow?" Still Lin insisted on breaking into his brother's thoughts. "I'd like to keep that little redheaded Morgan. We can use another man up here pretty easy."

"You an' me an' Windy an' Sacatone will be enough," John said shortly. "No use in the extra expense."

Lin grinned. "You're the boss," he said easily.

The following morning John wrote checks for the extra hands and paid them off. Sacatone he directed to go to town with the hands and bring back the horses. Beds were piled in a buckboard borrowed from the Patricks. Windy was directed to drive the buckboard, and the crew, hired only to move the steers, bade Lin and John good-by, said "So long" to Carl Yetman and pulled out.

With the leave-taking of the crew, John and Lin prepared to make a general inspection of the lease and to look at the cattle. Bobby had disappeared immediately after breakfast. When the brothers saddled and came by the house, Yetman told them that Bobby had gone down to Patricks' and would soon be back. So John and Lin rode off, and the little clump of houses was deserted save only for the cook.

Bobby had gone down to the Patrick house. That long

log structure intrigued him, and in all his eleven years Bobby McCord had never met a stranger. Nor did he meet one now. Eleanor Patrick, working in the kitchen, heard a dragging step on the porch and, going to the door, saw a dark-haired, bright-faced youngster standing there.

"I'm Bobby," the young man announced. "I was with Dad an' Uncle Lin when we came. You remember?"

Eleanor smiled and said that she remembered and was glad to see him. "Won't you come in?" she invited. "I'm baking cookies."

"I smelled 'em." Bobby came toward her, dragging his leg. The girl, noting that dragging gait, felt a sudden pang of pity. Bobby must have seen the hurt in her eyes.

"Don't mind my leg," he said cheerfully. "I don't. Uncle Lin says that a fellow is all right as long as he's got two legs an' can fork a horse. I'm goin' to be a cowman an' a cowman does his work on horseback. Only farmers work afoot, anyhow. How do you make cookies?"

Eleanor pulled out a kitchen stool. "Wash your hands and you can help," she invited. "You cut them out and I'll put them in the pan."

For half an hour Bobby helped, then the first cookies came from the oven and he had a handful. Sitting still had palled, and when Eleanor came back to the kitchen after a brief visit to her room Bobby was gone. The girl smiled and went on with her work. She liked Bobby McCord. In fact—and here her deft hands ceased their motions and were quiet—she liked all the McCords. Lin McCord—Eleanor blushed although there was no

69

one in the kitchen—Lin McCord, she admitted to herself, she might come to more than like.

Bobby, munching cookies, circled the house. When he reached the front porch he stopped. There was a man sitting on the porch, his knees wrapped in a blanket and his face turned toward the western vista. Bobby came cumbersomely up the steps, braced leg dragging, and gave greeting.

"Hello."

Dan Patrick turned his head and looked at the boy. "Hello," he returned, a little interest flickering in his eyes. "Who are you, young man?"

"Bobby McCord. Who are you?"

For the first time in a good many months Dan Patrick chuckled. The brightness of the boy, his serene indifference to matters of age, ownership or anything else, pleased the older man. "I'm Dan Patrick," he answered.

"Oh," Bobby said, and then with a wave of his hand: "You own this place, don't you?"

"Yes," Patrick admitted. "I own it."

Bobby came closer, pulling his leg along. "Are you sick?" he asked.

"Why . . ." Patrick looked down at his blanketed knees. "I've been sick."

"You're con-va-les-cent then," Bobby announced, pronouncing each syllable of the big word carefully. "That's what mother told me I was."

Patrick nodded. "I guess I'm convalescent," he answered. "Is your mother with you?"

Bobby shook his head. "Mother's dead," he said briefly.

70

"Oh. I'm sorry."

"Uncle Lin says that it was hard luck but that a man has got to stand up to hard luck," Bobby explained. "I miss her though. It's all right to miss her as long as I don't play baby and cry."

"I see," Dan Patrick said.

"An' sittin' around feelin' sorry is just cryin' without bawlin'," Bobby continued. "I used to do that but I don't now."

"And what do you do now?"

"I ride an' look after cattle an' exercise my leg." Bobby placed his hand on the steel brace. "I can make four steps without the brace now. Want to see me?"

Patrick turned his head away. There was hurt in his eyes. Bobby spoke cheerfully. "You needn't if you don't want to. Mother used to say that it distressed people sometimes. Are you distressed?"

"I'm not distressed, Bobby," Dan Patrick answered. "Come over and sit down and we'll talk a while."

Bobby moved toward a vacant chair. "Want a cookie?" he asked. "They're good cookies. I helped make 'em."

Gravely Dan Patrick reached out a hand and took a cookie.

Eleanor, coming into the living room perhaps an hour after Bobby's departure, heard voices on the porch and then a man's laugh. Not believing her ears, she hurried to the door. Dan Patrick and Bobby McCord, the best of friends, were talking.

"Sacatone said I looked just exactly like a jay bird," Bobby completed the story he was telling. "He said I sailed up clear over the barn. I didn't, of course, but I never carried anything on Chub again."

"But you rode Chub?" Patrick asked.

"Sure I rode him. I had to show him he didn't have me bluffed, didn't I?"

"Being what you are, I guess you had to show him," Dan Patrick agreed. "I guess you did, Bobby."

Very softly, careful not to make a sound, Eleanor Patrick retired from the open door. There was just a glint of tears in her eyes. Once more Dan Patrick's laugh echoed on the porch.

When Bobby, summoned by Carl Yetman's call, made ready to leave Eleanor came to the door again. There was a big sack of cookies in her hand. "These are for you," she said, extending the sack. "You'll come back, Bobby?"

"Thanks." Bobby took the sack. "You bet I will. You come to see us."

"We'll come up," Dan Patrick said. "Be sure and come back, son."

"Good-by." Bobby hobbled down the steps, taking them one at a time; then, leg dragging, he started to the camp. "I'm comin', Carl!" he called shrilly.

On the porch, after the boy's departure, there was silence. Dan Patrick broke it. "He'll go through life crippled," Patrick said slowly. "All his life he'll drag that leg. He's never had the use of it, he told me."

"But he won't know he's crippled," Eleanor said softly, "or if he does know he won't admit it."

"Brave," Patrick said, not answering his daughter but following Bobby with his eyes. "That's real bravery."

The girl was silent. Patrick pushed himself up from his chair and she took a swift step to aid him.

"No," Dan Patrick said, and there was a ring in his voice, a tone that the girl had never heard before. "I don't need help, daughter. I'm all right. I can make it."

Eleanor stepped back and Dan Patrick, alone and unaided save by the chair back, straightened and then slowly moved toward the door.

CHAPTER VI
TO LIVE AGAIN

FOR ALMOST TWO WEEKS JOHN McCORD HELD HIS interest in the lease. He rode the pastureland, he ate heartily, he was jovial with Bobby and jocular with Lin and Sacatone and Windy. Lin, noting his brother's interest with satisfaction, felt that this plan of his was worth while, that this scheme of running steers was more than paying for itself, no matter what the market might be in the fall. But at the end of the second week John McCord's interest began to flag, and before the third week was over it had failed completely. He no longer rode with the others. He was faultfinding and querulous. Lin, having lent Eleanor a horse and ridden with her, was told tartly that company horses were for company business. Windy took a sharp reproof over the minor matter of not closing a gate, although he had but gone through intending to return immediately. Sacatone was roundly taken to task; Carl Yetman's cooking came in for some criticism, and Bobby was tersely told to

73

keep still when he was in the midst of an eager recounting of his day's exploits. One man can cause plenty of trouble, can make plenty of hell in a little camp, and John McCord devoted considerable time to his attempts.

The others took it. Lin, worried and distracted, talked placatingly to Windy and soothed that big man's feelings. "What he needs," Windy stated with conviction, "is a right damned good lickin' to take his mind off hisse'f, an' I'm just the button that can give it to him."

There was no doubt that Windy was right on both counts. John did need a beating and Windy was perfectly capable of administering the medicine, Windy having gained his gold teeth and broken nose in a few seasons spent in the prize ring. But Lin shook his head and talked soothingly, and Windy's ruffled feathers were smoothed.

Sacatone, under John's sarcasm, became more and more reticent. To Sacatone, John could do no wrong, and so instead of becoming angry with his idol Sacatone vented his spleen on the others. Carl Yetman went right ahead with his chores and cooking, muttering Dutch expletives under his breath. And then the tension eased. John McCord went to town and when he came back he was cheerful.

His brother's good humor did not allay Lin's worry. He knew what made John cheerful, had caught the odor of whisky when John came back, and Lin's anxiety grew. Before his wife's death John McCord had not been a drinking man; he had turned to whisky only after his wife was gone. A little whisky made John forget, cheered him, buoyed his spirits; but John would not stop with a little liquor. A slow start and a strong finish, that was John McCord, and when he had more than a drink or two he was ugly, quarrelsome and strange almost to the point of insanity. There was no foretelling John McCord when he was drunk.

Still Lin did not voice his fears, either to John or the others, hoping that this was a brief flurry that would soon be over. He tried to interest his brother in the lease and the cattle once more, with no success. John went back to town the following Saturday and did not come in until Sunday night, and when Lin spoke to him concerning his absence, reminding him of what had happened on preceding occasions, John's temper flared.

"I'm no damned kid!" he snapped. "I know what I'm doing. If you don't like it, get out. You don't have to stay!"

Lin did not remind John that it was not his place to get out, that he, Lin McCord, owned most of the cattle and held the principal interest in the partnership. Instead he turned and walked away, leaving John to himself. Usually when the whisky was out of him John became contrite and more himself, and Lin waited for time to do what he himself had failed to accomplish.

But John had brought some liquor back with him. He drank it, not all at once but steadily, a little at a time, and in place of its cheering him, John became more and more morose with unexpected outbreaks of cruelty. On Wednesday John went to Adelphi again.

The social center of Adelphi for those men who had no wives was the Exchange Saloon. Fred Lyten ran the

Exchange and, to all appearances, was the owner. In reality the Exchange, like everything else in Adelphi, excepting only the railroad, belonged to Otis Melcomb. John McCord, reaching the little town late in the evening, dropped into the Exchange for a drink before supper. Melcomb was at the bar talking to Lyten when John came in.

"That one of the McCords?" he asked the saloon man, noting John's similarity to Lin.

"Yeah," Lyten answered, watching his bartender serve John's drink. "John McCord. He's been in a couple of times."

"What does he do?" Melcomb's eyes did not leave John.

"Drinks some, plays a few cards," Lyten said. "He was in that little game that Ed Draper runs last time he was here. Won a few dollars, Ed said."

"Treat him right," Melcomb snapped. "Make him like to come in here."

"Sure," Lyten agreed.

Melcomb, leaving Lyten, moved along the bar. Beside John he stopped and signaled the bartender. "Sunnybrook," he ordered when the bartender approached, and then, turning to John and with much good fellowship in his voice: "I'll buy a drink."

John McCord, at the moment, was feeling lonely and abused. A man is apt to feel that way when he knows that he is doing the wrong thing, and John was remembering what Lin had said. He turned to Melcomb. "Don't care if I do take one," he said, returning the smile on Melcomb's face. The bartender set the Sunnybrook bottle on the bar and John poured his drink.

"Here's to crime," Melcomb said, and tossed off his drink. John also put his whisky down and replaced the glass on the bar.

"My name's Melcomb." The big man held out his hand.

"John McCord." John took the extended hand. "I've got some cattle on Rough Mesa."

"Oh yes," Melcomb said. "I've met your brother. Nice fellow."

"Lin's all right." John McCord's tone left some doubt that he meant exactly what he said.

"He seemed to think I was trying to put one over on him when he first came," Melcomb said, watching John narrowly. He did not know how much John McCord had been told, did not know where John stood.

"Lin always thinks somebody's tryin' to put somethin' over on him," John answered. "I'll buy this drink, Mr. Melcomb."

Again the glasses were filled and emptied. Melcomb sensed a little feeling of elation. Evidently this McCord was no enemy. "Have supper with me," the big man invited cordially. "I just dropped in for a drink before I ate."

"So did I." John smiled at a kindred spirit.

Together the men started for the door. Before they reached it the shutters opened and a tall man, thin to the point of emaciation, came into the Exchange. Stopping inside the door, he greeted Melcomb. "Hello, Otis."

"Why, hello, Walter," Melcomb returned, and then, his hand on John's arm: "Mr. McCord, I want you to meet the smartest lawyer that ever put one over on a jury. This is Walter Yawl. John McCord, Walter."

Yawl shook hands. "I've met your brother, Mr. McCord," he said. "In fact, I drew a legal paper for him some time ago. I'm glad to meet you."

"Thanks," John McCord replied.

"We're just going to supper, Walter," Melcomb said. "Will you join us?"

"I came in for a drink," Yawl replied, "but I suppose that can be postponed."

"Never postpone a drink," Melcomb boomed. "How about it, McCord? We'll take one with him, won't we?"

John was agreeable. The drinks were taken and the three men went out of the Exchange.

At the hotel, where Melcomb declared that he was buying the meal, they separated briefly, John going to the washroom, Melcomb and Yawl remaining in the lobby. Until the moment of the lawyer's declaration, Melcomb had had no definite plan in mind. He had made himself agreeable to John McCord, thinking only that he might get some information, might have a friend in the enemy's camp. Now he had another idea.

"Did you draw that lease on Rough Mesa for the Patrick girl, Walter?" Melcomb asked when McCord was gone.

"Yes," Yawl answered.

"What was in it?" Melcomb spoke hurriedly. "Anything about the timber?"

Yawl frowned as he tried to recall the terms of the lease. "I don't think so," he said. "There was no specific mention of the timber. As I recall, there were only two specifications besides the regular form. The girl reserved the house and a small tract that contained her mother's grave."

"If I got a sublease on it, would that include the timber?" Melcomb demanded.

Yawl shrugged. "You could at least take it to court," he said. "I think that, properly handled, you might win a case like that."

Melcomb nodded. "And it would make work for the lawyers," he said. "All right. You stay with me, Walter. There'll be some money in this for you."

"What are you planning?" Yawl asked. "Are you . . . ?"

"Stick around," Melcomb said. "And don't talk. He's coming back."

John McCord rejoined the two, lumberman and lawyer, and the three went into the dining room together.

During the meal Melcomb was expansive. He talked to Yawl and he talked to McCord. He asked John McCord's opinion concerning various matters and seemed to defer to it. John McCord was made to feel that he was a big man, confidant of other big men. Under that treatment he expanded.

After the meal the men repaired to the Exchange, going to a table in the rear of the room, and sat together. Melcomb was entertaining, he was agreeable, and he bought drinks. John took them. He did not know that after the second round Melcomb's drink was heavily watered and that Yawl took a highball and stretched it out for two or three rounds. Ed Draper came in, accom-

79

panied by Spike Samms and two of the straw bosses from the camps. The boss sawyer and two men from the planing mill were at the bar. It was a good night in the Exchange. Melcomb excused himself momentarily and went to talk to Draper.

"I want you to run a game tonight," he instructed the brown-faced marshal. "John McCord's back there and I want him in it."

Samms pushed forward. "You—" he began.

"I don't want any trouble," Melcomb interposed swiftly. "This is John McCord, the other one's brother. We'll be in the game and I want him to win a little right along. I want him feeling good."

Draper's face was impassive. "You've had some ideas," he said slowly. "Most of 'em no good. What's this one?"

"Never mind what it is, it'll work!" Melcomb snapped. "Remember, McCord wins some money." Draper nodded and Melcomb returned to his companions.

After a time Draper and Spike Samms drifted back. Melcomb, John and Yawl occupied the only card table. Draper was friendly and asked if they might have the table as they wanted to play poker. Melcomb was agreeable and suggested that he take a hand himself. Yawl was declared in and John McCord, not to be outdone by the others, said that he would also take a hand. Cards and chips were brought from the bar, the stakes decided upon and, with Melcomb banking, the game began.

The drinks had warmed John, mellowed him. Taken

on top of a big meal, they had not yet so affected him that he became ugly. Indeed, the whole world was friendly to John McCord and when he began to win, when the chips in front of him grew in number, he was more than friendly.

The other players in the game flattered him, backed out of pots when he was bluffing, built up pots when he had a hand. It seemed to John McCord that he could do no wrong, that whatever he did was right.

The men in the game were voluble. Melcomb kept up a rumbling and humorous conversation; Yawl chipped in with thin-lipped humor. Even Draper added his bit. Only Spike Samms glowered and was silent. Somehow the talk veered to timber. Melcomb made humorous comment about the scarcity of good stands. Yawl suggested that there was plenty of timber in the world and not much whisky. They had another drink. The talk went on, John McCord doing his full share and more.

"But I tell you that timber's scarce in this country," Melcomb continued. "Good timber, that is. We've got a year's cut ahead of us and then we fold up, like that." He snapped his fingers.

"Nonsense, Otis," Yawl refuted; "there's plenty of timber. Look at McCord's lease. There's a stand of timber for you!"

"Lots of trees on the lease," John agreed. "Lots of timber."

"But you own it and I don't." Melcomb made a wry grimace. "That's the hell of it."

"Sure I own it," John McCord nodded confidently, "but it's for sale. I'll sell anythin' if I can see a profit.

That's the way to do. Always take a profit."

"You're sure right," Melcomb agreed heartily. "But you just lease that country; you can't sell it."

"Got a lease with renewal option." McCord looked exceedingly wise. "Always make a lease that way. Might just as well say I own it."

"Well, how about it, then?" Melcomb demanded. "You don't want the timber and I do. I'll give you a profit on it."

John McCord did not know just how it happened, but suddenly Yawl had produced paper and a pen and was writing. Melcomb was beaming and producing a checkbook, and he, John McCord, was agreeing to sell a sublease and the timber rights on Rough Mesa.

"I wish I could make money that easy," Melcomb stated complacently, folding the lease and putting it in his pocket. "Here's your check for five hundred. I call you a smart businessman, Mr. McCord."

"Always take a profit," John McCord advised owlishly. "Always."

"Sure," Melcomb agreed. "Always."

For two days John McCord stayed in Adelphi. The first day he spent drinking. On the second day he found a marvelous opportunity for investment. Under Walter Yawl's suggestion he bought two hundred acres of cutover land for two dollars and a half an acre. Yawl showed him just how Adelphi would grow and his newly purchased property become very valuable city lots. John endorsed the check to Melcomb and received a deed. On the morning of the third day the hostler at the livery barn poured John McCord into his saddle and started him toward the mesa. John was riding Redskin and Redskin knew the way home. He took his master there. Carl Yetman was at the camp alone when John arrived, and Carl helped John dismount and put him to bed. When Lin came in Carl greeted him gloomily.

"Come home drunk," Yetman said. "I put him to bed."

Lin went in and found his brother asleep. "How did he talk when he came in?" Lin asked the cook.

"He don't talk," Carl answered. "He jus' went to sleep."

Frowning, Lin kicked at the corner of the door and then went out. He was going to have to do something about John. Just what, he didn't know, but something had to be done.

In the afternoon John got up, still logy, still feeling the effects of the liquor. Lin's efforts to talk with him brought no response. Lin demanded to know what had happened in town, and finally, because John had to say something, he learned of the land purchase. John, however, made no mention of the lease. Lin left his brother, searched John's coat pocket and found the deed. It made him angry all the way through that John should have wasted money in such a fashion, but there was no use of talking, no use in recriminations. Lin got out the checkbook and deducted five hundred dollars. The balance was pitifully small. Outside he could hear John being sick. Lin was thankful that Bobby was not at home.

Bobby was with Eleanor and Dan Patrick. There had

been a picnic that day, a gala occasion. Sandy Donald had hitched the Patrick team of bays to the buckboard, and Dan and Eleanor and Bobby had driven to the head of Loblolly Canyon. To Bobby it was just a picnic and a mighty good time, but to Eleanor Patrick it was the end of an epoch; it was a high mark, a pinnacle, for Dan Patrick had suggested the picnic, Dan Patrick had made the plans and given the orders and Dan Patrick drove the team.

Since the day of Bobby's first visit a change had come over Dan Patrick; something that was dead in the man had come to life. Eleanor had watched her father's resurrection with unbelieving eyes. Perhaps it was the gameness of the boy, his courage, his contempt for his affliction; perhaps it was Dan Patrick's love for the boy. Whatever it was, the man who had had no life, who had dragged heavily about the house or sat inertly apart, had changed definitely. He refused aid where before he had demanded and expected it. He did for himself. His interest aroused, he entered once more into living. The awakening had not been instantaneous; a man does not break the habits of three years in a night. There were relapses and backslidings, but Bobby, visiting the Patricks daily, seemed intuitively to know what to say and what to do. The day Dan Patrick sat down as though he would never rise again, no matter what happened, Bobby's bad leg tripped him on the porch steps and he fell sprawling to the ground. He got up laughing, and after a little time Dan Patrick arose and walked again. The day that Dan Patrick's chest pained so badly that his face was a wan gray mask, Bobby removed his

84

brace and took his four steps before witnesses, stretching them out to a fifth step, after which he toppled and fell, and laughed. The day the whole world was black and there was no use of trying, Bobby came in with plans for a bow and arrow to take on a bear hunt. That day closed with Dan Patrick's promising to make the bow and go along. And now had come this culmination, this final achievement, this graduation as it were: the picnic.

The three of them ate their lunch in the glen above Loblolly. They drank from the little spring that sent a trickle down the canyon. They talked. They sat very still while Eleanor held out her hand, a cracker on its slender palm, and a chipmunk, bolder and braver than all the rest, risked his life and happiness by dashing across her skirt and snatching the morsel. And in the afternoon they drove home.

Lin heard the buckboard coming and went down to the Patrick house. He did not want Bobby to come home, not as yet. Later, when John was asleep, he would bring Bobby in and put him to bed, but not now. Bobby would ask questions and shrewdly get answers.

"Oh, but we had a good time!" Eleanor Patrick exclaimed as the buckboard stopped. "Bobby and I tamed a chipmunk and raced water bugs in the spring. Are you worn out, Dad?"

"I'm tired," Patrick said deliberately, "but I'm not worn out. This youngster is a bundle of barbed wire and rawhide, McCord."

"Bobby's a hand," Lin agreed, advancing to help Eleanor from the buckboard. "Have a good time, kid?"

"Swell!" Bobby's one word was an accolade.

Dan Patrick got stiffly from the buckboard, almost falling as he came down over the wheel. "I've had some ideas today," he announced, looking at Lin. "When you have some time free I'd like to talk to you about them."

"Sure," Lin agreed. "Can I talk to you a minute, Miss Patrick?"

Her curiosity showing in her eyes, Eleanor followed Lin aside. "I hate to ask you," Lin said, "but can you keep Bobby down here a while? His dad's back from town an' he's not feeling good. Could you keep Bobby?"

"Why, of course!" The curiosity changed to concern. "What's the matter with your brother?"

"He just isn't feeling good," Lin equivocated. "I'm obliged about Bobby. I'll come down for him—and thanks a lot."

He spoke pleasantly to Patrick, told Bobby that he could stay a while longer with the Patricks and walked back toward the camp. When he was gone Eleanor bustled Bobby into the house with the picnic basket.

"It just isn't fair!" she told her father when Bobby was out of sight. "Lin does everything, looks after Bobby and the cattle and everything, and John McCord comes home drunk. I know he's drunk!"

Dan Patrick looked at his daughter with quizzical eyes. "Lin?" he said.

"Yes"—in her anger Eleanor lost the meaning of Patrick's question—"Lin! He does everything, and it isn't fair!"

Dan Patrick's lips twitched. "I guess not, when you look at it that way," he said. "No. I guess it isn't fair."

CHAPTER VII
CHEAT!

WHEN HE RETURNED FOR BOBBY ABOUT NINE O'CLOCK that night Lin did not see Dan Patrick. Dan had gone to bed and was sleeping healthily. Lin thanked Eleanor for looking after the sleepy boy and took Bobby home. It was not until the next day that he talked to Patrick again.

The next day was a hard one. John, sick from the whisky, was savage and surly. Nothing went right, nothing could be done right. Lin, knowing why John was in this humor, tried to keep the peace but failed. Finally, his own temper frayed to shreds, Lin took John aside and laid down the law.

"Listen," he commanded forcefully, "you've blowed off all you're going to. I've had enough of it! You and me are pardners in this business an' I'm your brother, but that doesn't give you license to act the way you are. You've got Windy so mad he's ready to quit. You've got Carl the same way. Sacatone sticks with you, but he's about fed up too. Now you quit actin' like a damned baby an' get a grip on yourself!"

"Or you'll make me, I suppose?" John McCord snapped. "Let me tell you, Lin—"

"You're through tellin'. I'm doing it now! You've got five thousand dollars in this deal; I've got eleven. Either you come into your milk, or you can buy me out or I'll buy you out; but I'll have no more of this damned funny business!"

That was laying it on the line. Lin turned and walked away, and John McCord stood staring incredulously after his brother. He had never seen Lin so worked up, had never before met so directly the force that was in Lin McCord, the thing that drove through, come hell or high water. Lin turned the corner of the bunkhouse, and John McCord sat down on the old bench outside the house. He put his elbows on his knees and, with chin on his cupped hands, John McCord indulged in some serious thinking.

Instinctively Lin made his way to Patricks'. He needed the calming influence he knew he would find at the rambling log house. Eleanor was sweeping the porch, and when Lin saw her he knew that he had found what he sought. He sat down on the porch directly in the path of her broom, and the girl laughed and stopped her work.

"You look as though the whole world was wrong today," she said. "You look as though you'd eaten something sour and seen something you didn't like and heard something that didn't suit you. What's the matter? It's a fine large morning!"

"I guess I am goin' around like a bull that's been pushed out of the herd," Lin answered. "Things aren't suiting me too good."

"Aren't the steers doing all right? Is there something wrong with the lease?"

"The steers are puttin' on weight an' the lease is fine. It might rain a little an' make things better, but outside of that it's all right. It's just me, I guess." Lin studied the toes of his boots intently.

Eleanor laid her broom aside and came down to sit beside Lin. "It's your brother, isn't it?" she asked softly.

Lin nodded, not looking at the girl.

"I knew last night." There was compassion in Eleanor's voice.

"You can't exactly blame John," Lin said, still not looking toward his companion. "He's had some pretty hard things happen to him. His wife was sick a long time, an' John went in debt an' spent money an' worried, and finally she died. Bobby's been crippled for seven years, and John's spent a lot on him too. Then there was a drought an' the market dropped and John lost the ranch. He's had a run of hard luck, all right."

Silence followed the explanation. Lin had not mentioned the money he had given his brother, or the anxious hours he had spent at John's side, or the treatments that he had financed, the brace he had bought for Bobby's leg. There was no need to speak of them.

"But he had her," Lin said suddenly. "He had ten years with her that nobody can take away from him. They were mighty happy together, John an' Molly were. I guess they had their heaven. And that makes the hell he's going through now all the worse."

There was a soft hand on Lin's sleeve. He looked down at the hand and then at the girl that owned it. "I shouldn't be telling you my troubles," Lin said.

"I'm glad you did, Lin."

Again the silence hung, pregnant, between them. Eleanor Patrick's eyes were wide and there was a light in them that Lin had never seen before in a woman's eyes. Perhaps his own reflected that light, for the girl turned her gaze away. Behind them the door opened and Eleanor sprang up. Lin got slowly to his feet and looked around. Dan Patrick had come out on the porch.

Patrick came deliberately down the steps, one at a time, stopped and looked down at Lin. Eleanor was sweeping again, moving the broom hurriedly as though to hide the emotion she had shown so fleetingly. Patrick stood a long moment and then spoke. "Lin," he said, "I want to start the mill again."

"Good for you!" There was no mistaking Lin's sincerity. "That's fine, Mr. Patrick!"

Dan Patrick sat down heavily, holding his cane between his knees. "Sit down, Lin," he commanded. "I want to talk to you."

Lin sat down.

"I've been idle long enough," Patrick said. "I've sat around and felt sorry for myself and brooded on my grievances. Now I'm through with that. I'm going back to work."

"Any way I can help, Mr. Patrick?" Lin asked quietly.

"That's what I want to talk about. I've got to have some help." Both men were quiet while Patrick collected his thoughts, ordering them into what he wanted to say.

"I can't operate the mill right away," he announced finally. "I've got to spend some money on it first. Before I can spend the money, I've got to make some. We were in debt before you bought this lease, Lin, and we've paid those debts and been living on what you paid us. There isn't enough left to put the mill in shape."

"I've got enough to squeeze through till fall," Lin said

90

regretfully. "That's all, Mr. Patrick. We owe about eight dollars a head on the steers. They're goin' to bring some cash. As soon as we sell 'em, I can let you have what you need, but that won't be till November."

Patrick shook his head. "I don't want to borrow money," he announced. "I've got another plan. I can get a crew in here, a few men, and cut ties and mine props and perhaps some piles. There's a market for them, and if I operate that way I won't touch the saw timber. In three or four months I can have a little stake. Then I'll put the mill in shape and go to sawing. No, it isn't money I want."

"Then what?" Lin asked.

"I've got to get my props and ties to the railroad," Patrick said. "We've a few wagons that might do with a little work, but I haven't any horses. What I need is transportation." He looked expectantly at Lin.

For a long moment Lin studied the ground. "I've got cow horses," he said slowly, turning to Patrick again. "They're not work stock. They wouldn't do."

Disappointment came into Patrick's face. "Well . . ." he said, shifting the cane as though to rise.

"Wait a minute," Lin commanded. "My horses wouldn't do you any good, an' working 'em would ruin them for me. But I've got something else."

"What?" Patrick demanded.

Lin pointed out across the vista that lay before the log house. There in the deep grass of the park were bunches of steers, fifteen or twenty of them, grazing. "You're lookin' at some of the finest oxen you ever saw, Mr. Patrick," he said. "I don't guess you care how fast those props an' ties ride, do you, as long as they get there? Carve out some oxbows, round up some steers an' turn me an' Windy loose a while. There's your transportation!"

Patrick's hand came down on his leg with a resounding slap. "I would never have thought of it," he exclaimed jubilantly. "Of course. Oxen! That's the perfect answer."

"Well," Lin drawled, excitement in his own voice, "you can do most anything with a steer. I just happened to think of that."

"I'll pay you," Patrick said. "We'll make a deal."

"We'll get the oxbows an' the goosenecks an' some more stuff first," Lin answered. "We're goin' to have to spend a little money, Mr. Patrick."

"We can spend a little. I'm going to send Sandy out tomorrow. He'll get a crew of choppers. I tell you, Lin, it will work!"

"Sure it'll work," Lin agreed. "You watch us make it work."

Excited and happy as two boys, the men made plans. Eleanor, beaming, proud of her father, prouder of Lin, listened and presently hurried into the house. She returned carrying three small glasses and a bottle.

"Wine," she said. "It's some that I bought for you, Dad, when you were ill. We'll drink a toast to the new firm: Patrick and McCord!"

"We'll drink it standin' up," Lin said, and once again his eyes sought the girl's own.

It was not so simple as it had seemed there on the

92

porch; the business of breaking steers to haul, of getting oxbows and chain, goosenecks and the other paraphernalia. It is one thing to plan and another to accomplish. Sandy Donald, dispatched by Dan Patrick, drove away in the buckboard and was gone for three days. When he returned he had hired eight men, experienced choppers.

Lin, talking to Windy and Sacatone, with Carl Yetman and John silent listeners, explained his idea. Sacatone put a spoke in the wheel.

"You ever break any steers?" Sacatone asked.

"No," Lin answered.

"Nobody knows how." Sacatone looked around the little group. "That's fine for a start."

Lin looked his astonishment. He had seen oxen at work, had seen them used; it had never occurred to him that breaking steers to the yoke was not a simple process.

"Nobody knows how to make yokes; nobody knows a damned thing about it." Sacatone drove his point home.

Silence, prelude to gloom, descended upon the circle. Carl Yetman broke it. "Except me," Carl said.

Every eye turned toward the fat cook. Carl nodded. "In Luxemburg I haff driven oxen," he said solemnly. "I haff also made the yokes. In Luxemburg."

Lin grinned, first at Sacatone, then at Carl. "I guess it won't be any different here," he said. "Looks like we'll have to take you off the cookin', Carl. There'll be wagons to fix up an' one thing an' another to do, but Patrick can hire that, I guess. I . . . What's on your mind, Windy?"

"Away back in my misspent youth," Windy drawled reflectively, "I was a blacksmith's helper. I run a shop for a year one winter. I reckon I can fix the wagons."

"How about our own stuff?" Sacatone demanded. "You talk like we're goin' to let everything drop. What do you think of this, John?"

Lin looked at John McCord. So did the rest of the men. Here was a chance for dissension, here was where John McCord came in.

"I guess Sac an' me can look after the ridin' an' do the cookin' for a while, anyhow," John McCord said quietly. "How about it, Sacatone?"

Astonishment was in Lin's eyes. He stared at his brother, scarcely believing what he had heard. John read Lin's eyes and smiled faintly.

"I been doin' some thinkin', kid," he said gravely.

So, on Rough Mesa, events marched forward. The crew of choppers came in: Manuel Portillos, his seven sons and their families. Once more Rough Mesa rang to the sound of axes as the Portillos went to work.

Windy, having made his boasts, went to the mill shop. There was a disused forge in the shop, and behind the shed a litter of scrap iron and castoff machinery. In that pile of junk Windy found a plow, an old fresno, the shell of a donkey-engine boiler; but, better than these, there was half-inch iron rodding and lengths of chain. Windy lighted the forge, using coal from the pile that had stoked the donkey engine, unearthed hammers and tongs and fell to work, adding the clangor of the anvil to the sound of the axes.

Carl Yetman, supplied with oak brought from Junction and a spokeshave and handsaw, joined Windy in the shop. There, whistling, he turned out three ox yokes and steamed and bent the bows; and Lin and the dubious Sacatone, riding the mesa, brought in six steers, big and rawboned and the gentlest they could find. They necked the steers in pairs with stout three-quarter-inch rope and when the yokes were finished began the education of their oxen. Events moved swiftly on Rough Mesa, heading toward a common goal.

At the end of ten days they had their first test. Lin's steers, under Yetman's direction, had pulled and tugged at logs, not yet trustworthy of a wagon. But now, with a pile of ties cut and hewn, the steers, all three yokes of them, were hooked up to a wagon and another wagon fastened as a trailer behind the first. Carl Yetman strode beside the steers, a long gad in his hand, and the clumsy animals and the vehicles trained out across the park to the tie pile.

All hands loaded ties. All hands accompanied the wagons back to the house. All hands, except Bobby, had a drink of wine, finishing the bottle. The thing was a success. It worked. Every man on Rough Mesa was jubilant. In the morning Carl, with Lin accompanying him, would haul these loads, the first fruits of their painstaking effort, down the hill. In two days they would be in Adelphi. The McCord crew went back to their camp in high good spirits; the Patricks went into their home feeling just as elated.

Both parties to the triumph sat down to supper knowing that achievement was theirs. Dan Patrick, at the head of his table, looked fondly at his daughter. "Well, Eleanor?" he said.

The girl got up and, coming to her father, put her arms about his neck. "I'm so proud of you," she said, her cheek against his temple.

Turning his head, Patrick looked up at her. "And . . . ?" he suggested.

"And of the others too, of course."

"And Lin?" Patrick persisted softly.

For answer Eleanor dropped her face against his cheek. Dan Patrick's long hand came up and rested on her bright hair. "I know," he said. "I expect—"

There was a step on the porch where booted feet struck the planks. Patrick stopped in midsentence. This was Lin coming. This . . . A knock sounded on the door. Leaving her father, Eleanor answered that summons. Opening the door, she stepped back. "Come in . . ." she began. Sam Rideout, small, gray, neat, appeared in the doorway, hesitated and then entered.

"Hello, Rideout." Patrick arose at the end of the table. "Eleanor, get another place. You're in time for supper, Sheriff."

"I ate supper," Sam Rideout said shortly. "Patrick, I don't like this any better than you do, but I'm sheriff an' I've got to do my duties. I've got a paper here to serve on you."

"On me?" Patrick's voice was incredulous. "Why, Sheriff?"

Rideout came across the room, left hand dipping into the inner pocket of his coat. "It's an injunction," he announced. "Otis Melcomb's got out a restrainin'

96

injunction against you cuttin' any more timber."

"I don't understand," Patrick said, taking the folded paper that Rideout placed in his hand. "How can I be restrained from cutting my own timber? Sheriff, there's something . . ."

"There's somethin' fishy, all right." Rideout's eyes were hard. "You leased the mesa to the McCords an' McCord has sold a sublease an' the timber rights to Otis Melcomb."

Very slowly Dan Patrick sank back into his chair.

Lin McCord, finishing his supper, got up from the table, pushing back his chair. "I'm goin' down to Patricks'," he announced to the others. "I want to talk to Mr. Patrick about the trip to town. He's got the ties sold an' I want to make arrangements about deliverin' 'em."

As he reached the door Lin stopped. Taking the comb from the shelf, he ran it through his hair, then, replacing the comb, he went on out.

"Yeah," Windy drawled, "he's goin' to see *Patrick*."

Carl Yetman, literal soul, failed to interpret the accent that Windy placed on the last word. "Me," Carl said, "I think he goes to see that girl." He was surprised when all the others, even Sacatone, laughed.

Lin went blithely along the path to the Patrick house. He could see the light flooding through the open door and fanning across the porch floor, and when he reached the porch steps he took them in one stride. As he came to the door he hesitated and then called "Hello! Can I come in?" following the question with a quick

97

step that took him through the opening.

He had expected to hear Dan Patrick or Eleanor bid him enter, but there was no answer to his call. Just inside the door Lin stopped. Dan Patrick, his face gray, sat at the head of the table, his head tilted until his chin rested on his chest. Beside Patrick stood Eleanor, her eyes angry, head lifted, face defiant, as though she dared the world. Between Lin and the girl was Rideout and, as Lin stopped, Rideout stepped aside and faced the doorway.

"Why . . ." Lin began, astonishment and anxiety in his voice, "what's the matter? What's happened?"

Patrick did not lift his head. Rideout remained blank-faced and silent. It was Eleanor Patrick who answered the query. "You know what's happened! I could kill you, you cheat!"

CHAPTER VIII
ORDER OF THE DOUBLE-CROSS

LIN STOOD STOCK-STILL. HE COULD NOT MOVE, COULD not speak. It was impossible that this should happen, and yet it had happened. Motion became possible once more, and he advanced another step. And then Sam Rideout drawled from where he stood: "If I was you, McCord, I'd get out."

Lin faced the officer. He had found his voice again. "Maybe you can tell me what this is all about," he said.

"I could," Rideout drawled, "but I don't waste my

time on skunks. You ain't welcome here, McCord. You'd better git!"

Hot anger flooded Lin. He snarled at Rideout: "I suppose you're giving orders. I'll go when I find out what all this is, and not before." Lin was unarmed, but there was rage so plain upon his face that Rideout took a step back.

"McCord . . ." he began.

Eleanor Patrick dropped words into Lin's anger, cold, cutting words. "You pretended to be our friend," she said levelly. "You took a lease on Rough Mesa. Now we've found you out. You sold a sublease and the timber rights to Otis Melcomb. There's no need of telling you; you know. Now will you go?"

For a long minute Lin stood poised, then gradually his muscles relaxed and he slumped, sagging, in his clothing. Wordlessly, with no defense, no denial, he turned and walked through the door, and as he cleared it Eleanor Patrick flung herself down into a chair beside the table and dropped her head on her arms.

Lin went back to the camp, walking slowly, a man in a daze. When he entered the cabin the others—Sacatone, Bobby, Windy and Carl—noted with amazement the expression on his face. John, issuing from the bedroom, looked at his brother and stopped short in the bedroom door. It was Bobby who spoke. Dragging his crippled leg, he hurried to Lin's side and caught his hand.

"What's the matter, Uncle Lin? What happened?" Bobby's voice was filled with concern.

Lin sat down in a chair. Unseeingly he looked at

Windy. "I went down to Patricks'," he announced, lowvoiced.

"Somethin' wrong down there?" Windy was on his feet. "Has somethin' happened?"

Lin made no answer. Windy, perceiving that there would be no reply, snatched up his hat and hurried out. John came on into the room and walked over to Lin. He put his hand on his brother's shoulder. "What's the matter, kid?" he asked. "Somethin' wrong?"

Lin looked up at him, lifting his head slowly. "She told me to get out," he said.

John jerked his head around, caught Sacatone's eyes and nodded toward the door. Sacatone, already on his feet, said: "Let's get out of here, Carl," and walked over and took Bobby's hand. The men and the boy went out.

"Come on, kid," John urged. "Tell me. What happened?"

"It just ain't so," Lin said slowly. "It couldn't be so."

Windy, running down the path to the Patricks', found Sam Rideout coming down the porch steps. Windy hauled up, confronting the sheriff, his face concerned and anxious there in the light from the open door. "What happened down here, Sheriff?" he demanded. "Lin come back to camp lookin' like a ghost. What's wrong?"

Rideout drew back from the tall man. "I guess he didn't let you in on it, Tillitson," Rideout said levelly. "Your boss sold the Patricks out."

"Sold 'em out?" Windy was incredulous.

"Yeah." The little officer stared up at Windy. "That's what I said. He sold a sublease an' the timber rights on the mesa to Melcomb. I'll say McCord sold the Patricks out!"

Windy's big hand shot out and caught Rideout's arm, the fingers biting in. "He never done it!" Windy snarled. "Lin McCord couldn't pull a trick like that. It ain't in him!"

Rideout jerked his arm free. "I served an injunction on Patrick so that he wouldn't cut any more timber," he snapped. "I seen the sublease. Don't tell me it didn't happen!"

Windy drew back a trifle. "I don't believe it," he said flatly.

"Makes no difference; it's so." Rideout's voice carried anger. "I thought you was pretty good fellows. I was mistaken. You'd better get back with the rest of your bunch, Tillitson. I want no part of any of you." Turning, the sheriff stalked away toward his horse.

"Wait!" Windy called. "Wait a minute. Come up to the camp!"

Rideout did not even turn his head. Untying his horse from the fence, he mounted and rode off. Windy took two steps after the mounted man, turned and ran back toward the camp.

Sacatone, Carl and Bobby were in the yard when Windy returned. Sacatone tried to stop the big man, but Windy brushed him aside. He went into the room, stopped and looked down at Lin who was sitting very quietly, John beside him.

"Rideout," Windy snarled, "says that you sold the Patricks out, Lin. He says that you sold Melcomb a sublease on the mesa an' the timber rights. How about it?"

Lin looked up at his friend. "You know," he answered slowly, "I didn't do it, Windy."

"Rideout said he'd seen the lease," Windy snapped. "Did you . . . ?" Abruptly he stopped his question and, slowly turning his head, looked fully at John. John's face was white.

"So it was you done it, huh?" Windy said very quietly. "So it was you?"

Lin, too, was looking at John. There was no mistaking the play of expression across John's face. He glared up at Windy. "It's none of your damned business what I did!" John snapped defiantly. "Where do you get off, comin' in here an' accusin' me? Get out, Tillitson, you—"

"John!" Lin said, his voice level. John stopped his tirade, and Windy stood waiting. Lin looked at the big man. "Let me talk to John," Lin ordered. Wordlessly Windy turned and went out.

When the tall man was gone Lin looked at his brother. "Well, John?" he said quietly.

John was still defiant. "Sure I sold the lease," he admitted. "It was a good deal. Melcomb wanted it, an' we ain't lumberjacks. Why shouldn't I sell him the timber?"

"Because it wasn't yours to sell." Still Lin kept his voice level, steeled himself against the surge of anger. "No wonder the Patricks think I sold 'em out. That's where you got the money to buy that land, was it?"

John nodded wordlessly. Lin got up from the chair. "John," he said, "I've stood for a lot from you, but this tears it. I'm done." He turned abruptly and walked out the door. In the yard Windy came to him swiftly.

"It was John, wasn't it?" he demanded.

Lin nodded.

"What you goin' to do?" Windy asked.

"I don't know yet," Lin answered. "I've got to think."

"He couldn't do it!" Windy's voice rose with his anger. "He hadn't no right to do it. You signed that lease. This is your lease. He couldn't sell it."

"He's my pardner," Lin said quietly. "Let me alone a while, Windy. I've got to think about this."

"I'm goin' down there an' tell 'em," Windy declared hotly. "John ain't goin' to get away with this. I'll tell 'em—"

"Windy!"

Windy subsided.

"I've got to get that sublease," Lin said slowly. "Maybe if I took it to Eleanor an' told her what happened . . . I've got to get it, Windy."

Windy put his hand on Lin's shoulder. "We'll go down to Adelphi tomorrow," he said. "An' if Melcomb don't come across . . ." He left the threat unfinished. Then: "That damned John!" Windy snarled. "You ought to let me tell 'em, Lin."

Lin made no answer. He walked out from under Windy's hand, going back toward the house. Bobby, leaving Sacatone, came to him. "Is there anything I can do, Uncle Lin?" Bobby asked.

"I don't think so, Bobby. Thanks," Lin said kindly. "I've got to talk to your dad a while. You'd better go to bed pretty soon." Bobby released Lin's hand, and Lin went on to the house.

In the yard Windy stood undecided, then, turning abruptly, he strode off toward Patricks' again. Reaching the porch, he mounted the steps, went to the door and knocked. For a long time he waited and then knocked again. This time the summons was answered.

Rufina Vara, the native woman, opened the door and looked at Windy with beady, expressionless eyes.

"I want to see Eleanor," Windy announced. "Her or Mr. Patrick."

"*No está aquí,*" Rufina answered flatly, and closed the door in Windy's face.

Lin got nowhere with his brother. John was defiant. He maintained that he had a right to do what he had done, that he had made money for the partnership, that Lin was taking the whole thing too seriously. Lin controlled his temper with an effort and finally, words proving futile, he left John and went outside to sit on the bench close by the door and stare out toward the Patrick house where no lights showed. The dreams that he had dreamed, the plans he had made, everything that he held dear, had been tossed carelessly away for Lin McCord. Finally, with a sigh, he got up and went inside.

In the morning, with no word to John, Lin saddled a horse and started toward Adelphi. Windy, not to be left behind, went with him. All the ride in, Lin looked straight ahead, his face set in harsh, firm lines. Windy knew that his friend was thinking, making plans, and so respected his silence. When they reached Adelphi they tied their horses to the hitch rail in front of the store and, with Windy flanking him, Lin walked to the company office. Melcomb was in. Indeed, Otis Melcomb was expecting this visit.

"You wait out here, Windy," Lin directed when he was in the outer office, and then, turning to the book-keeper: "I want to talk to Mr. Melcomb."

"I'll tell him," the bookkeeper answered, and went into Melcomb's office. He returned, and Melcomb appeared in his office door.

"Come in, McCord," he said heartily. "What brings you to town?"

"I want to see you," Lin said quietly, and followed Melcomb into the office.

Inside, with the door closed, Melcomb gestured toward a chair. "Sit down," he invited. "What's on your mind, McCord?"

Lin sat down. "That sublease," he said shortly. "John had no business selling it to you."

"Why, I thought he made a very good deal," Melcomb said. "You boys can't use that timber and I can. It seemed to me that we both ought to make a profit."

"John had no business sellin' it," Lin said stubbornly. "I want it back, Melcomb. I'll pay you back your money, but I want that lease."

Melcomb laughed. "I can hardly do that," he said. "I'm planning on cutting that timber; in fact, Samms, my woods boss, is going to move a camp up there right away."

Lin shook his head. "The timber belongs to Patrick," he announced. "He didn't lease it to us. You can't buy the timber, Melcomb."

"I think I bought it," Melcomb said. "There's no use in getting your back up about this, McCord. I bought the timber and I'm going to have it. You can fight me in court, of course, but I've had legal opinion on this and you can't win."

"The lease is in my name," Lin said. "John couldn't sell you a sublease."

"But he did." Melcomb leaned forward across his desk, enjoying the situation immensely. "You and your brother are partners, McCord. You don't deny that, do you?"

"No. We're pardners."

"And your brother has been acting as agent for the partnership." Melcomb smiled thinly. "He's paid your bills here in town and he has done the purchasing. I think that you're barking up the wrong tree, McCord. I've bought the timber and I'm going to keep it."

"That's your last word?" Lin got up.

"My last word." Melcomb was triumphant. "Samms will be moving a camp in there this week."

Lin McCord's eyes held an odd look. "Don't have him do it," he said slowly. "He won't get there."

"What do you mean?"

"You know what I mean. There's one way to the top of Rough Mesa, Melcomb. It ain't open." Lin turned abruptly and, without another look at Melcomb, pulled open the door and walked out. "Come on, Windy," he ordered.

Windy got up. "Do any good?" he asked.

Lin shook his head and they left the building together.

Melcomb, alone in his office, thought briefly after Lin's departure, then, rising, he went to the door and spoke to the bookkeeper. "Hunter, you go out and get Draper and Samms and bring them here. Hurry up!"

"Yes sir." Glen Hunter pushed the ledger aside and got off his tall stool. He reached for his hat, looked toward Melcomb's door and went out. Back at his desk, Melcomb sat tapping the desk top with his fingers. "So that road's closed, is it?" he mused. "We'll see about that, McCord."

Within ten minutes Hunter came back to the office. His return was closely followed by the advent of Spike Samms and Ed Draper, who came in together, went directly to Melcomb's office and closed the door. Hunter bent over the ledger again, his ears alert. Melcomb's office door was closed, but the transom above the door was open a crack. Sometimes Glen Hunter had heard interesting things through that transom.

"What's on your mind?" Draper asked after he had closed the door.

Melcomb gestured toward chairs. "Sit down," he commanded. "McCord was just here, Ed."

"Which McCord?"

"The young one. He wanted to buy back that sublease I've got on the mesa."

"An' you didn't sell it," Draper drawled. "So then what?"

"So he told me that we couldn't move a camp up there; that Pinál Canyon was closed."

Samms grunted scornfully. Draper said nothing. "I'm going to put a camp up there," Melcomb declared.

Draper's drawl came smoothly. "One good man with a Winchester could hold down Pinál Canyon till hell freezes over. You're in tough luck, Otis."

Melcomb's voice lowered in tone, and Hunter moved

the ledger toward the end of the desk near the office door. "I don't think I'm in tough luck," Melcomb refuted. "Young McCord wants trouble and we'll accommodate him. Now you boys go up there . . . ." Hunter lost the rest of the sentence. Nervously he moved the ledger back to where it belonged.

After a time Melcomb's door opened, and Samms and Draper came out. Draper, stopping in the doorway, turned and spoke again to the man inside. "I don't like it," Ed Draper said. "It ain't my way of doin' business an'—"

Melcomb's voice blotted out the rest of the sentence. "I don't give a damn whether you like it or not!" Melcomb roared. "You'll do what I say or I'll—"

He stopped. Draper had held up his hand. Draper's voice was thin and full of menace. "Don't talk too much, Otis," Draper warned.

"Come on, Ed," Samms growled from the middle of the office. "Come on."

Draper turned back slowly, as though reluctant to leave, and joined Samms. They went out together. After a few minutes Hunter heard the drawer of Melcomb's desk slide open, a clink and then a gurgle. Otis Melcomb was taking a drink from his private supply.

Lin McCord and Windy, leaving the company office, walked silently back toward their horses. When they reached the hitch rail Lin looked at his companion. "You go on an' get the mail," he directed. Windy nodded and walked off toward the post office, and Lin went into the store.

When Windy came back with the little bundle of mail, Lin was coming out of the store carrying a box. When he saw the end of the box Windy grunted approval. Stenciled in black letters across the wood were the words: UNION METALLIC CARTRIDGE COMPANY, and down below the big black letters formed a design: UMC.

"I'll pack it on my saddle," Lin said quietly. "Here, hold this gunny sack while I put the box in."

Windy held the sack and Lin slid in the box. When he finished Windy knotted the top of the sack. "Now what?" he asked.

"Now I've got to go to the hotel an' write a couple of letters," Lin said, "an' I've got to send a telegram. Maybe you'd better stick with me, Windy."

"Uh-huh," Windy agreed. "I think . . . Say, there's Donald."

Both men looked up the street. Sandy Donald, driving the Patrick buckboard, was coming along toward the store. He passed the two men without a look in their direction, stopped the team below the store and, climbing out of the buckboard, tied the off horse with a neck rope to the hitch rail. Then deliberately he looked at Lin and Windy, no recognition in his eyes, turned his back and walked toward the millinery store.

"Let's go to the hotel," Lin said. Windy followed him along the walk.

When the letters were written and mailed, when a telegram had been sent from the depot, Lin McCord and Windy rode out of town, heading back toward the lease. They kept a good pace, traveling steadily.

As they entered Pinál Canyon they passed Sandy Donald. On the seat beside Sandy sat plump Cora Ferguson, her hat a little awry from the jolting of the buckboard.

Lin said "Hello" as they passed the vehicle but received no answer. Donald did not look up but kept his eyes on the backs of his trotting horses. Cora freed a hand from the iron grip on the seat and settled her hat more firmly on her head.

Near the head of the canyon, well past the buckboard and its silent occupants, Lin reined in. "Melcomb said he was goin' to put a camp up on top," he announced to Windy.

"So?" Windy drawled. "An' you told him . . . ?"

"That he wasn't," Lin finished.

"An' that's why the cartridges?"

"Part of the reason. I wrote Judge Nesbit back home, Windy. I need some help on this."

Windy nodded. "Judge is a good man," he agreed.

"And I'm goin' to need some more help," Lin continued.

Windy grinned. "Well," he said, "you got me, ain't you?"

"I figured I had you." Lin returned Windy's smile. "Now, up there might be a good place. A man can see a way down the canyon from up there." He pointed to a ledge reaching out from the canyon wall.

"Gimme a Winchester, plenty of shells an' a canteen an' I could stay there quite some time," Windy drawled.

"Maybe we'll both stay there," Lin said. "All right, Windy."

CHAPTER IX
DEATH COMES AT SUNDOWN

AT CAMP THAT NIGHT JOHN MCCORD KEPT TO HIMSELF. He had nothing to say to Lin, nothing to say to Windy. Sacatone hauled a chair over and sat beside John, plainly stating, in his action, where his sympathy lay. Bobby, torn between two affections, was unhappy. Bobby had gone on his usual visit to the Patricks' during the day but had not seen Dan Patrick at all and had found Eleanor silent and distrait. It was an unhappy situation for Bobby, the whole affair.

The following morning Lin and Windy went out together. John idled about camp and finally saddled a horse. Sacatone made it evident that he intended to accompany John, but the older McCord brother would have none of his company.

"You take Bobby an' go over to Red Lakes Spring," he ordered. "I saw a steer over there yesterday that's wire cut. You'd better take a dope bottle an' fix it up." Sacatone shook his head in protest but obeyed nevertheless. He and Bobby rode off together, and when they were gone John McCord mounted and started down Pinál Canyon, bound for Adelphi.

A very sober, serious John McCord made that trip to town. He had seen the effect of his foolhardiness on Lin. He had been defiant and stubborn with his brother, but underneath the exterior there was a great deal of good as well as a great deal of weakness in John McCord. Now he was determined to ride in to see Otis

Melcomb, recover the sublease and undo the damage he had wrought. He was late in awakening, but now that he was aroused he was determined on action.

Due to Sacatone's desire to accompany him, McCord got a late start. Still he was in Adelphi by twelve o'clock, and at one o'clock he went to Melcomb's office.

At one-thirty John McCord came from Melcomb's office, the cords in his neck bulging and his jaw muscles tight with anger. He stopped at the Exchange Saloon, took one quick drink and went on to the depot. There, while Pop Vicars looked on, McCord wrote a telegram, paid for it and dispatched it. "How long before the answer comes on that?" he demanded.

"Three or four hours." Pop looked around, located the coal bucket and spat juicily.

"I'll wait," John McCord announced, and plumped himself down on a bench in the waiting room.

"Want a paper?" Pop inquired, selecting the least ancient of a pile of newsprint.

"No!" snapped John. "I don't want anythin' but an answer to that wire."

Cora Ferguson came to Rough Mesa because Eleanor Patrick needed her. Good soul that she was, Cora could not, would not even think of denying the request of a friend, and when Eleanor Patrick sent word by Sandy Donald that she needed help Cora packed a battered grip and turned her shop over to her trimmer. All the way up Pinál Canyon she plied the taciturn Donald with questions and when she reached Patricks' she had a good idea of what had happened.

Dan Patrick, all his carefully built props knocked out from under him, had suffered a slight stroke. Eleanor and Donald, helped by Rufina, had put him to bed following the sheriff's brief visit and had worked over him, but Patrick remained almost in a coma, certainly in a daze. Eleanor tried without avail to rouse her father and finally, because there was no doctor nearer than Junction, had sent for Cora. Cora, arriving, took immediate charge. She sent Eleanor to bed, for the girl was worn with her nightlong vigil, and then, the decks cleared, Cora went into action. Possessed of boundless vitality, she found an outlet for it here. There was a stir and bustle such as the Patrick house had not seen in years.

Cora shifted furniture, she looked after Dan Patrick, she cooked supper and, when the meal was ready, called Eleanor. The girl was listless. Despite the excellence of Cora's cooking she ate very little and, having eaten, repaired to her father's big chair in the living room and sat down. Cora, directing Rufina's operations in the kitchen, looked in and saw Eleanor lying back in the chair, staring vacantly at the wall. It was impossible for Cora to leave her friend alone to brood; she came in the room and launched upon a one-sided conversation.

"I think it's a shame the way you've been treated," she announced. "It's enough to make a body want to kill a person. Red Indians ain't mean enough for them McCords, the way they treated you!"

Eleanor had nothing to say in answer, and Cora continued her monologue. She dealt in battle, murder and sudden death with Lin McCord and, to a lesser extent, his brother as the recipients. In full action, verbally, Cora cheerfully suggested boiling in oil and a few of the lesser high lights of the old Inquisition. She was well into her theme when Rufina appeared at the kitchen door and called: "Mees Cora?"

"Now what is it?" Cora snapped, not relishing the interruption.

"Can you come here a meenet?" Rufina asked, and Cora bustled off to attend Rufina's wants.

When she was gone Eleanor sighed wearily. She had hardly listened to Cora, and yet the rapid fire of words had made some impression. All her hopes dashed to earth, all her desires vanished, the girl in the chair was left with nothing. But there was a spirit in Eleanor Patrick, a steel that had carried her along through adversity, and with that spirit there was a temper. As she sat brooding in the chair she lifted her head. In the corner of the room Dan Patrick's deer rifle, a .38-.55 Winchester, rested across deerhorns. Eleanor glimpsed the gun as she looked at the wall, and gradually it became plain to her. Cora's talk of revenge, of the punishments that should be visited upon the McCords, was there in Eleanor's mind, latent but firmly planted. Gradually the temper of the girl changed. Gradually her shoulders squared and her back came erect.

"I think your papa wants you, Eleanor," Cora said from the doorway. "He's tryin' to talk."

Eleanor sprang up and hurried into her father's room. Dan Patrick lay on the bed, and as the girl bent down she could hear his muttering voice. "Oxen!" Patrick murmured. "The oxen . . ."

There was no more, and despite her efforts Eleanor could not rouse the man. Her attempts proving useless, the girl sat there by the bed, her eyes dry and hot, her face serious with her thoughts.

"You'd better go to bed, dearie," Cora said. "I'll set up with Dan."

"I wouldn't sleep," Eleanor answered.

"You'd rest, though," Cora declared guilelessly. "You go lie down, dearie."

Eleanor allowed herself to be led from the room.

Under Cora's urgings she did lie down, resting on her bed. But she did not sleep; there was too much in her mind for sleep. Thoughts churned there, crazy, vicious thoughts moving in an endless circle. There was no stopping the thoughts, no answer to them. When she got up early in the morning they still obsessed her. Eleanor Patrick, that first morning, was close to hysteria.

During the day Patrick was held by the stupor and he did not rouse. He breathed, his heart beat, he lived, that was all. That night he roused somewhat, looking at Eleanor with knowledge in his eyes. Then he sank into the stupor again and the girl, sleepless, worn out, nerves at a breaking point, refused to leave him. When morning came she was on the verge of collapse, and Sandy Donald was dispatched to Adelphi to call the doctor from Junction.

Cora, noting her friend's condition, tried vainly to get Eleanor to sleep. Failing that, she tried conversation, but the girl would not talk.

"You need to get tired out," Cora diagnosed. "You've been sittin' worryin' until your brain is all wore out, but you can't sleep. You need to get tired. You go outside a while an' I'll watch your papa."

Listlessly Eleanor agreed and left Cora with her father.

The girl walked for a while, taking the path that led to the pines and the little graveyard. She did not linger there. It was as though the grave reproached her, and she returned to the house. There, entering noiselessly, she peeped into her father's room. Cora was sitting leaned back in her chair, almost asleep, and Dan Patrick had not stirred upon the bed. The girl went out again.

Once more she sat in her father's chair and stared at the corner, and as she sat there gradually the rifle stood out above all else. It was almost as though the gun spoke to her, called to her temptingly. Resolve formed in Eleanor Patrick's disordered mind. She got up, crossed to the corner and lifted the gun from the horns. It lay there cold and heavy and deadly in her hands. For a long time she stood there holding the weapon and then, stooping, she picked up a box of shells from the table below the horns and, clutching them, tiptoed out of the room.

That morning Lin McCord and Windy had ridden out on the mesa; that morning John McCord had ridden to town after having sent Bobby and Sacatone to Red Lakes. The sun was high now, for it was noon and past when Eleanor Patrick stepped down from the porch carrying the rifle. She walked away from the house toward the park and, at the edge of the timber, circled toward the north. She stayed in the shadow of the trees, moving along the edge of the park, seeing the big steers grazing on the grama, watching the dry grass ripple in the sun. How far she walked she did not know, but presently she found herself at the northern edge of the open space and high on a knoll. And, so finding herself, she looked down at the gun in her hands and suddenly sanity returned to her.

The knoll on which she stood was bare-crowned. Opposite her, to the west, was another higher rise of ground with cedars on its sides and top. The girl rested the weapon on the ground. What had she meant to do? Why had she come? Why was she carrying the gun? A revulsion of feeling flooded her. She had been insane, crazy, a madwoman. There was movement below. Down there in the park Lin McCord crossed between a bunch of cattle and the knoll. He rode like an old man, humped over in his saddle, his head bowed, not looking as he rode. He was alone. There, below her, was the man that Eleanor Patrick had meant to kill! She shuddered at the thought, the gun falling to the barren, weathered shale of the knoll. Then, from the hill to her right, a report sounded, a thunderclap against the silence of the mesa. Lin McCord's horse jumped and Lin was down!

The girl whirled, catching up the rifle and turning, all in one swift motion. There was movement among the cedars on the higher slope, and Eleanor Patrick threw the gun to her shoulder, her hand racing on the lever of the action. Again thunder smote the mesa, and the heavy slug from the Winchester at the girl's shoulder kicked up gravel among the cedars. She levered in another cartridge and fired again, and then a horse, the rider bent in the saddle, came crashing out from the trees and pounded down the slope toward the north. There was a second crashing sound that told of another horseman riding. Eleanor Patrick lowered the weapon and stared toward the knoll. There was no movement other than the wind among the trees.

She poised there, vibrant, tense, and suddenly, from below her, she heard a horse threshing its way up the slope. Turning, she faced that sound. Lin McCord, face tense and eyes flaming, came into the open space atop the knoll, pulled his horse down and threw himself from the saddle.

Dropping the rifle, Eleanor turned to run. She took three steps, and then Lin's strong hands had caught her arms, stopping her. Wordlessly she struggled against that grasp. She could not free herself, and then she was released and, turning, stood defiantly facing the man.

The anger had gone from Lin's eyes, the tightness from his muscles. For a long moment the two confronted each other, and then he spoke. "I don't blame you," Lin McCord said quietly. "I guess you thought I had it comin' to me."

Eleanor was speechless. Lin, turning, went back, picked up the rifle and, returning, held it out to her. "Here," he said. "Take it an' go on an' finish the job."

His words broke the tension. The girl snatched the rifle from him and, turning, ran blindly down the slope. She was at the bottom of the knoll before Lin moved, and as he reached the edge of the bare top he saw her come out into the park and, still running, still carrying the rifle, go toward the camp. Lin stood stock-still for a moment and then walked slowly to his waiting horse.

He mounted then and rode down the slope and out into the park. Eleanor had disappeared in the timber at its eastern edge. Lin let Jug carry him along. When he reached the houses he turned Jug into the corral and went up to the camp.

Carl Yetman, busy as usual, looked up when Lin came and noted the expression on the man's face.

"What's the matter?" Yetman demanded.

Lin made no answer but went out, sat down on the bench and stared off toward the Patrick house, part of which was discernible. Carl had followed him to the door. He saw Lin, just sitting there, looking off into distance. Noiselessly Carl went back to the kitchen. He was putting his bread in the oven when Lin came in.

"You want some cinnamon rolls?" Yetman asked. "I got some fresh, an' some coffee. You sit down, huh, an' eat some?"

"I don't think . . ." Lin began.

"Sure," Carl urged. "I got it all fixed."

Lin was still at the table, toying with his coffee, when Windy, Sacatone and Bobby arrived, all together and in a hurry. They had heard the shots, ridden toward the sound and, finding nothing, headed for camp. Windy, dropping from his horse outside the door, came running in and, seeing Lin at the table, stopped short.

"I heard some shootin'," Windy announced breathlessly. "I thought—"

"I took a few shots at a coyote," Lin interrupted. "Missed him. I didn't think about you fellows or I wouldn't of done it."

He grinned apologetically. Sacatone and Bobby had reached the door in time to hear his announcement. Now they came in. "Where's John?" Sacatone asked.

"He hasn't come back yet," Yetman answered.

Sacatone went out, and Bobby sat down and reached for a fresh cinnamon roll. Windy was eying Lin speculatively. There was something fishy about Lin's explanation of the shots. Windy could not be sure of the cause of the trouble but he sensed that there was something wrong. Lin, noting Windy's quiet survey, elaborated on his theme. "That was sure a big dog coyote," he said. "Wish I'd got him."

Windy said "Uh-huh" skeptically and took a cinnamon roll.

Sacatone called from the outside: "Are we done with the horses, Lin? If we are I'll turn 'em out."

"Leave Jug up for a wrangling horse," Lin directed. "I guess we're through."

"You fellers," Yetman complained, "eat up all my cinnamon rolls an' you don't get an appetite for supper. You get oudt now. I got supper to fix."

Windy went to the bedroom. Lin followed him, and Bobby, helping himself to another roll, walked out and looked off toward the corral where Sacatone was unsaddling. There was nothing in particular to interest Bobby at the corral and he set out for the Patricks', munching his roll as he went. Bobby wanted to satisfy himself that his friends were all right. He had not seen either Dan or Eleanor for two days, and what with the dissension at camp and no visits with the Patricks, Bobby was worried.

When he reached the house he knocked politely at the back door and was greeted by Cora. Bobby had seen Cora on his visits made the day before and had tried to establish a liaison with her. Cora had not responded. Now he asked if Eleanor was in.

Cora, thoroughly aroused against all the McCords, large and small, spoke sharply to the small boy who stood on the back porch. "She's gone out," Cora snapped. "You go on home now an' don't bother us down here. You McCords have done enough damage!"

Hurt to the quick, Bobby turned and slowly limped down from the porch. Passing around the corner of the house, he stopped and looked up at Eleanor's window. He would show that fat woman! Bobby pulled and hauled himself into the small cottonwood beyond the window. There, perched on a branch, he peered into the room. Eleanor lay face down upon the bed. The window was open.

"Eleanor," Bobby said softly.

There was no movement of the woman on the bed. Bobby tried again. "Eleanor."

The girl raised her head. To the boy in the tree it seemed that she looked straight at him. How could Bobby know that her eyes were too tear filled to see, her ears deaf except to the pounding of her heart? The girl flung herself down again.

His best friend had denied him! Bobby climbed down from the tree and, like any small animal, took his hurt into the solitude of the trees.

The sun dropped out of sight behind the Brutos,

notching itself in the V between Las Mujeres for a last shot at the mesa. Carl Yetman came to the door of the camp and called toward the corral: "Come on, Sac. Supper!" Lin and Windy, appearing at the door, poured water into the washbasin and made their toilets. Sacatone came up from the corral.

"Bobby!" Carl called. "Bob . . . bee!"

"Buckboard's comin' to the Patricks'," Sacatone commented. "They . . . It's comin' here."

Lin, drying his hands, stood holding the towel. Windy poised the comb above his forelock and turned. A buckboard, two men on the seat, was coming along the road. It was beyond the Patrick house, plainly heading for the camp. The buckboard stopped. Sandy Donald, face white, held the lines, and beside him was another man, a stranger. But it was not Sandy nor the stranger that caused Lin to take a hasty step forward, that made Windy gasp and drop the comb, that brought one quick startled exclamation from Sacatone.

They could see into the bed of the buckboard and there, clothing torn and tattered, bloody head beaten until it was almost unrecognizable, was John McCord.

"Good God!" Lin exclaimed.

"You—" Windy began.

"We found him down Pinál Canyon," the stranger announced. "His horse had dragged him. He was dead when we found him."

Sacatone, face flat and expressionless, stared up at the speaker. "Who are you?" Sacatone demanded.

"I'm Doctor Vorfree from Junction," the stranger said. "I was coming up to see Mr. Patrick. We—"

"Where was he?" Lin asked.

Donald answered. "About three miles down the canyon. He was in a pile of rocks. His horse is still there. We thought we'd better—"

"Get him inside," Lin said quietly. "Help me, Windy."

Vorfree and Donald got out of the buckboard seat. Windy lifted John McCord's booted feet and Lin the head. Together they carried the tattered torn thing that had been John McCord into the house. The doctor and Donald followed them and behind those two came Sacatone. Sacatone watched the two men narrowly, watched their every movement, their expressions. His own face told nothing.

Once inside, Lin turned. "Now tell me again," he ordered.

Methodically Vorfree recounted his tale, how he had been called from Junction to attend Dan Patrick, how Donald had met him in Adelphi, how they had driven up the canyon; then the discovery of John McCord, lying beside the road, of his horse, strayed off and grazing; of loading the body in the buckboard. "Donald said he was your brother," the doctor completed, looking at Lin, "so we brought him here."

Lin nodded slowly. "Thanks," he said, heavy-voiced. "I guess . . . There's nothin' we can do about it. Those things happen."

"John was ridin' Redskin," Sacatone said flatly. "He don't spook so easy. John was a good rider."

Lin looked at the speaker. "Redskin ain't exactly gentle, though," he reminded, "an' John had been to town." He left it there. John had been to town and the

123

last time John had gone to town he had come home drunk. Sacatone, without a word, turned and walked out of the room.

Lin looked at Windy. "Somebody's got to ride in an' tell the law about this," he said wearily. "There 'll have to be an inquest. I guess you'd better go, Windy. Sacatone can go with you an' pick up the horse. An' somebody's got to find Bobby an' keep him out of here a while. The Lord knows where we'll keep him. At one of the Portillos', I guess. Carl, will you get him an' take him down there?"

Carl Yetman nodded silently. Windy had not gone as yet. "You'd better go, Windy," Lin urged.

Windy turned and went out, Carl Yetman following him. Lin looked at Donald and then at Vorfree. "I'll cover him up," he said. "I . . . I guess we can't do anythin' for him till Windy brings a deputy. I'm . . . well, I'm obliged to you."

Vorfree said: "We couldn't leave him lying there," his voice gruff. Donald said nothing. The doctor turned to his companion. "I'd better go and take a look at Patrick," he said briskly. "After all, that's what I came for." Turning back to Lin, he spoke again. "If I can help you, call on me."

"Thanks." Lin nodded, and Vorfree and Donald went out. When they were gone Lin sat down beside his brother. He looked at the tattered clothing, the bruised and bloody head, and then he lowered his own head to his hands. This was the end of it. This was what it had all come to. There was nothing left for Lin McCord. Nothing!

CHAPTER X
"NOT YOU, REDSKIN!"

SACATONE, HAVING GONE DOWN THE CANYON TO PICK UP John's horse, came back after dark. He put Redskin in the corral, pulled off John's saddle, then came to the house. Windy came back from Adelphi about midnight. He had talked to Ed Draper, the deputy sheriff in Adelphi, and Draper and a justice of the peace had assured him they would come out to the camp early the following morning.

"Draper said that he'd telegraph the sheriff," Windy reported to Lin. "He was mighty decent. Kind of surprised me. I didn't want to go to him, but he's the only deputy in Adelphi!"

Lin nodded.

"An' Draper said that John had been in town an' that he'd been drinkin' pretty heavy," Windy continued, not looking at Lin. "I guess that was it, Lin."

"I guess so," Lin said dully.

"I'll set up with John," Windy offered. "You'll have to get some sleep, Lin. You're goin' to take John back home, ain't you?"

"Bobby an' I'll take him back," Lin said. "Sacatone is in with John now. I told him that I'd stay, but he said he'd ruther. Sacatone thought a lot of John, Windy."

Windy said, "Uh-huh," and then: "Where's Bobby?"

"Carl took him down to the Portillos."

Again Windy grunted. "Well," he drawled, "we won't sleep, but we might as well get what rest we can."

"John's in the house," Lin announced needlessly. "Carl pulled our beds outdoors. He's made camp outside, around in back."

Windy led the way around the house. Carl Yetman had placed the beds on the ground back of the house. He was sitting on his own bed, smoking his heavy curved pipe.

"Which one of the Portillos did you leave Bobby with?" Lin asked the cook.

"Manuel," Carl answered, and puffed slowly.

Lin looked down toward the houses that the chopping crew occupied. There were no lights. "Manuel's a pretty good Mexican," Lin said. "I guess he's got Bobby taken care of. There's no lights down there, an' I won't bother him."

"You lie down a while," Yetman urged. "You get some rest, Lin."

Bobby McCord was not at Manuel Portillos'. Bobby had gone with Carl dutifully when Carl had called him from his retreat among the trees. The fat cook had talked slowly to the boy, and Bobby knew that his father was dead. He had accepted that fact bravely. He had cried in Carl's arms but after a time had straightened himself and forced his tears back. At Portillos', Rosa, Manuel's motherly wife, had taken Bobby in and assured Carl that she would look after him. Bobby stayed in the kitchen with Rosa while Yetman, his duty done, returned to camp. But Rosa was busy, and Bobby, after having gone to bed at her behest, had lain awake. Presently he got up, pulled on the small boots his father had given him and slipped out. Rosa, in the excitement, did not miss him. Bobby went down to the Patricks'. There were lights at the Patricks' house and people talking in the big front room.

When Dr. Vorfree and Donald first reached the house Vorfree immediately went in to examine Dan Patrick, working over the man for some time, testing heart action, temperature, reactions. He would give no definite report following that first examination. It was not until night had come and he had made a second examination that he spoke his mind to Eleanor Patrick.

"Your father," the doctor told her, "has had a slight stroke. It has affected his right side. I think that he will get better. His heart is strong and his pulse good. I've given him some medicine that should help him. Paralysis is caused by hemorrhage in the brain. Sometimes a clot forms. If the clot absorbs there need not necessarily be any bad aftereffects. But I don't want to hold out too much hope to you. A second stroke may follow this first one immediately. That would be disastrous. What happens, I would say, depends on how he reacts to treatment within . . . oh, perhaps the next five or six days. It's difficult to say what will happen. All we can do is wait."

There was some assurance in the doctor's speech. Eleanor accepted it. She left Cora with her father and showed the doctor a room, the same room that Lin and Windy had once occupied. Then, with the necessity of thought and quiet heavy upon her, she went out to the porch to be alone for a few minutes.

She sat down on the steps and rested her arms laxly across her knees, staring off into the darkness. Gradually her eyes became accustomed to the night and beyond the porch she saw a small huddled figure. "Who is that?" Eleanor said, sharp and low-voiced. "Who . . . ?"

"Me," a small voice answered out of the gloom.

"Bobby!" Eleanor exclaimed.

The huddled figure stirred, straightened, and Bobby moved toward her. Eleanor went down the steps and, stooping, collected the small boy in her arms. Bobby pressed his face against her shoulder, and beneath her arms his body shook with his sobbing.

Lin McCord, stretched out on his bed behind the cabin, heard Carl Yetman begin to snore. Windy was twisting and turning on his bedding, but presently that motion stopped. Lin said "Windy" softly, and, getting no answer, knew that Windy slept. He turned on his back and looked at the stars. They were high and glittering. He turned on his side, then, sitting up, he put on his hat. The light burned steadily in the house and, rising, Lin walked around the building, entered the kitchen softly and looked into the bedroom. Sacatone sat there, brooding, beside the blanket-wrapped body on the bed. Lin tiptoed from the house.

Restless, he could not remain. He walked slowly along the path toward the Patricks', reached the corner of the porch and stopped. Above him a rocker creaked slowly on a loose board. Lin moved again, and from the porch Eleanor Patrick's voice came, soft but clear:

"Who is there?"

"Lin."

The creaking of the rocker stopped. Lin hesitated beneath the porch steps. "Bobby is with me," Eleanor said. "He's asleep."

Lin came up the steps. A match flamed in his hand. In its light he could see Eleanor Patrick seated in the rocker. Bobby was in her arms, and Dan Patrick's old blanket was pulled around her shoulders and arranged to cover the small boy.

"He's asleep," the girl said again.

"I . . ." Lin began.

"I'm sorry about your brother." Eleanor's voice was still low. "I heard. Doctor Vorfree told us."

"I'll take care of Bobby now," Lin said. "I can take him with me."

"I'll look after him." There was possessiveness in the girl's reply. "He'll stay here."

The match had gone out. Lin made no answer. The board creaked as the rocker began its motion again. Lin turned and tiptoed from the porch.

Ed Draper arrived from Adelphi well past sunrise the next morning. With him was Tom Barton, storekeeper, and Adephi's justice of the peace. The two men questioned Vorfree and Donald, talked to Lin and the others, and then Draper drew Lin aside.

"You don't like me, McCord," Draper said bluntly, "any more than I like you, but that don't come into this. You say you're goin' to take your brother back to Texas to bury him. I expect you want to get goin'. It's hot weather, an' you'll want to get to an undertaker. I'll get Barton to hold the inquest right here. We can get a jury

129

from the Portillos boys, an' it won't take long. It's open an' shut: Your brother got drunk in Adelphi an' started home. His horse spooked an' throwed him. He got a foot caught an' was drug to death. Is that the way you think it happened?"

Lin could only nod his agreement. Draper had voiced Lin's own version of the death.

"Suit you if we get at it?" Draper asked.

"Yes," Lin agreed.

"All right, then." Draper turned away. "I'll get some of the Portillos boys an' we'll get through." He walked off toward Manuel's house.

Draper's program was followed. Vorfree and Donald gave their testimony, Barton acting as coroner. The jury, with Manuel, the leader of the Portillos clan, acting as foreman, rendered a verdict and Barton wrote it out for the jurymen's signatures. Vorfree made out a death certificate and gave it to Lin.

"I'm going back to Junction," he said when he gave Lin the paper. "If you'd like me to, I can take your brother to Adelphi. Donald is going to take me in. You can get the train out of Adelphi this evening."

"I don't know . . ." Lin began.

"Donald made the offer himself," Vorfree informed.

"Well, then . . . all right," Lin agreed. "We've . . . I've got to fix John up some, Doctor. I . . ."

"Your man Thomas is taking care of that," Vorfree said. "He went to work as soon as the jury had viewed the body."

"When are you going, Doctor?" Lin asked.

"Right after dinner. I want to examine Mr. Patrick

again and I can't get a train from Adelphi until four o'clock."

"How is Mr. Patrick?" Lin asked.

Vorfree's face brightened. "Better," he said. "There's a young fellow down at the house that's done more for Dan Patrick than all the medical profession could do."

"Bobby?" Lin asked, startled.

Vorfree nodded. "He came into Patrick's room this morning," the doctor said. "Patrick had wakened and was conscious. Bobby went over to the bed and sat down beside him. They didn't talk, but the boy took Patrick's hand. Before I came up here they were both talking and Patrick was asking to sit up. Of course I wouldn't let him. Rest and quiet are imperative, but the boy cheered him up immensely. He was mighty good for Patrick. Is Bobby your boy?"

"John's boy."

"Oh . . . I see."

"I guess he's my boy now," Lin said slowly. "I'm all he's got left."

"He's a manly little fellow," Vorfree said. "I . . . well, I'll be glad to help you, McCord."

Lin said, "Thanks, Doctor," and Vorfree turned and walked away toward the Patricks'.

When the doctor had gone Lin went into the house. Sacatone had wrapped John's body in a blanket and put a bed tarp around that. He and Lin talked a little concerning plans. It was agreed that John would be buried beside his wife in Duffyville. Bobby would go with Lin. It would be necessary for Sacatone Thomas, Windy and Carl to stay at the lease. They would need another man, and Lin promised to send one out from Junction. Carl was already packing the clothing that Bobby would need.

Leaving Sacatone, Lin sought Windy. They talked together a long time, Lin unburdening his mind to his friend and confidant. Windy listened, nodding from time to time and interposing a few words.

"I'll look out for things, Lin," Windy promised. "Say, if you can get hold of that redheaded Morgan, send him up. He's all right."

"I'll do that," Lin agreed. "And remember, Windy, I'm counting on you. It will be up to you and whoever I send up here."

Carl Yetman came out to where the two men stood. "I got some dinner ready," he announced diffidently. "You want to eat before you go, Lin?"

"I'll get Bobby," Lin answered and walked away toward the Patrick house.

After the meal, where good food went begging, the buckboard came up from Patricks', Donald driving. Windy and Sacatone put the blanket-wrapped body of John McCord in the bed of the buckboard, together with grips for Lin and Bobby. The buckboard rolled away, stopping briefly at the Patricks' for Vorfree to climb up beside the driver. Sacatone came from the corral, leading horses for Lin and Bobby and a horse for himself. Good-bys were said to Windy and Yetman and, Bobby and Lin mounting, the riders followed the buckboard. Draper and Barton were already gone. By half-past one the camp on Rough Mesa was deserted save for Windy and the cook.

Sacatone left Lin and Bobby in Adelphi. Sacatone was stolidly silent on the ride in and had equally little to say on reaching town. Lin was occupied there, sending telegrams and making arrangements for shipping the body to Junction. Sacatone said a brief goodby to Lin and to Bobby and left, heading back for the lease.

Sacatone rode slowly, taking his time up Pinál Canyon where now the shadows of afternoon were collecting. In his mind Sacatone reconstructed another ride up the canyon. He could visualize John McCord leaving Adelphi, filled with whisky, uncertain in his saddle and yet riding with the natural seat of the man who has learned to ride as he learned to walk.

Pinál Creek wandered down the canyon, the road crossing and recrossing the stream. Sacatone went along, the hoofs of his horse splashing in the fords, sending up dust from the road between the fords. Pinál Canyon was dry. The whole country was dry, for there had been no rain. Even the pines looked parched. Sacatone paid but little heed to the pines; he watched the road.

From Donald's description he knew about where the tragedy had occurred. Some three miles from the last steep ascent to the mesa top Sacatone pulled his horse to a halt and looked all around. This was the place. Here, or near here, something had frightened John McCord's horse; there had been a sudden lunge, a man unseated, and then the wild run of the horse dragging a screaming man across the rocks. Just about here! Sacatone Thomas rode forward slowly.

The creek crossed the road just ahead of him, the last crossing in the canyon. Sacatone's horse and his lead horses stopped in the creek to drink. Grulla, Sacatone's mount, stretched out his mouse-colored neck and nosed the water, and Sacatone, looking down, saw something bright wink beneath the limpid trickle of the creek. He stared at it, catching its distorted image through the water. Grulla snuffed and drank and snuffed and drank again, and then splashed out of the creek. Sacatone stopped the horse, dismounted and, thrusting his hand down into the water, lifted out a spent cartridge. He stared at it.

The shell was a .38-.55, not particularly bright, not dull. It had, from its color, been recently fired. Sacatone's black eyes were sharp. He looked up and down the creek and just beyond the ford saw a splash of darkness on a rock. He walked to that rock and looked at it; then, tying his lead horses to trees, he mounted Grulla again and went back across the ford.

Down the road a hundred feet he stopped again. Carefully he examined the road and the small area about it. The horses had gone along the road; the wheels that had marked it, the dryness and the dust, obscured the sign, but Sacatone Thomas could trail a snake across rock. He dismounted and on foot walked around, stopping now and then, examining a broken stick, a bunch of dry grass that had been crushed, a displaced pebble. Again he mounted Grulla and now, briskly, went back up the road again.

Collecting his lead horses, he went along up the ascent of Pinál, out to the top of the mesa and through the lower gate. He did not go to the cabin where Windy and Carl awaited him but on to the corrals. There he left his horses and walked briskly to the barn. The saddles were kept in the barn, resting on a long pole against the wall. Windy's saddle was there; Carl Yetman's old battered hull, thrown across a discolored blanket, rested beside Windy's. There was another saddle on the pole, a saddle that was new compared to the others, a saddle just broken in, the sheen of the saddlemaker's shop still upon it: John McCord's saddle. Sacatone dragged it from the pole and carried it outside. There in the sunlight still streaming in from the west he examined the saddle, seat, swell, skirts, jockeys, latigos, cinches, stirrup leathers and stirrups. Once more he went over it carefully, searching for something. And where the right jockey pressed against the skirts he found the thing he sought. There was a thin line of rust color at the edge of the jockey. Sacatone lifted up the leather. The rust color had seeped beneath it. With his fingernail he scraped the rust. It flaked and broke and rested on his finger. Sacatone straightened up from the saddle and slowly pulled the .38-.55 cartridge from his pants pocket.

That was blood on the saddle, blood that had been wiped away but that had seeped down under the jockey to lie hidden against the blond leather of the skirt. Blood on the saddle. A man dragged along the ground might bleed; there might be blood upon the cinches, spattered there from a kicking hoof, from a jagged rock, but not upon the saddle.

Sacatone walked over toward the corral. There were horses in the pen, and outside his own Grulla and the lead horses stood, heads drooping, waiting to be relieved of the saddles. At the gate Sacatone stopped. Redskin moved out from the penned horses, coming toward the fence. He stopped and looked at Sacatone, ears pricked forward, head raised.

"Yeah," Sacatone said, his voice dry and cracking, "you never done it, Redskin. It wasn't you."

Redskin turned and trotted back to the other horses, and Sacatone opened the gate and pulled Grulla through.

"Not you, Redskin," he said again. "He was shot. Blood on his saddle. He was murdered!"

CHAPTER XI
AMATEUR DETECTIVE

WINDY HAD COME BACK FROM ADELPHI LATE IN THE evening. He had no particular news. Sacatone, with the taciturnity of an Indian, kept his discovery to himself. There was much on Sacatone's mind. His code was the old Biblical precept: "An eye for an eye; a tooth for a tooth." Someone had killed John McCord; therefore, reasoned Sacatone, that person must be apprehended and killed. Simple enough reasoning and deadly. The morning after Lin's departure Windy and Carl talked, and Sacatone ate breakfast and, when the meal was over, went with Windy to the corral and got a horse.

Windy did not try to tell Sacatone what to do. He knew Sacatone well, and there was an equality between

136

the two men. Sacatone knew what to do, so Windy believed and, accordingly, saying that he was going to ride the west fence, he rode out across the mesa top. Sacatone watched Windy go and then, mounting, rode back toward Pinál Canyon.

He spent a good part of the morning in the canyon, re-examining the ground, going over it carefully. Slow rage seethed in Sacatone, not so much toward the person who had killed John McCord as toward the fools that had messed up the tracks. It was impossible to read trail accurately, but from his investigations Sacatone became sure of one thing: Whoever had shot John McCord had come from the mesa. He reasoned this from the position occupied by the shell he had found. The shell had lain in the gravelly creek crossing in the ford. John McCord had been coming up the canyon. The spot where he had fallen, the first blood-stains, were below the crossing. Then John McCord and his murderer had met face to face. Sacatone was sure of that.

Toward noon he rode back up the canyon road and as he traveled he formed a plan. There were only a few men on the mesa, a few people all told. There were the Patricks, the McCord crew and there were the choppers. True, someone might have reached the mesa top by another route, or even by this one, but the first people to be eliminated in his search were those who lived on the mesa.

When Sacatone reached the top he went to camp. There he pulled his Winchester from its scabbard and carried it into the house. It was necessary, as a part of his plan, that he appear without a weapon. Substituting for the Winchester a short-barreled Colt which he secreted in the pocket of his chaps, he grunted to Carl Yetman and went out again. From the camp he rode to the houses occupied by the Portillos.

Here he began his search. At the house occupied by Manuel Portillos he dismounted, and when Manuel came to join him Sacatone produced papers and tobacco, offered them and, while Manuel rolled a cigarette, began a guileless conversation. In the course of that talk Sacatone mentioned the fact that Lin had seen a big dog coyote. Perhaps Manuel had also seen coyotes. No? Well, then, would Manuel lend Sacatone his rifle? Sacatone was riding every day and he might stumble upon coyote sign, or even a den.

Manuel was desolate but he had no rifle.

Did any of the Portillos, to Manuel's knowledge, own a rifle?

There was Adolfo, a younger brother. He had a gun.

Sacatone bade Manuel good-by and went to visit Adolfo.

Adolfo's rifle turned out to be a twenty-two single shot. A *"Veintidós."* It was too light for coyotes. Sacatone politely declined its loan. From one Portillos to another he took his way, and found no rifle.

That, of course, was just the first step. Sacatone did not believe any of the Portillos boys. If they had killed John McCord they would certainly deny possessing a rifle; but, having been questioned, they would be anxious if they were guilty. Anxiety betrays itself. Sacatone would watch and search.

Having temporarily eliminated the Portillos, Sacatone went to the Patrick house. There he encountered Sandy Donald and in Donald he struck ore. Telling the same story of the dog coyote and the wish to borrow a gun, he met with an answer. Donald himself had no rifle but Dan Patrick had one.

"Dan's got a deer gun," Donald said. "I think you could borrow it, but I hate to bother Eleanor right now."

"What's the caliber?" Sacatone asked. "Do you know?"

"A thirty-eight fifty-five," Donald said. "I'll go in an' get it. I think it'll be all right to loan it to you."

Sacatone made no protest, and Donald went into the house. He returned empty handed. "I couldn't find it," he said. "Dan always kept it over some deer horns in the corner, but it ain't there. I guess Eleanor's put it away."

"Well," Sacatone drawled, "I don't need a gun right today, anyhow. Thanks, Donald."

Leaving Donald, Sacatone went to camp and ate a lunch with Carl, Windy not yet having come in. The dark little man was abstract and silent as he considered his next step. Donald he eliminated from the scheme of things, at least temporarily. Donald, he knew, had been in Adelphi waiting for the doctor to come from Junction when John was killed. At least that was the supposition and could easily be checked upon. Inquiries could be made in Adelphi and the truth learned. And with Donald eliminated, that left but one person: Eleanor Patrick. Certainly Dan Patrick was too sick to have taken his rifle, gone down the canyon and committed murder. So Sacatone reasoned.

He left the camp before Windy came in, and returned to his quest. Riding down to the Patrick house, he went to the front door and knocked. Fortunately for Sacatone it was Cora who answered.

"I'd like to see Miss Patrick," Sacatone announced when Cora opened the door. "I want to borrow her daddy's rifle if I can. Could I see her?"

"I don't like to bother her," Cora said. "She's layin' down an' the poor thing's had no rest all night. She was out yesterday for quite a while an' last night she sat up with her father. I'll go see if she's asleep."

Cora left him then, and Sacatone waited on the porch. So the Patrick girl had been out yesterday! He filed that information.

Cora came back to the door. "Eleanor says they haven't got a rifle," she reported. "I'm sorry. What did you want one for?"

"There's a big dog coyote hanging around," Sacatone replied. "I wanted to get a shot at him."

"You can get a rifle in Adelphi," Cora informed. "There's lots of men got them there. I know you can borrow one. You go see Jake Smith or one of the Loftus boys an' they'll loan you a rifle."

"Thanks," Sacatone said briefly, and left the porch. Walking back toward the corral, he thought over what he had learned. Donald said that the Patricks had a rifle, a .38-.55. That was the proper caliber. When Donald had gone to get the gun it was missing. That, to Sacatone, meant that Donald had been sure the gun was in the house. Either he really hadn't found it or he had lied. Now, applying to Eleanor Patrick, Sacatone had learned through Cora that Eleanor had been absent from the house the day before and that she said there was no rifle. It didn't look good to Sacatone. He got his horse from the corral and started north. He would cut a circle around the Patrick house. There would be tracks, undisturbed by others, and from those tracks Sacatone might learn where Eleanor Patrick had gone. The weather was dry and tracking difficult; and still, with absolute faith in his own ability, Sacatone clung to the idea.

The paths he crossed were marked by numerous feet. Horses, steers and men had passed along the trails. But trails are not the only pathways. Following along north and west of the settlement, Sacatone saw where someone had come into the main-traveled trail. He got down and led his horse and within fifteen feet of the path identified the person who had entered it. Here, plain in the leaf mold under the pines, was the deep imprint of a narrow foot. The toe was pressed deeply and the heel barely touching. Eleanor Patrick had come by here and she had been running.

Sacatone went on. He found other prints, a broken twig crushed by a running foot, brown pine needles disturbed and scuffed, a little patch of shale that had been scattered, and when he neared the edge of the timber and approached the open grassland of the big park he stopped short. There beside the trail he followed was the thing he sought. The .38-.55 cast hastily aside by Eleanor Patrick, when she realized in her terror that she still carried the gun, lay heavy and blue and brown beside the trail. Sacatone stooped and picked up the gun. He looked at it. The initials "DP" had been burned in the stock. When he shoved down the lever and looked through the barrel he could see the fouling, the residue left by a recent shot. The cartridge ejected when he worked the lever was a UMC. The cartridge that Sacatone had picked up bore that same marking. Sacatone put the rifle in the scabbard under his right fender and, mounting, rode back the way he had come. His problem, so Sacatone believed, was answered.

As he rode, Sacatone reconstructed events. Eleanor Patrick had gone down Pinál Canyon with the gun. She had met John McCord and shot him, probably waylaid him and killed him from ambush, so Sacatone reasoned. Then she had come back to the mesa top and, from where the road crowned out of the canyon, had circled, intending to return to the house from the northwest rather than the east. That would be logical. It would hide the fact that she came from the canyon, should anyone observe her. Somewhere along the way she had become frightened and, throwing the gun aside, had run. The chances were, Sacatone thought, that she had intended to return and get the rifle after dark but had been delayed by the arrival of the doctor and the discovery of John's death. Sacatone scowled as he rode. He had solved his problem but now another confronted him.

According to Sacatone's reasoning, the girl had killed John McCord. With a man Sacatone would have known what to do. With a man he would simply have made direct accusation and abided by the consequences. A man he would have killed. But this was a woman. What should he do? You don't kill women; only the law can

142

do that. It was apparent to Sacatone that this was a matter for the law.

He ran in the horses after reaching the camp, rode out into the horse pasture and brought them in. Deliberately he changed horses and then, with no word to Carl Yetman or to anyone else, Sacatone mounted and started for Adelphi.

Sacatone reached the little town just before five o'clock. He rode slowly along the street, debating his next move. Sacatone did not want to turn this evidence he had found over to Ed Draper. There was, to Sacatone's simple mind, a feud between Draper and the McCords. Sacatone remembered how Lin had gone to get the crew free from Draper and, too, he remembered the night vigil when Draper and Samms had come along the road and been stopped by Lin and himself. Draper wasn't the man he wanted. It must be some officer other than Draper. Stopping at the store, Sacatone dismounted and went in. As he hesitated in front of the counter a clerk came to ascertain his wants.

"Who's sheriff here?" Sacatone asked the clerk.

"Ed Draper is the deputy," the clerk said, staring at the weathered little man.

"But who's the sheriff?" Sacatone persisted.

"Why . . . Sam Rideout's the sheriff."

"Where does he live?"

"In Junction."

Sacatone scratched a bushy, itching eyebrow. "Thanks," he said and went out. On the sidewalk again he debated. Junction, he knew, was fifty miles away. He could ride in to Junction all right, but he wouldn't get there for seven or eight hours. That would be midnight or after. Sacatone knew the schedule of the Polly. He untied his horse and, mounting, rode back to the depot. He did not want to go to Sam Rideout in Junction; he wanted Sam Rideout to come to him in Adelphi. Sacatone arrived at the depot and once more dismounted and tied his horse.

Pop Vicars was in the office when the dark little man appeared at the window. Vicars left his work and approached this potential customer. "What's it cost to send a telegram to Junction?" Sacatone inquired.

"Half a dollar," Vicars answered.

"Telegrams is secret, ain't they?" Sacatone pursued his inquiry. "Nobody knows what's in 'em except the fellow that sent 'em an' the man that gets 'em?"

"I know what's in 'em," Vicars answered. "I have to know, to send 'em."

Sacatone's black eyes were sharp as he looked at the agent. "You in the habit of puttin' out what's in 'em?" he asked bluntly.

Pop bristled. "I've been here thirty years an' nothin's leaked out of this office yet!" he snapped.

Again Sacatone studied the station agent narrowly. He shook his head. "You give me somethin' to write a telegram on," he directed.

Vicars brought a pad of blanks and a pencil. Sacatone took them. He wet the pencil copiously, chewed on it and then scrawled words on the message blank.

It took Sacatone a long time to write his telegram. A man with a fourth-grade education is not prolific in written words. Sacatone wrote and scratched out and

144

wrote again and presently pushed the message across to the waiting Vicars. "If that gets out around town," he stated mildly, "I'll kill you dead enough to skin."

Vicars was angry. He glared at Sacatone and then, noting the expression on the little man's face, the hard glitter of the black eyes, Pop Vicars' anger was supplanted by alarm. This black-eyed man meant exactly what he said. Pop Vicars counted words hastily.

"That's more 'n fifty cents," he said. "You got twenty-four words. That'll be a dollar."

"You said fifty cents," Sacatone reminded. "It'll go for fifty cents."

Once more Pop Vicars examined his customer. "All right, give me fifty cents then," he said surlily. "The sheriff can't get here till mornin'. There ain't any train."

"I'll wait for him," Sacatone announced and put half a dollar on the window counter.

He remained at the window, watching Pop Vicars sit down at the desk and tap the worn black knob of the key. He heard the staccato clicks as the words he had written went on the wire. Vicars stopped and looked up.

"Well, she's gone," he announced.

Sacatone grunted and disappeared from the window. Vicars moved from the telegraph desk to his worn desk. After a time, passing the window, he looked out. Sacatone was ensconced on the bench in the waiting room.

"You ain't waitin' for an answer, are you?" Vicars asked, leaning out.

Sacatone shook his head. "Just waitin'," he replied.

Vicars grunted and went on about his work.

At six o'clock, when the depot closed, the agent, key

in hand, went into the waiting room to lock the door. Pop Vicars lived upstairs above the depot. It was time for him to close the station and cook his lonely supper. Sacatone was still on the bench.

"I'm goin' to lock up," Vicars announced.

"Not tonight," Sacatone said.

Eye met eye. Pop Vicars shrugged and put the key in his pocket. He was not going to lock up tonight. All right, he wasn't.

Later, cooking supper, he thought of the man downstairs. Vicars sliced more bacon and made extra coffee. He took the bacon in a thick sandwich, together with a cup of coffee, down to his self-invited guest. Sacatone received them gratefully. He ate and drank. With the coffee cup empty, Vicars asked a question.

"Goin' to stay all night?"

"Till the train gets in," Sacatone announced.

"Want to come up an' visit a while?"

"No."

Pop Vicars took the empty cup and went back upstairs. When he opened the depot the following morning Sacatone was still on the bench; Sacatone's horse, head hanging, was still at the hitch rail. There was nothing about either man or horse that spoke of sleep. Sacatone's beady black eyes were wide awake and alert. Vicars said, "Good morning," and got no answer. He went on about his work. Still, when he cooked breakfast he again fried extra bacon and made two extra cups of coffee. These he carried downstairs.

Sacatone accepted them, ate slowly and drank the coffee. Finished, Sacatone wiped his mouth with the back of his hand. "Mebbe there wasn't no reason for me to stay all night," Sacatone admitted slowly, "but a man never knows, does he?"

"I guess not," Pop Vicars agreed.

"That's good coffee," Sacatone said. "Thanks."

"It's all right," the depot agent said.

The train from Junction came in at one o'clock. Pop Vicars, his official cap perched on his head, was on the platform when the engine came steaming by. Sacatone stood close by. When the accommodation car slid to a stop and Sam Rideout got down stiffly, Vicars spoke to Sacatone for the last time.

"There's your man," he said. "That's the sheriff."

"Yeah," Sacatone said and then, grudgingly, "You're all right." With that recommendation he went to meet Rideout.

On the morning of the second day after Lin McCord's departure with his brother's body, Ed Draper walked into Otis Melcomb's office. Hunter, the bookkeeper, raised his watery brown eyes as the deputy arrived and answered Draper's question. "Mr. Melcomb's in his office," Hunter informed. "Samms is with him."

Draper nodded to the bookkeeper and walked on into Melcomb's office, not knocking, simply pushing open the door and walking in. When the door had closed Glen Hunter reapplied himself to the ledger upon which he worked.

He was a bald-headed man, Glen Hunter, with a fringe of sparse hair circling his head and a few stragglers on the crown which he combed back to make thin lines across his scalp. To compensate for the lack of hair on top of his head Hunter grew a mustache. That hirsute adornment resembled nothing so much as the whiskers of a cat. Added to the feline antenna was a pug nose, a pair of full and sensuous lips that drooped at the corners and ears that stood out from the side of his head like the open wings of a butterfly. In all Adelphi Glen Hunter was the only man of fashion. He bought his clothes from a mail-order house in Chicago, and his coats with the padded shoulders, his peg-topped trousers and the knobby-toed, brown-buttoned shoes he wore set him apart aside from all the rest of the town.

When a safe time had elapsed after Draper's entrance, Hunter slipped down from his high stool and went to the end of his bookkeeper's desk, the end nearest Melcomb's private office. Unknown to Otis Melcomb, but of old acquaintance to Hunter, was the crack in the transom above Melcomb's office door. Sounds seeped out through that crack, words and sentences. Glen Hunter had acquired much information through the transom crack. Standing there at the end of the desk, he was a picture of sartorial splendor and of innocence, and yet there was something pathetic about Glen Hunter. With a book open before him and a pen in his hand he advertised to anyone who looked that he was at work. And while he advertised he listened.

"I guess you won't have to worry any more, Spike," Draper was saying. "They swore out a warrant for the Patrick girl. Arrestin' her for murder."

Hunter did not hear Samms' reply; it was indistinct,

but Draper must have been standing just inside the door, for his voice came plainly.

"Yeah. That fellow Thomas found a gun that belonged to her old man. It had been shot. It's a .38-.55, just like yours. I guess that puts you in the clear."

Again Samms' reply was lost but Melcomb's voice came clearly to the listener. "I don't give a damn! You killed the wrong man, Spike. I needed John McCord in this business. It was his damned brother I wanted out of the way."

Hunter hunched his shoulders. So Spike Samms had killed John McCord. Now Samms had moved; at least his voice was audible. "I tell you I couldn't help it! I run square into him. He knew we'd been up there. I had to down him."

"If you'd stuck with Ed you'd have been all right!" Melcomb snarled. "Ed didn't get caught. I needed John McCord. Now you've—"

Draper interrupted. "It's done, Otis. Let it go. No need of crawlin' on Spike. He's done plenty for you before this."

"You're both a pair of bungling damned fools." Melcomb was wrathy. "You went up there to kill Lin McCord and the girl scared you away. Then Samms kills the man I needed most. I've a mind to—"

"Now wait," Draper interposed once more. "Don't say what you don't mean, Otis. This killin' will be hung on the girl. From what Barton told me, they got the dope on her all right. Rideout's got the warrant an' he's goin' to serve it. He's gone back to Rough Mesa now. That ought to be some help. You can crowd her now,

Otis. If she's in jail she's goin' to listen to reason about the timber."

Melcomb's reply was a pacified rumble. Draper, too, lowered his voice and Samms apparently had nothing to say. Glen Hunter toyed with his pen and pushed the ledger away and then pulled it back. In Melcomb's office the voices rose again.

"I won't do it!" Melcomb flung the words out angrily.

"Yes you will." Draper's voice had risen a note but was still smooth. "You've had the pickin's off this other country, but Spike an' me get a third each for this Rough Mesa deal. We each get a third of the profits."

"I've already cut you in," Melcomb said hotly. "I—"

"But not enough," Draper interposed. "Look here. It was Spike that crippled Patrick for you in the first place. I've done your dirty work around here. I know that you've got it on us, Melcomb, but we've got it on you too. You're goin' to cut us in for a third each."

There was movement in the inner office. Hunter hurriedly closed the ledger and, slipping softly around the high desk, opened the gate in the railing. There was a chance that some one of those three men would open the office door. When that happened Glen Hunter did not want to be in evidence. It was too dangerous.

CHAPTER XII
TIME ELEMENT

TEN SHORT DAYS AFTER HIS DEPARTURE LIN MCCORD returned to Junction. In that thriving little city he first went to the hotel where, registering, he left Bobby. Exacting Bobby's promise that he would stay either in his room or in the lobby, Lin left the boy and went to the courthouse. He entered that red brick memorial to an architect's nightmare and, striding down the corridor, walked into the sheriff's office. Sam Rideout, appraised by the thump of boot heels of an arrival, turned in his swivel chair and, recognizing Lin, got up.

"I got your telegram," Lin said. "I came back as soon as I could."

"Sit down," Rideout invited. "I want to ask you a question, McCord."

Lin sat down. Rideout reseated himself in his chair and, swinging it so that he faced Lin, spoke slow-voiced and earnest. "McCord, on the afternoon of your brother's death did you see Eleanor Patrick? Did you see her when you were riding your pasture? Were there shots fired at you?"

Lin sensed that here was trouble. He thought swiftly. He, and he alone, knew of the girl's action there on Rough Mesa. Lin believed, could do nothing but believe, that she had shot at him. He dismissed that thought. He loved Eleanor, knew that he loved her, and in his heart he could not blame her for firing those shots. Since the first shock of John's death had passed

Lin had thought a great deal about that meeting on the knoll. Now he lifted his eyes to Sam Rideout's face. "No," he said abruptly, "I didn't see her. I wasn't shot at."

Rideout sighed and leaned back in his chair. "Then I guess it's all up with her," he said. "She killed your brother, McCord."

"Killed John?" Utterly astonished, Lin started to his feet. "Why, you're crazy!"

"I wish I was," Rideout said. "I sure wish I was. Lissen, McCord, I'll tell you. Sit down an' let me talk."

Lin reseated himself, taking the edge of the chair, his hands resting on the sheriff's desk top.

Rideout swung the chair away from Lin and then back so that he faced the man again. "There was a mix-up," Rideout said shortly. "When you left here you thought that your brother had been drug to death, didn't you?"

Lin nodded.

"Well"—Rideout's face showed his discomfort "he wasn't. I was gone out to Holtrace the day that happened. I didn't get back till a day after you'd left. My chief deputy was gone to Colorado after a prisoner, an' José Aragon was here in the office. When you come in you took your brother to Ray Evans' undertakin' parlor. You wanted him fixed up so that you could ship him."

"I know all that," Lin said impatiently. "What's that got to do with—"

"Wait," Rideout interposed. "I'm tryin' to tell you how this happened. Ray has got a young fellow workin' for him, an apprentice, an' it was the kid that worked on

152

your brother. When Ray come back the two of them put your brother in the coffin you'd picked out an' closed it up an' packed it in the shippin' box. Ray had the death certificate an' all, an' it was all in order. The box went to the train an' you pulled out. It wasn't till later that Ray an' the kid got to talkin', an' somethin' the kid said made Ray think that things wasn't right. So they went back down to the parlor an' looked over things, an' Ray found this." Rideout opened the drawer of his desk and took a misshapen lump of lead from it. He held it out to Lin.

"The kid had taken this out of your brother's back. It's a bullet."

Lin took the lump of lead and turned it slowly in his fingers.

"Ray asked the kid some questions an' found out some things, an' then he come hotfootin' it up here to get me. An' I was gone." Rideout's voice was bitter. "That fool deputy of mine didn't know what to do. He couldn't get hold of me, so he let things set till I got back."

"Well?" Lin said.

"Well, by that time your man Thomas wired me. He'd found the shell for the lead an' he'd done some trackin'. There was sign where a rider had come down the canyon an' met your brother. There was the shell: a .38-.55. The Patrick girl had gone out of the house an' left Cora Ferguson lookin' after her dad. Thomas scouted around an' found a rifle in the timber below the house. It was Patrick's gun an' it had been fired. Eleanor told a wild cock-an'-bull story about goin' out carryin' the gun an' seein' you. You come across the flat beyond the house, she said, an' she was on a hill, an' somebody on the next hill took a shot at you. She said that she shot into the hill an' two men rode out. Then she said that you came up the hill an' she ran home. She said she'd throwed the gun away while she ran."

"She—" Lin began.

"Wait till I get done!" Rideout said harshly. "That story wouldn't wash. It didn't stick. There's been a rain on the mesa, an' I went up there. Of course I didn't find any tracks. But I'd heard her tell you that she could kill you. Now I been investigatin', McCord. I know that it wasn't you that sold that lease. I saw the sublease that Melcomb's got, an' your brother signed it. Tillitson said that you didn't know a thing about it, that you was upset an' sore because your brother'd sold it, an' that you went down an' tried to buy it back. I figure that the Patrick girl found out that your brother sold that sublease an' she killed him for it."

"No she didn't," Lin said quickly. "Maybe John was shot. I don't doubt that. There's evidence to prove it. But Eleanor didn't do it. She was right, Sheriff. She *was* up on the mesa when I had a shot taken at me, an' I found her on the hill, like she told you. I thought she'd shot at me an'—"

Lin stopped. Rideout was shaking his head. There was a friendly expression on the officer's face but his voice was stern. "It won't do, McCord," he said. "When you came in here, before you knew anything about your brother's bein' shot, I asked you an' you said 'no.' You're tryin' to protect the girl, McCord. Thomas said that you'd fallen for her. I don't like you none the worse for it, but it won't go down."

"Sacatone seems to have given up plenty of head," Lin said bitterly. "Look, Rideout, I know she didn't shoot John."

"How do you know?" The sheriff was eager.

"You won't believe me, but that story about her bein' on the hill an' shootin' is true," Lin said. "I was tryin' to keep her out of trouble when you first asked me, an' I lied. She was there, all right. I thought she'd took a shot at me—" Seeing the expression on Rideout's face, he stopped in midsentence. As Lin had said, Rideout was not believing him.

"Anyhow," Lin said desperately, "I'd swear to it in court. An' the night that John was killed I went lookin' for Bobby an' she had him on the porch. She was holding him on her lap an' she'd rocked him to sleep. Do you think she could kill Bobby's dad an' then do that?"

Slowly Rideout shook his head. "*I* don't think so," he said, "but it ain't evidence, McCord. Here's what's evidence: she said she could kill you when she thought you'd sold that lease. That was a threat. Patrick's gun, with the barrel fouled from shootin', was in the timber below the house. The gun's a .38-.55. The slug that killed your brother was a .38-.55. Eleanor went out an' she had the rifle with her. She admits that. She don't know what time she got back, or else she won't tell the time, an' Cora Ferguson don't know when she come in either. There's the motive an' there's the proof she done it, an' that's what the judge an' a jury are goin' to look at."

"Then we'll get something else for them to look at," Lin snarled. "I know she didn't kill John."

Rideout stood up wearily. "I hope you can," he said. "I like that girl. I've always liked her. But—"

"But hell!" The anger in Lin's voice lashed at the sheriff. "You won't believe me when I tell you the truth an' you'd sit here an' not look to find the real killer. Well, I won't sit, Rideout. I'll find him!"

Lin left the sheriff then and, going to the street, stood undecided for a moment. He was upset, alarmed and angry. He wanted to get to the lease, wanted to talk to Sacatone and to Windy, wanted action. But there was no train for Adelphi until morning. He had time to kill.

Desiring action as he did, he thought of another matter: the injunction that had been issued against Dan Patrick. Here was something that he could immediately attack. In Duffyville Lin had talked to his old friend, Judge Nesbit, who had given him legal advice and the name of a lawyer in Junction. Now Lin drew a letter from his pocket, read the name scrawled on the back of the envelope and, stopping a passer-by, asked the location of Rafael Watts's office.

Rafael Watts had his office above the post office and he was in. Lin, having introduced himself to the chubby, pink-cheeked man, spoke of Judge Nesbit and Nesbit's recommendation. Watts nodded and was pleased. From that beginning Lin plunged into his business. Watts listened, hands locked across his pursy middle, eyes half closed. When Lin finished Watts

156

brought his feet to the floor, tilted his chair forward and asked a question.

"You want me to handle this for you?"

"I want you to handle it for the Patricks, but I'll pay you," Lin said.

Again the lawyer indulged in thought. "All right," he said at length, "I'll do it. We may not win, but at least we'll make things interesting for Walter Yawl and Otis Melcomb. This isn't the first time I've had to do with them."

"Yawl?" Lin asked.

"The company lawyer," Watts explained.

"But he drew the lease," Lin began. "He—"

"No doubt!" Watts's voice was dry. "Now go over it again, please. I want to make some notes."

Lin repeated the story, with occasional interruptions from Watts as he asked questions. The lawyer was particularly insistent concerning the partnership agreement between Lin and John, was pleased to find that there was no written agreement and more than pleased when he learned that, despite John's activity around Junction and Adelphi, it was Lin who had contracted for the steers, who had done the shipping and signed the Rough Mesa lease.

"I think we'll whip them," Watts said at the end of the conference. "I'll set things in motion here, Mr. McCord, and I'll write to you in a few days."

Lin went back to the hotel. There he found Bobby sitting on the edge of the desk and entertaining the clerk.

Early the following morning the two, man and boy, got up and dressed and, although the train to Adelphi did not leave until an hour later, went to the depot. When the Polly pulled out they were on it, and all the way up the hill Lin fumed with impatience. As they climbed down from the accommodation car at Adelphi they saw Windy awaiting their arrival with the buckboard from the lease.

Windy shook hands, first with Bobby and then with Lin, and Lin was about to plunge into questions when Pop Vicars came from the depot waving a yellow envelope. "Telegram for you," Vicars announced. "It came in last night."

Lin took the envelope, ripped it open and, having read the address, looked at Pop in surprise. "Why," he said, "this is for John."

Vicars nodded. "I know it," he answered. "But he's—" Pop broke off.

"Yeah," Lin said, knowing what Pop had intended to say. Again he looked at the telegram and then, having read it through twice, turned to the agent again. "I don't *sabe* this," Lin said. "It's . . ."

"Your brother sent a telegram the day he was killed," Vicars explained seriously. "I got it an' the answer he got in the depot. Do you want 'em?"

"Maybe they'll tell me what this is all about," Lin answered. "I'd like to have them."

Lin followed Pop into the station, Bobby and Windy trailing along. Vicars searched through the messages on his spindle, pulled off a few and handed two yellow blanks to Lin. "There's the one he sent an' here's the answer he got," the agent explained.

Lin read through the messages.

158

"You want copies?" Vicars asked.

"I'd like to have them," Lin agreed, and Vicars, pulling a pencil from under his cap, fell to writing.

"When John came in here," Lin asked carefully, "was he . . . had he been drinking?"

Vicars looked up from his labor. "Not that I could tell," the agent replied. "He was mad. He wrote that message an' asked how long it would take to get an answer. I told him about four hours. He sat down on the bench in the waitin' room an' stayed there. He never left till his answer come in. Then he pulled out."

"I see," Lin said, and Vicars resumed his writing.

So then John had not been drunk. That was some consolation to Lin, and, according to the messages, John had wanted money. The first telegram that John had sent was to an old friend in a bank in Galveston, asking for a loan. The reply stated that the man John had telegraphed was out of town. Mr. McCord's request would be referred to him on his return. The third message was from his friend Wimberley himself, saying that John's message had been forwarded to him in Chicago.

"Here you are," Pop said, pushing out the copies he had made.

"Thanks," Lin said and took the messages.

"Any time I can do you any good you let me know," Vicars said.

"Thanks, I sure will. So long." Lin nodded to the agent and, with his two companions, left the depot.

When they were in the buckboard Windy asked a question. "Say, I got to deliver a message here in town.

Will that be all right?"

"Sure," Lin agreed.

Windy drove the buckboard down the street and stopped in front of the millinery shop. Giving Bobby the lines to hold, he went in.

Windy was gone about ten minutes. During that time men and women, passing by, stared curiously at Lin and Bobby who occupied the buckboard seat. Windy came back, climbed up and took the lines. Turning around in the street, he started the buckboard back toward the west.

They were out of town before Lin spoke. "How are things at the lease?" he asked.

"Cattle are all right," Windy answered. "We need some rain. We had one little shower after you'd gone, but it's dry now. Red Lakes went dry. The steers are waterin' at the spring an' at the creek."

Lin nodded. "How about the rest of it?" he asked quietly.

Windy spat over the wheel. "We've had a hell of a time," he announced. "Sacatone is a damned fool, Lin. He says that Eleanor Patrick killed John."

"The sheriff told me." Still that ominous quiet in Lin's voice.

"He tell you they arrested her an' that she's out on bail?"

"He told me all about it." Lin looked at Windy. Windy watched the road. "He told me about findin' the gun an' about the shell an' the slug they took out of John, an' the whole case they had against her. I made it worse, Windy. Rideout asked me if I'd seen her that afternoon.

160

He asked me if I'd had a shot taken at me. I told him 'no.' I thought I was protectin' her." Lin's voice was bitter.

"How does that make it worse?" Windy asked.

"Because I had seen her and I had a shot taken at me," Lin admitted. From there he went on, detailing the happenings on the knoll the afternoon of John's death. "She ran," he completed. "She threw that rifle away when she saw that she was carryin' it. If I'd known a damned thing about it I'd have told Rideout the truth. Now, when I do tell him the truth, he thinks I'm tryin' to protect her an' he won't believe me. I'm sure a fool, Windy. All I've done is make trouble for her."

"Is Eleanor in trouble?" Bobby asked.

"Kind of, kid," Lin answered. "Don't you worry about it; we'll get her out. Have you seen her, Windy?"

"I been down there," Windy answered. "She don't say much. Sacatone an' me damned near fought over it. Sacatone says she done it, an' I told him he was crazy. We had a pretty poor time."

"Sacatone is crazy," Lin said.

"Uncle Sac?" Bobby looked at Lin. "Is he crazy? Will he have to go to the aslyum?"

"No, kid," Lin said, "he won't have to go to the asylum. He isn't crazy that way. I guess we'd better not talk till we get home, Windy."

Windy nodded and tapped the team with the buggy whip. The team trotted.

As they neared the top of the canyon Windy said "Here's where it happened," and pointed with the whip. Lin looked at the creek, barely a trickle now, and at the canyon all about. He made no comment. Further along Windy pointed up with the whip.

"Shorty Morgan an' me kind of kept lookin' out from up there," he said, indicating the outcrop in the canyon wall. "We thought mebbe Melcomb would try to move a camp up here. He didn't, an' we ain't keepin' watch no more."

"Why?"

"Because Melcomb's workin' another way now. He knows that Eleanor's in a tight an' he's puttin' the pressure on her. He's tryin' to buy the mesa."

Lin said, "Ummm."

"Patrick wants to sell," Windy continued after a time. "He's up an' around now an' kind of takin' an interest. Eleanor won't let him sell to Melcomb. She says she'll go to jail first."

"You know a lot about what she says an' what's going on," Lin said sharply.

"I went to see her." Windy did not look at Lin. "I told her it was John sold that sublease an' how you tried to get it back. Rideout told her about the sublease too. She ain't sore at you, Lin."

"You shouldn't have done that!" Lin's voice was sharp.

Windy turned his head and looked his employer in the eyes. "I was damned if I was goin' to see you get all the rough edges," he snapped. "You think a hell of a lot of that girl, an' I know it. Cora says—" Windy broke off.

"Cora?"

"Cora Ferguson. She was up here a while lookin' after Patrick when he was so bad. I kind of got acquainted with her." Hot color flooded Windy's brown face.

"I see," Lin said. "What did Cora say?"

"Never mind," Windy answered. "You'll find out, I guess. Here we are, on top."

The buckboard emerged from the canyon and rolled on into the trees. Past the Patrick house it went, and on to the camp. Carl Yetman came to the door as the buckboard stopped, and Shorty Morgan walked up from the barn. Lin got down, lifted Bobby out and turned to shake hands with Carl and Shorty.

"How's it goin'?" he asked.

"Pretty good," Shorty said. "The cattle are in good shape."

"I got some cookies, Bobby," Carl Yetman said. "You like some?"

Bobby went eagerly to the kitchen with Carl, and Windy drove the buckboard off toward the barn. Lin stood in front of the door and talked with Shorty Morgan, whom he had sent to the lease to help while he and Bobby were gone.

"I'm going to want you to stay right here, Shorty," Lin announced. "We'll need you. Can you stay all right?"

"You bet," Shorty said heartily. "Sacatone is out in the pasture. He'll be in after a while."

Lin bent and, picking up his grip, carried it into the camp house. When he came out again Shorty was at the corral helping Windy unharness. Lin watched them for a moment, absently listening to the voices from the kitchen where Carl Yetman and Bobby talked. Bobby was telling Carl about Duffyville. Abruptly Lin turned from the house and started down the path to the Patricks'. He had to see Eleanor.

He hesitated briefly when he reached the Patrick house; then, taking his courage in his hands, he mounted the steps and, crossing the porch, knocked. He waited nervously. The door opened, and Eleanor Patrick stood before him.

Neither the girl nor man spoke for a long moment, then Eleanor stepped back. "Won't you come in?" she said, small-voiced.

Lin went into the living room, deserted save for the two of them. He stood holding his hat in his hands, unsure of himself, not knowing how to begin what he had to say.

"I don't want you to think I believe you did it," Lin blurted suddenly. "Rideout telegraphed me to come back as soon as I could. I saw him yesterday. I told him you had nothin' to do with it." Lin looked at the floor and twisted his hat in his hands. "I had to come and tell you," he concluded.

Following that brief speech there was silence. Then Eleanor said: "Thank you for coming, Lin."

There was something in her voice that made Lin look up. The girl was watching him, a small hesitant smile trembling on her lips. Lin dropped his hat and forgot it.

"An' I'm going to clear this thing up," he stated firmly. "John was killed. I'm going to find out who killed him."

The little fleeting smile disappeared. "They say I did," Eleanor said soberly. "I was arrested, Lin."

"I know that!" The girl thrilled to the surge of anger

that came to Lin's face. "It wouldn't have happened if I'd been here. I'm afraid I made it worse for you, Eleanor."

"Sit down and tell me," the girl urged. "How did you make it worse, Lin?"

Lin sat down. "Rideout asked me if I'd seen you that afternoon," he said, looking at the floor. "I thought I was helpin' you an' I told him 'no.' I didn't know then about how John was killed. I thought—" He stopped.

"I know you were trying to help me," Eleanor said. She was sitting in a chair across from Lin, watching him with steady eyes. "Lin, that day when I left here I was mad. I intended to kill you. Then I came to my senses up there on the hill when I saw you ride across the park. I knew that I'd been crazy. Do you believe me, Lin?"

"I believe you."

"There was someone on the other hill. I heard the shots and I saw you go off your horse." The girl's hands were clenched on her lap, the fingers so tight that the knuckles were white. "I shot into the timber," she went on. "I heard the men ride out. Then you came up the hill and . . . you thought I'd shot at you."

"I was crazy," Lin said gruffly. "But if you had shot at me it was all right. I guess—"

"I know that you didn't sell the lease," Eleanor interposed quickly. "I know that now. Windy told me and so did Mr. Rideout. Will you forgive me, Lin?"

"There's nothin' to forgive."

Quiet hovered over them. Lin studied his tightly clasped hands and the girl watched him with steady,

165

level eyes. Suddenly Lin looked up.

"John tried to make it right," he said, apology in his voice. "He went to Adelphi. He'd spent the money he got for the sublease and he wired to a bank in Galveston to borrow some. He was coming back from that when he was killed. Here's the telegrams he sent."

Lin produced the messages from his pocket and, rising, carried them to the girl. Eleanor took them, glanced at their contents and passed them back.

"I'm glad," she said. "I thought . . . It doesn't matter what I thought."

"We're goin' to clear this thing up," Lin said strongly. "They'll believe me when I tell them I saw you on the mesa, and you can account for all your time that afternoon except that. I—"

"But I can't," Eleanor said quietly. "Cora didn't see me come in and neither did Rufina or Sandy. I didn't answer Cora when she called me to supper. I was here at home, but there's no way to prove it. I—" She stopped. Bobby's dragging step sounded on the porch.

"Can I come in?" Bobby asked from the door.

"Come in, Bobby," Eleanor invited.

The boy limped into the room and stood looking at the girl and at his uncle. "Where's Mr. Patrick?" he asked.

"He's gone out right now," Eleanor answered. "He walks a little every day. Won't you come here and say hello, Bobby?"

Bobby gravely crossed to the girl and shook hands. In the last ten days Bobby had shaken hands with a good many people, had women weep over him and men regard him with sympathy. He had learned to be solemn when he shook hands.

"I'm glad that you're back," Eleanor said, releasing Bobby's hand. "Is it good to be home, Bobby?"

The boy nodded. "Is Mr. Patrick all right now?" he asked.

"He's a great deal better."

Solemnly the boy regarded Eleanor. "Were you cryin' about Mr. Patrick?" he asked.

"Crying?" Eleanor questioned. "When was that, Bobby?"

"The day that Dad was killed," Bobby answered.

Eleanor wrinkled her brows as she tried to remember. Bobby helped her. "I came down to see you," he said, "an' that woman wouldn't let me in. So I went around by your window and climbed a tree. You were on the bed and you were crying. Don't you remember?"

"When, Bobby?" Lin's voice was sharp.

Bobby looked at his uncle. "In the afternoon," he said. "Right after Sacatone an' me came in. I wanted to talk to Eleanor an' find out what was the matter."

"And you climbed a tree and looked into her window and saw her on the bed?" Lin insisted.

Bobby nodded. "Yeah," he said.

A grin, wide and boyish, broke over Lin's face. With one swift step he reached Eleanor's side and caught her hand in his. "There's a witness that can prove you were at home!" Lin exclaimed. "Bobby! That proves it!"

The girl's cheeks were flushed and her eyes were bright. "But . . ." she began.

The telegrams were in Lin's hand. Hastily he opened

167

them, studied them, his eyes eager. "Look here," he exclaimed.

Eleanor turned so that she was looking over his arm at the yellow message blanks. Lin's big forefinger pointed out a line. "John stayed in Adelphi until this message came in," he said. "The agent at the depot told me so today."

"But . . ." the girl broke in once more.

"This message came at four thirty-five"—there was exultation in Lin's voice—"and John was in Adelphi at the station. He didn't leave until after four-thirty, and Bobby knows that you were here at the house. It doesn't make any difference if Rideout believes me or not. You couldn't have done it."

Lin's hands shot out and caught the girl's shoulders. "I'll get Rideout up here! I'll show him this message. He can talk to Bobby. It's perfect. There's not a hole in it."

Eleanor's eyes were shining. Her hands were on Lin's arms. Bobby, unnoticed, watched the two of them. From them he caught the excitement.

"Is everything all right?" Bobby asked. "Lin said that you were in trouble, Eleanor. He said . . ."

"She's not in trouble any more!" Lin looked down at his nephew. "Everything's all right now, Bobby."

There was a tremor in the girl's voice as she echoed Lin's words. "Everything's all right now, Bobby," she said.

His hands still holding her shoulders, Lin looked down at Eleanor Patrick. He saw the moisture in her eyes, the trembling of her lips. Once more Lin McCord spoke to his nephew.

"Suppose you go out an' find Mr. Patrick, Bobby," Lin suggested. "You skip on out, son."

Obediently Bobby turned and limped to the door. Out on the porch he stopped. There was absolute silence in the room he had left. Silence and then a small sound. Bobby went on down the steps to find his friend.

CHAPTER XIII
A MAN OF IMPORTANCE

LIN TALKED WITH SACATONE THE NIGHT OF HIS RETURN to the lease; he talked reasonably, his voice quiet but insistent. He had been angry with Sacatone but that anger died. Getting mad and cussing and raising hell was no way to handle Sacatone. At first the dark little man held out that he was right; that, regardless of what Lin said, Eleanor Patrick had killed John McCord. Lin talked and showed the telegrams and strove to keep his temper, and still Sacatone was obdurate. And then Bobby took a hand. When Bobby said that he had climbed a tree and looked into Eleanor Patrick's bedroom and had seen the girl lying on the bed—all this during the time when she should have, according to Sacatone's reasoning, been in Pinál Canyon waylaying John McCord—the old man blinked his eyes and reluctantly agreed that Eleanor must be innocent. When, late that night, Lin McCord went to bed he felt as though the whole world was his oyster and he had a good knife.

In the morning Lin rode the pasture, taking Eleanor with him. Bobby was visiting Dan Patrick, and Windy, Shorty and Sacatone went upon their various businesses. As they rode, the man and the girl talked about the next step in their campaign. Lin told Eleanor about his visit to Watts, about the measures he had taken to have Melcomb's injunction removed and to regain the sublease that John had sold to Melcomb.

"Watts says we can prove that I was agent for the partnership," Lin told the girl. "He says that Melcomb bought a pig in a poke an' that I can let him whistle. He'll get a hearing set, an' we'll go down an' clean things up. I want to give Melcomb back the money he paid John, then after Watts gets through we'll be clear."

The girl, new-found happiness shining in her eyes, looked at her companion. "You don't have to pay him, do you, Lin ?" she asked.

"Watts says not." Lin frowned. "But I'm goin' to."

Eleanor rode close. Her hand reached out and touched Lin's arm. "You have to be fair, don't you?" she said softly. "It's just the way you're built. You're fine, Lin."

"If I can keep you thinkin' so for the next thirty years or longer, I'll be satisfied," Lin said, his frown supplanted by a smile. "This afternoon we'll harness up an' go to Adelphi. We'll take the train down to Junction and see Rideout an' Watts. I want to clean this up, Eleanor."

The girl knew that he spoke of the charge that had been laid against her. She smiled and agreed. "We'll go."

But there was no need for them to make the trip. After dinner, when Lin was changing clothes, Yetman called:

170

"There's somebody to see you, Lin," and Lin, going out of the bedroom, found Sam Rideout waiting for him in the kitchen.

"I thought I'd come up an' see you," Rideout announced shortly. "I run into your man Thomas down in the canyon. From what he tells me, there's a different look to things."

"You bet there is," Lin said heartily. "You saved me a trip, Sheriff. Eleanor an' Bobby an' me were going down to Junction to talk with you. Eleanor didn't have anything to do with John's death. She was at home. Bobby saw her that afternoon, and John didn't leave Adelphi till after half-past four."

Lin plunged into his story, Rideout listening and occasionally asking questions. The telegrams were produced, and Rideout scrutinized them, nodding as Lin pointed out the "4:35" that was written below the signature of the telegram from the bank. Bobby, called in, told his story again, and when he had finished and gone out the sheriff leaned back in his chair and beamed at Lin McCord.

"You proved that point, didn't you?" he said. "Well, McCord, this takes a load off my mind. I'll see Pop Vicars when I go back an' get copies of these and an affidavit from him as to the time your brother left the depot in Adelphi, an' when I talk to the district attorney he'll throw the whole thing out. It won't ever be presented to the grand jury."

It seemed to both men to be an occasion for celebration. They shook hands gravely, drank coffee that Yetman brought and then went down to the Patricks' to

171

tell Eleanor and her father and include them in the celebration.

Rideout stayed that night at camp. Indeed, he not only stayed the night but most of the next day, riding out with Lin to look at the steers and comment on their weight. When the sheriff left, Sacatone accompanied him. They were going to look through Pinál Canyon again; not with much hope of finding anything, but just on a chance.

Just before he rode off with Sacatone, Rideout talked to Lin once more. Standing beside the house while Sacatone saddled, Rideout looked up at the tall man beside him and asked a question. "You proved the girl innocent," he said. "Now what, McCord?"

Lin's eyes narrowed as he faced Rideout. "Now we can go on from that," he said quietly. "Eleanor's in the clear, but there's others that ain't."

"What do you mean?" Rideout asked.

"I told you," Lin said slowly, "that I was goin' to find the man that killed John. I'm going to do it."

Sam Rideout had the same breeding as Lin McCord. He knew just how Lin felt, knew with certainty how Lin would react. Lin's code was Sam Rideout's code, but Rideout was an officer. "I'll be workin' too, McCord," he said slowly. "I want you to promise me one thing: we'll find out who killed your brother, but it's a business for the law, not for private parties."

Lin turned his face away, and Rideout's voice drawled on. "I know how you feel," he said again. "You think that the whelp needs killin'. So do I. But the law is for that, not you, McCord."

Still Lin said nothing. His face was rock hard and his lips thin, while his eyes were simply narrow slits through which blue steel shone.

"You got some ideas as to who done it," the sheriff drawled. "So have I. Maybe we're mistaken."

"There's no mistake!" Lin blurted. "I could ride to Adelphi and inside of ten minutes be lookin' at the man that killed John."

"Now wait . . ." Rideout interposed.

"Oh, maybe he didn't do it himself," Lin interrupted swiftly. "He's got money an' he could hire a thing like that. But Otis Melcomb's the man I'm talkin' about, an' you know it!"

"You'll have to prove it," Rideout said softly. "I like you, McCord. I'll side any man that rode with Truett. But I'm an officer. If you kill Otis Melcomb I'll do what I have to do, an' that is to see you hung."

"Have I asked you different?" Lin said levelly, his voice barely a murmur.

"No," Rideout agreed, "you ain't. But I've told you, Lin."

"You told me," Lin said expressionlessly.

"Look, Lin." Rideout was sympathetic and there was a plea in his voice. "I've got an idea how you feel about Eleanor Patrick. You're in love with her, is that right?"

Lin nodded wordlessly.

"An' she's in love with you." Rideout's voice was gentle. "How do you think she'd feel if you killed a man? Supposin' even that you come clear on it, how'd you think she'd feel? You've got to think of that."

Lin made no answer but his stern face softened.

173

Rideout drove his blows on home. "An' it ain't as though he'd get away," the sheriff said softly. "If we can prove this on him he won't go free. I'll promise you that."

For a long minute neither man spoke. Then Lin lifted his head and looked steadily at the sheriff. "All right," he said brusquely. "I'll go slow, Rideout. I won't jump into it. I'll let the law do it."

"That's the boy!" Relief and heartiness flooded Rideout's voice. He slapped Lin on the shoulder. "That's the right thing to do. An' you can bet I'll be workin' on this deal, Lin. You can bet I'll cover the country."

"So will I," Lin said thinly. "I didn't promise I'd just sit still, Rideout."

"I didn't ask you to sit still," the sheriff said heartily. "I want you to help. But I want you to tell me whatever you find out. Here comes Thomas. I guess it's time to go. So long, Lin. You won't be sorry. You're doin' the right thing."

Sam Rideout, traveling back toward Adelphi down Pinál Canyon, was well satisfied with his visit to the mesa. Two things had happened that pleased him. First was the absolute proof of Eleanor's innocence in the death of John McCord. Rideout had been worried over that. He had believed the girl innocent, had protested to the district attorney that she was not a likely murder suspect; but a strong case had been built against the girl, a case to which Rideout had unwillingly contributed. Now with that evidence against Eleanor shredded by Bobby and the telegrams,

Rideout was pleased. The second reason for Rideout's satisfaction was Lin's reluctant agreement to let the law handle matters. Lin McCord was the kind of man who very readily turns bad; the kind of man who, once he has taken a course, will go through with it. The fact that he had consented to co-operate with the sheriff's office was a concession to Rideout's personality and power of persuasion.

Like Lin, Rideout believed that John McCord's death hinged and fitted into the difficulty over the timber on Rough Mesa. Sam Rideout wanted no man murdered, but now that this had happened he was pleased that he was on the right track to solving the crime. Since he had taken office he had found trouble with Otis Melcomb and the Hoysen Lumber Company. Melcomb was a political power in the county and the state. He had money and he controlled a lot of votes. Melcomb had opposed Rideout's candidacy for sheriff and that had rankled. Then, since election, the Hoysen holdings had received especial consideration. The district attorney owed his place to Melcomb; the judge was indebted to Melcomb politically, and Sam Rideout had been forced, time and again, to forget things that otherwise he would have pushed to a conclusion: minor disturbances, petty crimes, things which individually were of small moment but in the aggregate mounted up. An officer from the crown of his Stetson to the toes of his boots, Rideout had fretted under the restraint placed upon him. But this was murder, and murder is too big a thing to be glossed over and passed by. If Rideout could connect the murder of John McCord with the Hoysen Lumber Company he could be sure of two things: re-election and a free hand in law enforcement. And Rideout wanted both of these. So it was that Rideout and Sacatone rode down the canyon, thinking, not talking.

Below the creek crossing where Sacatone had found the spent shell the two men stopped. They scouted the canyon around that point, discovering nothing, adding nothing to the knowledge they already possessed. Rideout had not expected to find anything but had taken Sacatone's suggestion that he accompany the sheriff simply to humor the old man. Their brief search finished, Sacatone went back up the canyon and Rideout pushed on toward Adelphi.

When he reached the little town Rideout sought Ed Draper. Draper was in the Exchange Saloon playing solitaire when Rideout walked in and, spying his deputy, came on back to the card table. Greetings were exchanged and Rideout sat down, waved the bartender away and spoke to Draper.

"Well," Rideout said, "we've got a murder case open in the county now, Ed. A real one."

Draper laid aside the deck and looked inquiringly at the sheriff. "Another one?" he asked.

Rideout shook his head. "Same one," he answered. "The Patrick girl didn't kill McCord. It was somebody else."

Draper's face remained expressionless. "Got some new evidence?" he asked.

"Yeah." Rideout had as good a poker face as Draper's. "New evidence. Guess the district attorney will dismiss the charge. It'll never get to the grand jury."

Draper did not ask what the new evidence was. He looked expectantly at Rideout.

"Been quite a little criticism of you, Ed," Rideout drawled. "Folks think it's funny that you overlooked that gunshot wound in McCord when you was up there an' held the inquest. They kind of had Doc Vorfree on the pan too. But it seems like you hurried things a little. That body should have come down to Junction an' been gone over real good."

Draper's brown face slowly turned red. "Who's doin' all this talkin'?" he demanded. "I was tryin' to help Lin McCord out. I pushed things along . . ."

"Too fast," Rideout completed. "As for who's doin' the talkin'—I been doin' some of it. I'm responsible, Ed. I have to stand good for what my deputies do. I guess I'll have to ask you to resign your commission."

The red still suffused Draper's face, but aside from his color he showed no emotion. "Are you askin' for it?" he demanded.

Rideout nodded.

Draper reached under his coat and, unpinning his shield, he placed it on the table. Removing his pocket-book from his hip pocket, he extracted a card, his deputy's commission, and placed it beside the badge. Rideout picked them up. "Kind of puts things on an even footing," he drawled. "I'll see Gilberto Gil and send him up here to hold things down until I get around to appointin' a regular deputy. Well"—he arose—"I'll see you, Ed." With that Sam Rideout left the Exchange.

When he was gone Draper collected the cards and stacked them deliberately. Then, coming to his feet, he settled his hat with a savage tug and walked out of the saloon. Rideout was walking along toward the depot. Draper scowled at the small man's back and, turning, went down the street to the company office.

He walked in, passing Hunter with no word, and on to Melcomb's office. Melcomb, reading a letter, looked up when Draper arrived. Draper reached back and slammed the door and stood scowling at Melcomb. "I just turned in my deputy's commission to Rideout!" he snapped. "He asked for it."

Melcomb sat staring for a moment and then growled an answer.

"Rideout's too damned fresh. We'll see about him. You'll have that commission back in a week, Ed."

That was solace. Draper came on across the office and sat down. "Rideout was sore about that McCord thing," he announced. "Said I worked too fast. That we should have taken the body to Junction for the inquest."

"You don't need to give a damn what Rideout says," Melcomb assured. "He's a two-bit sheriff that was elected on a fluke. We'll take care of him this fall."

Draper grunted. "The Patrick girl is in the clear," he announced. "Rideout just told me."

An expression of alarm came over Melcomb's face. "She's in the clear?" he demanded. "Why, I thought—"

"You thought the same as I did," Draper interrupted. "I didn't ask Rideout what had happened, but he said there was new evidence turned up. Mebbe . . ."

"Well, what?"

"Mebbe Spike had better take a little trip for his health."

"You get scared, Ed." Melcomb spoke loftily. "There's nothin' to worry about. I'm not scared."

"*You* didn't shoot McCord!" Draper was abrupt. "Spike did, an' I put his foot in the stirrup an' spooked his horse so it would look like he'd been drug to death. I don't like the looks of things, Otis. I think I'll pull out."

"Run an' confess," Melcomb snapped. "No you won't, Ed. You know you won't do it. You've got too many guts. So has Spike. Besides, there's the Rough Mesa timber to think about. You boys forced my hand, but I've made a deal with you. Remember?"

Draper sat silent for a time and then nodded slowly. "All right," he agreed, "we won't pull out."

"We're going to have to move up there." Melcomb picked up his letter again and frowned at it. "I heard from Yawl this morning. McCord an' the Patricks have hired Watts, and he's already started to fight us on that lease. Yawl says that if we have a camp up there it'll show good faith on our part and it will help. We're going to have to move a camp up there, Ed."

"We'll move one, then," Draper said flatly. "I'll go get Spike an' we'll figure what we'd better do."

"Bring him in," Melcomb agreed. "He went to Camp Two this morning, but he ought to be back by now."

Draper stood up and moved toward the door. Outside, at his long desk, Glen Hunter moved hurriedly away from his position near Melcomb's office door and the crack in the transom. He was working industriously when Draper came out.

At five o'clock that evening Hunter closed his ledger and put it in the safe. He removed the black sleeve protectors from his striped shirt, got into his coat with the wide padded shoulders and, taking his derby, left the office for the night. Melcomb was still in the inner office. Samms and Draper had come in and were closeted with the manager.

As he walked along toward the hotel Hunter spoke to various of Adelphi's inhabitants, gallantly lifting the derby to the women, nodding to the men.

In his room at the hotel he cleaned up, brushed the fringe of hair around his head, twisted fresh wax into his wispy mustache and then, having completed his toilet, went down to the lobby.

While he waited there for the dinner bell to ring he read his mail. This consisted of three advertisements, sent in reply to his requests, and the Junction paper. No one bothered him, no one spoke to him, although the regular occupants of the hotel were assembling in the lobby. Glen Hunter was left alone. He was always left alone. The bell rang and the men went into the dining room, Hunter taking his seat at the long table.

There, while the meal was in progress, talk passed back and forth among the boarders. Three times Hunter entered that conversation and three times received no attention. No one in Adelphi thought much of Hunter. Dress as he might, boast as he might, he was an outlander, not a member of the fraternity. Even the counterjumper who worked in Barton's store felt that it was

180

perfectly safe to snub Hunter. Only Bessie, the buxom waitress, showed him any attention. Bessie smiled at him and brought him a second cup of coffee. She had been paying him these small attentions for some time. Hunter thanked the girl gratefully.

Supper finished, the men pushed back their chairs and departed on their various occasions, some to go to the pool hall, some to the Exchange, each to his own affair. Hunter lingered in the dining room. Bessie, intent upon clearing away the debris of the meal, was surprised to find him still at the table.

"Aren't you through, Mr. Hunter?" she asked, pausing beside him.

"Ah . . . yes, I'm through, Bessie." Glen Hunter blushed fiery red. "I . . . ah . . . I stayed to talk to you a moment."

Bessie smiled and put down the dishes she had picked up. "You're kiddin'," she said. "You wouldn't wait to talk to me."

"Oh yes, I did," Hunter interposed hastily. "I . . . ah . . . Do you ever go to dances, Bessie?"

"Sometimes." Bessie tilted her head and looked archly at the man.

Hunter's face was still rosy. "There's a dance in Junction . . . ah . . . Saturday," he announced.

Bessie was enjoying herself hugely. "Are you goin' to the dance?" she asked innocently.

Hunter ducked his head. "I . . . ah . . . had thought of it," he answered.

"Gee . . ." Bessie was properly interested. "I wisht that I could go."

"Ah . . . would you accompany me?" Hunter still stared at the tablecloth.

"You're kiddin'," Bessie said. "An important man like you wouldn't go to a dance with a waitress."

The little bookkeeper looked up quickly. There was a plea in his eyes. Waxed mustache, loud suit, striped shirt, padded shoulders: these were camouflage for Glen Hunter's shyness. He wore them as a harmless grass snake may wear the diamond markings of the rattler. "Indeed I would, Bessie," he said earnestly. "I'd be honored to have you accompany me."

Bessie read the watery brown eyes. Just a girl on the make, Bessie, but she had to answer the thing that was in those eyes. "Sure I'll go," Bessie said gaily.

Once more Hunter blushed. "Thank you," he said.

"But I can't see why a businessman like you would want to take me," Bessie persisted. "Tomorrow's Saturday, ain't it? Gee! What'll I wear?"

CHAPTER XIV
DEFERRED PAYMENT

CORA FERGUSON EXPECTED COMPANY. BELIEVING implicitly that the way to a man's heart is through his stomach, she had baked a cake Saturday and made an assortment of cookies; and now, on Sunday afternoon, she wore her prettiest dress, first having pulled her corset so tight that her ribs were in extremity. All in all, Cora had done herself proud. Her mirror told her that she was at her best, and her sense of taste told her that the cake was a success.

Cora had met Windy Tillitson on the mesa, not under the most favorable of circumstances. Windy had gone to the Patricks' when Cora was helping Eleanor look after Dan. There had been but little conversation between the two on the first few meetings, but later—when Eleanor had been arrested, when she was in Junction arranging bail—during those stressful times, Windy had been in evidence. Somehow the tall, talkative gentleman with the two gold teeth had ingratiated himself with the Adelphi milliner, and now that Cora was at home and at work again, Windy was a frequent visitor. On this particular Sunday Cora was expecting him, and she was not particularly pleased when, answering a summons at her door, she found Bessie, one of the two girls that worked at the hotel, standing there waiting for her.

Bessie being a friend, Cora let her in. Many a juicy tidbit had been added to Cora's store of information by the waitress, but this time Cora was resolved to rid herself of her guest as quickly as possible. She forgot that resolution as soon as Bessie entered and the door was closed, for Bessie, palpitant with her news, threw her arms around Cores plump shoulders, burst into tears and blurted out: "I'm going to marry him, Cora. He asked me."

Cora immediately took measures. She patted Bessie's back, hugged her, propelled her to a chair and asked the logical question: "Who?"

"Glen," Bessie said, beaming through her tears. "Glen Hunter."

Here indeed was a surprise. Cora, figuratively, was set back on her haunches like a cow horse at the end of a rope. She had hold of something and she did not know what to do with it. Surprise rather than friendship inspired her next words:

"That little snip?" said Cora.

The light of battle replaced the gleam of happiness in Bessie's eyes. "He's not a little snip!" Bessie refuted. "He's as tall as I am, and he occupies a very important position with the company."

Before this spectacle of a female fighting for her mate Cora backed down. "I didn't mean that, Bessie," she placated. "You know I didn't. I'm just as happy as I can be. When did he ask you?"

Bessie was not to be so easily cajoled. Her fighting spirit was aroused and she poured on more steam. "You aren't a bit pleased!" she flung at her whilom friend. "You're jealous, that's what you are. Mr. Hunter is a big man in the company. Mr. Melcomb never does anything that he doesn't talk it over with Glen."

"Now, Bessie . . ." Cora meant to be placating but had the opposite effect. Bessie flounced out of her chair.

"I didn't come here to have you insult my future husband," she cried. "I thought you'd be happy. I thought you were my friend. I thought . . ." Bessie began to cry afresh. Through that barrage of words and tears Cora moved forward.

"Of course I'm happy, dear. Of course I didn't mean to hurt your feelings. Why, I'm so glad for you!" Cora put her hands on Bessie's shoulders and pushed her back into the chair. Bessie, not too reluctantly, allowed herself to be pushed.

"He asked me last night in Junction," Bessie said. "We went to the dance, and he asked me just after the orchestra played 'Home, Sweet Home' and he was taking me to the hotel. I know he's little, Cora, but he's a gentleman. And Mr. Melcomb does talk to him. Why, just this morning Glen was telling me that he and Mr. Melcomb had decided to put a camp on Rough Mesa right away because of the trouble they're having with the lawsuit. There now! Does that sound like he was a little snip, when Mr. Melcomb trusts him?"

Cora could hardly believe her ears. The announcement spilled the wind from Cora's sails. "A camp? On the mesa?" she gasped.

"Right away," Bessie said triumphantly. "You're the first one I've told, Cora. I want you to be a bridesmaid. We're going to be married in a month, just as soon as Mr. Hunter closes a big deal that he has on. We . . . you aren't paying a bit of attention to me, Cora!"

"Oh yes, I am," Cora assured. "It was just . . . I was so surprised, Bessie. You certainly kept it a secret."

Bessie giggled. "Oh, we wanted to surprise everybody," she said. "Listen, Cora, do you think I ought to have a big wedding or just something simple? Mr. Hunter wants a simple ceremony, but I thought maybe we'd have it in the church in Junction. What do you think?"

Determinedly Cora put aside the news that she had just heard and, sitting down, smiled at her friend. "I think in the church," she answered. "A girl just gets married once, Bessie."

"That's what I thought," Bessie said happily. "I told him I thought the church would be best."

"And I'll make your wedding dress," Cora announced. "White satin and a tulle veil. I think . . ."

Bessie leaned forward. "And a train . . ." In the room back of the millinery shop voices babbled happily.

Windy Tillitson, arriving like a knight of old on horseback, fastened Big Enough to the hitch rail and gave the bay rump a friendly slap. "Mebbe there'll be cake," Windy told the horse. "If there is, you git a bite, Big Enough." With which happy promise he tugged his belt up around his middle and advanced to the door.

Windy's knock was a signal for the voices inside to cease. Windy waited and then knocked again. The door opened, and Windy stepped back to let Bessie come through.

Bessie hesitated on the step. "I'll get that picture, Cora," she said. "I'll bring it over tomorrow."

"And I'll see if I can find that pattern," Cora assured. "Be sure to bring the picture. Good-by, Bessie."

Bessie said good-by and, with not a look at Windy, went on down the walk. Windy stood watching her departure. For a big woman Bessie walked mighty lightly, he thought.

"Come in," Cora bade from the doorway.

Windy went in. Cora led the way back through the shop to her living room. There, on the table, was a plate of cookies on which deep inroads had been made and a cake that had been cut. When Cora turned Windy stopped and looked at her.

"Lots of excitement," he drawled. "Must be there's

goin' to be a weddin'.' "

"How did you know?" Cora demanded.

"Women get excited over babies an' weddin's," Windy answered. "Who's the lucky man?"

"Come in and sit down," Cora ordered. "I want to talk to you."

Windy brought his long length into the room and found a chair. Cora seated herself on the couch that at night served for a bed. "My, but you look pretty," Windy drawled. "Just as pretty as a red heifer in a flower bed. Say, it's quite a ways from here to camp. If you ain't savin' that cake for anythin'—"

"Help yourself," Cora directed. "I made it for you."

Windy was already on his feet. At the frank admission he checked his motion toward the cake and looked at Cora. "For me?" he asked. "Say . . . !"

"Help yourself, and don't talk for a minute," Cora ordered. "Do you know what I just heard?"

"That your lady friend was goin' to get married." Windy, possessed of a wedge of cake, retreated toward his chair again. "That ain't surprisin'. People do it every day. I been thinkin' that I—"

"I heard that Otis Melcomb was going to put a camp on Rough Mesa right away."

Windy poised the cake halfway to his mouth. "Huh?" he ejaculated.

Cora nodded, lips firmly compressed. "That's what Bessie told me. The man she's goin' to marry told her. He works in Melcomb's office."

Windy took a bite of cake, and his Adam's apple bobbed as he chewed and swallowed. That bite down, he looked at the cake as though he had never seen it before and then helped himself to another bite.

"Windy Tillitson!"—there was wrath in Cora's voice—"are you going to sit there an' eat cake an' not do a thing about what I've told you? Are you?"

"They ain't goin' to move a camp there today," Windy drawled. "I've just come down the canyon, an' there's no sign of 'em. It's good cake. I reckon I'd better eat this piece, anyhow."

"You . . . you . . ." Cora fumed.

"But as soon as I get this cake et I'm goin' home," Windy said. "I'm goin' right back up the canyon an' talk to Lin. There ain't any chance of you bein' mistaken about this, is there, Cora?"

"I don't think so," Cora answered. "Bessie just told me. She was mad because I'd called her fiance a little snip. That's why she told me."

Windy shook his head. The ways of women were beyond his comprehension.

"Will there be any trouble, Windy?" Cora asked.

"There won't be no Sunday-school picnic," Windy replied, licking cake icing from a finger. "If Melcomb starts to move a camp up there he'll ask for trouble. Lin told him not to try that."

"Will there be shooting?" Cora was on her feet. Windy, the last of the icing gone, had risen.

"Somebody might bust a cap," he admitted. "It might just happen that-a-way. I got to go, Cora. I'd figured on takin' you to church tonight, but with this thing comin' up I guess . . ." Windy paused apologetically.

"You go right back and tell Lin McCord," Cora urged.

"I don't want to go to church tonight, anyhow. You can take the rest of that cake, Windy. Here, wait till I wrap it up. And you tell Eleanor that if she wants me to come up there, just to send word. And, Windy . . ." Cora bustled about as she talked, wrapping the cake in tissue paper and covering that with thick folded sheets of newsprints. "You be careful while you're up there. You're so tall that if you stand up you'll just be a target. Here's the cake and don't forget to tell Eleanor."

Windy accepted the cake. Cora stooped and, retrieving his hat, handed it to him. "Now don't forget to be careful," she warned. "If you got yourself killed I'd never forgive you."

"Me neither." Windy's hat was sitting jauntily on the back of his head. One hand held the cake. With the other long arm Windy Tillitson reached out and pulled Cora toward him. Cora ducked but the kiss landed on her ear, and Windy, already halfway through the shop room, called back a threat. "I'm comin' back when we get done on top an' give you a real one. So long, Cora."

Big Enough was three quarters mustang and a quarter Steeldust. There was a lot of horse connected with his fourteen-two height and nine hundred pounds. Big Enough widened on it going home, and when the two of them, horse and rider, crowned out of Pinál Canyon and made across the mesa top to the camp, Big Enough still showed symptoms of wanting to run. Windy held him down, slid the little horse to a stop in front of the camp and yelled for Lin.

Lin, so Yetman said, was at Patricks'. Windy loped on down and found his boss on the porch with Eleanor and

Dan Patrick. Somehow the misunderstanding about the lease had brought about a closer relationship between Lin McCord and Dan Patrick, or perhaps it was Eleanor that had effected that liaison. Every time Lin came to the house—and that was frequently—Eleanor looked at him, and when she looked at him the whole world could tell how matters stood. There was nothing mean or little about Eleanor Patrick. When she gave Lin her love she gave all of it, and the fact shone from her eyes. Lin, seeing that Windy was hurried and worried, came down the steps and stopped by Big Enough, laying his hand on the horn of Windy's saddle.

"What is it, Windy?" he asked.

"I just found out that Melcomb's goin' to move a camp up here," Windy answered, each word portentous, though he did not lift his voice from a level drawl. "Cora told me. She said to tell Miss Patrick that she'd come up if she was wanted."

Eleanor paid no attention to Cora's message to her. She was watching Lin, apprehension in her eyes. Lin looked at Windy, his face expressionless. "Right away?" he asked.

"There's nobody in the canyon now," Windy answered, "but Cora seemed to think it was goin' to happen right away."

Lin nodded. "Tomorrow, mebbe," he said thoughtfully. "They'll start about tomorrow mornin'. All right, Windy, thanks for tellin' me."

He was so at ease, so unalarmed, that the girl on the porch relaxed. Windy, who knew Lin better perhaps than anyone else, was not at all fooled by that easiness.

He had warned Lin and Lin was ready to act. The time was not yet; that was all. When the time came Lin would go into action with explosive force.

"I'll go on down to camp," Windy said, his tone as casual as Lin's own. "You comin' down after a while?"

"After a while," Lin agreed and went back to the porch while Windy trotted off to the corral.

"What are you going to do, Lin?" Eleanor asked anxiously when Lin rejoined her. "You can't stop Melcomb from putting a camp up here, can you? Isn't there some legal way? Oughtn't you to send for Mr. Rideout?"

"I don't think I'll have to send for the sheriff," Lin said. "I'll talk to Melcomb. I think he'll see the light. Don't you bother your head about it, honey." There was so much assurance in the man, so great a calm, that Eleanor Patrick lost her anxiety. Dan Patrick, watching Lin's face, kept silent. Dan Patrick had worked a lot of men and knew them. What he saw in Lin was strength and determination, a driving force that would not be stopped. Later, when Eleanor had gone into the house momentarily, Patrick spoke to Lin.

"How about it? Wasn't Eleanor right? Shouldn't you send for Rideout?"

Lin shook his head. "I don't know how he'd stand," he answered frankly. "Rideout's an officer. He's got to uphold the law. No, I told Melcomb not to try to put a camp up here. He knows the canyon's closed. I don't think he'll try very hard."

Eleanor returned from the house and went to Lin, and Dan Patrick, still worried, watched the two as they stood together.

191

"I think I'll go to camp now," Lin told the girl. "I won't be gone long. I'll be back after a while." And with a final pressure on the girl's hand he turned and walked down the steps. The two, Eleanor Patrick and her father, watched him stride away, tall and straight and with the swing of repressed strength in his walk.

At camp Sacatone and Windy, Yetman and Shorty Morgan were waiting. Windy had assembled them and told them his news. When Lin came in the men eyed him expectantly, and Lin did not disappoint them. He went to his bunk, reached underneath and pulled out the gunny sack that contained the ammunition box.

"You've got your rifle, Sacatone," he said. "I bought some shells for it. Here you are." Lin passed over three boxes of .30-.30 cartridges. "There's more," he continued, "but that ought to hold you a while. Carl, you dig out your old Springfield. I've got some shells for it too. I guess you and Windy and me will stay with the belt guns, Shorty. That is, unless you've got a rifle up here with you."

"I just got a Colt," Shorty Morgan answered. There was pride in Shorty. Lin had not asked if he was in this thing but had taken it for granted that he was. Shorty felt now that finally he was an accepted member of the McCord crew.

"How do you want to handle it, Lin?" Sacatone asked. Since Lin's return Sacatone had been aching for action. He wanted to prove to Lin, and incidentally to Eleanor Patrick, that it had all been a mistake, that he bore no malice toward the girl, that he was as loyal as any of the crew.

192

"I think that you'd better borrow Carl's rifle," Lin said, looking at Windy. "I've got a spare Colt that you can have, Carl. You and Sac," he addressed Windy again, "can take turns watching the canyon. You'll hold down the camp, Carl, an' keep Bobby in line. Shorty an' me will kind of be reinforcements. We'll stay on top. They might get smart an' try to come up Loblolly Canyon or Cedar Canyon. I don't believe we'll have to do anything until tomorrow; I don't think they'll start tonight."

Sacatone grunted. "Just the same, I'm goin' down to the canyon right away," he said. "Suppose somebody did come up? They could stand us off till the rest got here."

Lin nodded. "It's an idea," he agreed. "You want any help?"

"I'll take a canteen an' some lunch," Sacatone answered. "I don't need any help."

"We'll keep horses up," Lin decided. "We've got three places to watch. Shorty, you might ride out an' look at Loblolly an' Cedar canyons. And listen, boys don't hurt anybody. Stop 'em an' yell for me. Let me do the talkin'. I don't want anybody killed, either us or them. I don't want the law comin' into this. Wait a minute, Sacatone. I've got an idea."

Sacatone, who had been collecting his lunch, grunted and went on with his business. Lin, picking up the ammunition box, carried it to the table and began to pry off a side.

"What's that for?" Sacatone asked, slapping a big slab of meat between thick slices of bread.

"A sign," Lin said and wrenched the side of the box free. "Where's somethin' I can paint with, Carl?"

There was no paint. Carl brought a bottle of ink and, using a rolled paper for a brush, Lin made his sign. "Road closed. No Trespassing."

"What good is that goin' to do?" Sacatone asked scornfully.

"It might just put us on the right side of the fence," Lin said slowly. "They won't pay any attention to it, but that's all right. We'll give 'em warning, anyhow. Windy, you got a horse saddled; you ride down an' put this up in the canyon down below the hill. Shorty, you'd better run in the horses an' we'll pick out what we want to ride."

Windy departed, carrying the sign. He had fence pliers and staples on his saddle, and with those he would put the sign in place. Shorty went for the horses, and Lin walked with Sacatone down toward the canyon.

There, on a ledge that reached out from the canyon side, he ensconced Sacatone. There were rocks on the ledge, forming a sort of natural fort, and a line of timber running down toward the rocks assured a method of retreat. "An' remember, Sacatone," Lin warned sternly, "don' you cut anybody down! Not now; not yet! We want to stop 'em, not kill 'em."

Sacatone grunted, deposited the canteen and lunch behind a rock, sat down, squirmed until he was comfortable and could look down into the canyon, growing dark now in the fading light, and gave answer. "A man that's shot is stopped," Sacatone said, "but if you don't want 'em hurt, it's your party, Lin."

"I don't want 'em hurt," Lin assured. "All right, Sacatone. There'll be somebody along pretty soon to visit with you."

Sacatone said nothing, and Lin climbed back up the ledge.

Nothing happened. All that night, all through the following morning that reached out and presently was noon, Rough Mesa was quiet. Windy, with Carl Yetman's .45-.70, went down and relieved Sacatone who ate breakfast, slept an hour or two and returned to the ledge. Shorty and Lin rode to Loblolly and Cedar canyons, taking their horses down into those steep declivities and finding no activity. It was two o'clock, and Sacatone basked like a lizard in the sun, when from below him he heard the faint murmurs that told of moving men, of horses and wagons. Sacatone raised his head, and beside him Windy stirred and sat up.

"Guess I'll call Lin," Windy said after listening a moment.

Lin, warned of the approach, made rapid disposition of his force. "You go to Loblolly," he instructed Windy. "Stay there. They might try to come around us. Shorty's at Cedar Canyon. If you hear somethin' that ain't right, or see them comin', you shoot once, up in the air. You'll have help right away. I'll go down with Sacatone now."

Grumbling, Windy rode off, and Lin, mounting Jug, rode toward the head of Pinál Canyon. As he passed the Patrick house Sandy Donald called and came running.

195

Donald had a big Colt thrust in his belt. "Where do you want me to go, McCord?" he asked.

Lin grinned. "You stay here," he directed. "If I need help I'll yell—don't think I won't—but I don't believe I'll need help."

Donald, disgruntled, stood and watched Lin ride away, then sat down on the porch steps, pulled the Colt from his waistband and cradled it in his hands.

Lin rode down the canyon. Just below the ledge he stopped Jug and waited. Above him, when he looked up, he could see the sun wink from the end of Sacatone's gun barrel and knew that the old man was watching him. The sounds in the canyon grew more distinct. Around the turn below Lin a team appeared, another pair behind the first horses and then a wagon with Ed Draper riding beside the driver on the seat. Lin lifted his hand, and the driver pulled his horses to a stop. Behind the first wagon, out of sight, Lin heard other men calling to their horses, stopping their teams.

"Good evenin'," Lin drawled, looking at Draper. "Didn't you boys see the sign?"

For a moment Draper did not reply. Then: "We saw a sign. I tore it down," he said flatly.

Lin shook his head. "You oughtn't to of done that," he chided. "The road's closed, Draper. We want no trespassers."

"The Hoysen Lumber Company owns the timber on Rough Mesa," Draper stated. "We're movin' camp up there."

Again Lin shook his head. "Not today," he said. "Not for a long time, if you ever do. We'll let the court decide about your claims to the timber, but you won't put a camp up above."

Draper glared at Lin. Lin, sitting Jug easily, returned the stare. The driver beside Draper shifted uneasily, and up on the ledge Sacatone called savagely "You set on that wagon. Don't try that, you!"

"Friend Samms must be gettin' ambitious," Lin drawled. "Tell him to stay with his wagon, Draper, or my man on the ledge 'll kill him."

Draper lifted himself from the seat and looked back. "Sit still, Spike," he called and then, turning so that he faced Lin once more, climbed down over the wheel of the wagon. Standing on the ground, clear of the team, he spoke to Lin.

"Clear the road!" Draper ordered. "I'm an officer! Clear—"

"You'll have to show your authority," Lin drawled. "Show me a court order givin' you possession of the mesa. Show me any kind of authority." He waited. He was bluffing. Draper could call that bluff. Draper, so Lin believed, was a deputy sheriff. If he showed his commission, one of Lin's points was swept away. But Draper made no move, and Lin, suddenly elated, knew that either Draper had lost his appointment or intended to go on without it and ride roughshod over the opposition.

From the ledge above Lin a little rock rolled down and bounced in the road in front of Jug. Sacatone had shifted position and displaced that rock. Jug shifted nervously, and Lin reined in the horse. Sacatone, on the ledge, had seen the stone bounce. It gave him an idea.

From another point on the ledge a good-sized rock came slithering down, struck the road and came to rest just in front of the lead team. The driver of the lead team called: "Whoa!" and up above, Sacatone said conversationally: "Lawd, but there's a lot of rocks up here!"

"Where's your boss?" Lin demanded, looking squarely at Draper. "Are you still pullin' his chestnuts out of the fire for him? Don't do it, Draper. Like Sacatone says, there's lots of rocks up above. An' if the rocks play out . . ." Lin shrugged suggestively.

Draper's voice was choked. "Climb down off that horse an' take your chance," Draper commanded. "You an' me, McCord. How about it?"

Lin shook his head. "There's no percentage in that," he drawled.

"Yellow!" Draper snarled. "You yellow-bellied Texan! I thought you had guts."

Lin flushed. He moved, shifting his hand on Jug's reins, freeing his right foot from the stirrup.

From the ledge above, Sacatone snapped a command. "Stay on that horse, Lin! If you get down I'll let Draper have it right in the head."

Lin poised, halfway out of the saddle. There was quiet in the canyon save for the occasional stamp of a horse's hoof. Then Lin said softly: "He means it, Draper. Some other time."

Draper turned without answering. "You fellows behind turn around," he ordered, lifting his voice. "We'll go back down a ways an' make camp. Get your teams turned."

Lin dropped back into his saddle. Down in the canyon noise began once more as men obeyed Ed Draper. Jug stood, statuesque, and Lin watched. Wheels rasped against wagon beds, horses strained, men called hoarsely. Ed Draper looked up at the driver of the first wagon and nodded.

"There's room for you to turn now," Draper said.

The teamster, startled, lifted his lines and called to his teams. The wagon surged forward. At a wider spot just beyond the turn the driver swung his teams, making a narrow circle, going back to the road. Then, when the tail gate of the wagon had disappeared around the turn, Ed Draper looked once more at Lin McCord.

"Check," Draper said levelly. "Some other time, McCord."

CHAPTER XV
TRIPLE THREAT

LIN, ON JUG, KEPT HIS POSITION UNTIL SACATONE, calling from the ledge, informed him that the wagons were out of sight; then Lin turned his horse and rode back up the canyon. When he reached the top Sacatone was there, waiting for him. Sacatone was angry.

"You're a damned fool, Lin," the old man said bluntly. "You was all set to get off an' have it out with him just because he called you yellow. You kind of lost your head."

Lin scowled at Sacatone. The scowl bothered Sacatone not at all. "You'd of been shot," Sacatone continued. "As soon as you hit the ground he'd of pulled. Then I'd of had to kill him. I thought you said you didn't want anybody killed."

Lin made no answer to that. "I'll go pick up Windy and Shorty," he said gruffly. "There's no need of them stayin' out by the other canyons. They aren't goin' to try to come that way."

Sacatone nodded agreement. "They might come up them other canyons," he said, "but they got to get to the head of Pinál before they can bring up their teams. One of us will stay on the ledge an' another back in the timber, an' we can hold down the place."

Lin nodded and rode away, and Sacatone, his battered .30-.30 trailing, went back toward the ledge.

Windy and Lin came back to camp within half an hour. When they rode up Carl Yetman appeared and looked searchingly at them and then walked out to Lin. "You got trouble on your hands, Lin," Yetman said. "The Portillos boys was all down here. They . . . Here they come now!"

Lin turned in his saddle and, seeing Manuel Portillos and his sons coming from their houses, dismounted. He did not know just what was coming. Old Manuel drew to a halt, straightened impressively and addressed Lin.

"W'at for, Meester McCord, you leeve us out, huh? You theenk eet ees we cannot fight?"

Lin was astonished. He had not counted at all on the Portillos, and here they were, all of them, and apparently all wanting a piece of the trouble.

"Why . . . I . . ." Lin began.

"Theese Adolfo ees shooteeng the *cabeza* off thee

cheepmonk," Manuel announced. "Ees got a *escopeta,* Adolfo. Me, I'm w'at you theenk *bueno* weeth thee ax. Theese Huberto ees very good weeth the *cuchillo* an' . . ."

"Dispenseme," Lin said, lapsing into Spanish. "I did not think, *señores.* Forgive me."

Manuel bowed gravely, and Lin continued, his Spanish fluent and fluid. He was sorry that he had neglected the Portillos. It would not happen in the future. He needed their help, appreciated it, would use it. Gradually Manuel's austerity softened, and when Lin asked that the old man and Adolfo go to guard Cedar Canyon and so relieve Shorty Morgan, all of Manuel's hurts were vanished. He strode off with Adolfo, and the other sons, assured that they would be called if needed, went back to their homes. Lin watched them go and then looked unbelievingly at Windy. Windy chuckled. "Got lots of fightin' men," he commented. "I'll slip down an' spell Sacatone. Doggone him, him an' you had all the excitement!"

"I'm going down to Patricks' a minute," Lin said. "All we can do now is wait an' see what they try next."

"They won't try comin' up the canyon," Windy prophesied cheerfully. "Carl, you got anythin' to eat in that dugout of yores?"

Down in the canyon, a quarter of a mile below the first creek crossing, Spike Samms and Ed Draper made camp with their three wagons and six teams. Besides the teamsters, Samms had collected ten lumberjacks, hard-bitten men each of them, bound to him by some tie

201

other than that of wages. In those ten there were two escaped convicts, a man who had committed murder, another who, in a fit of drunken fury, had hopelessly crippled a mill hand and a fifth who had spent two years in the violent ward of the state asylum for the insane. The remaining five were of like caliber, lacking only the opportunity to add their names to the rest. The murderer was the cook. With his fire built, he proceeded to prepare a meal. Draper and Samms, overlords of their companions by virtue of superior ferocity, drew apart from the rest and, sitting on a log, watched the preparations.

"Fifteen men," Samms said bitterly, "an' there was one man sittin' on a horse an' another up in a pile of rocks. We're kind of losin' our grip, Ed."

Ed Draper shook his head. "McCord said somethin' that stopped me," he answered. "I wasn't scared of him, Spike. It was what he said."

"What did he say that was so bad?" Samms spat brownly at the dirt.

"He said that I was pullin' Melcomb's chestnuts out of the fire," Draper replied. "That's what he said."

"You knew that before you started up here." Samms watched three men spreading a blanket on the ground.

"But I'd never had it throwed into me," Draper retorted. "Look, Spike. Melcomb's cut us in on the Rough Mesa timber, ain't he?"

Samms nodded.

"An' we get a third after it's logged an' sawed," Draper continued, musing. "An' for a lousy third apiece we walk up against McCord an' that old son-of-a-gun

202

hid out in the rocks with a rifle. I dared McCord to come down off his horse an' shoot it out, an' that of devil up on top told him if he got down I'd get it right in the head. McCord stayed on his horse. He ain't afraid, Spike."

"Well," Samms stated flatly, "neither are you."

"No"—Draper shook his head—"I ain't afraid. But where is this gettin' us, Spike? That's what I want to know. Melcomb gets the grapes an' we take the chances."

"I ain't . . ." Samms began and then sprang to his feet, catching up the double-bitted ax that rested beside him. "You, Tony!" Samms bellowed, "drop that! Don't touch that knife. Any fightin' around here that needs to be done, I'll do it!"

Over by the blanket one of the three men looked around sheepishly. At the card game in progress on the blanket Sam had caught a glimpse of Tony's hand reaching back to a sheath knife that hung at his belt.

"Hell, Spike, Dobie was cheatin'," Tony excused himself surlily.

"I'll cheat you an' Dobie both," Samms warned, holding the ax as a lesser man might have held a hatchet. "You lay off now!" He sat down beside Ed Draper again.

"Well, what *is* it gettin' us, Ed?" Samms demanded.

"Nothing," Draper answered gloomily. "I can kill McCord, all right; I ain't afraid of him. But when I do I've just made money for Melcomb."

Samms shrugged. "You're gettin' awful soft," he observed. "Someday you an' me will take that money away from Melcomb, that's what we'll do."

Draper shook his head. "He'll outsmart us," he prophesied. "He knows more than we do, Spike. He's a coward but he's smart. . . . Here he comes up the road now."

Melcomb, driving his sorrel team hitched to a buckboard, came around a turn below the camp and, with the sorrels set at a brisk trot, approached rapidly. When he pulled the team to a stop the big manager of the Hoysen Lumber Company wrapped the lines around the whipstock and deliberately climbed down over the wheel. Both Ed Draper and Samms were apprehensive, but Melcomb, stopping in front of them, nodded briefly.

"I thought I'd find you down here," he said, a tinge of derisiveness in his voice. "McCord stop you?"

Samms nodded, and Draper said angrily, "McCord an' an old devil hid in some rocks with a rifle. I tell you, Otis—"

"Two men," Melcomb said slowly. "I send you and Spike and a crew up here, and two men stopped you." He laughed scornfully. "You've got quite a reputation, Ed. I wonder how you got it."

A slow red dyed Draper's face. He got deliberately to his feet. Standing, he yet lacked six inches of Melcomb's height and was forced to lift his head to look into Melcomb's eyes. "You know how I got my reputation," Draper said dangerously. "Maybe you want me to prove I earned it!"

Melcomb took a step back. "Now, Ed," he placated, "you know—"

Draper interrupted. "I ain't afraid of McCord!" he

snapped. "I ain't afraid of you either. I'm just all done pullin' your chestnuts out of the fire, that's all. You can do your own dirty business from now on, Melcomb. I'm through."

Melcomb glanced from Draper to Spike Samms. Samms' face was stolid, expressionless. Facing Draper again, Melcomb spoke quickly. "You get a third of the timber on top, Ed. Don't forget that. You—"

"You'd cheat me out of it," Draper said flatly. "I told you I'm through, an' I'm through." He turned abruptly, presenting the back of his square shoulders to Melcomb, and walked over to the log upon which he had been sitting.

Melcomb looked at Samms uneasily. "Spike . . ." he began.

"I stay with Ed," Samms stated.

Melcomb shrugged. "All right," he said. "If you're yellow I'll—"

"Don't call me yellow!" Draper snarled. "Me or Spike either. Anybody that's yellow around here is you."

Melcomb looked at Draper, at Samms and at the interested men clustered about the camp. Here was defeat and he knew it. He shrugged, turned and walked to his buckboard. Climbing up over the wheel, he settled into the seat and picked up the lines. "You'll come back to Adelphi tomorrow?" he said. "You'll bring the outfit in?"

"In the mornin'," Draper said shortly. "You can pay me an' Spike off then, an' what I mean is you'll pay us off." There was significance in the last words, a threat implied. Melcomb caught that threat. He swung the team, cramping the buckboard wheels, turned the vehicle and started back down the canyon. Ed Draper sat down on the log. Samms, coming over, sat down beside him.

"Damned yellow bastard!" Draper snarled. "He's goin' to payoff plenty in the mornin'."

Spike Samms nodded and sucked on his cigarette.

Otis Melcomb, driving down Pinál Canyon with twilight all about him, let the horses take their own speed along the road. Anger filled the man, anger and fear. The tools that he had used so often had turned against him. Here was an end to his aspirations, an end to his greed and his desire; not only an end to them but a threat to his position, to his very existence. He had gone too far with Draper and with Samms, had pushed them too greatly. They were a living threat, a menace to be dealt with. But how? That was the question that arose, that came to obsess him. There must be some answer, some scheme, something that he could use to avert the reckoning. Somehow . . . Otis Melcomb lifted his head. Perhaps there was a way; perhaps there was a plan that he could use. If he could throw Ed Draper and Spike Samms against Lin McCord, fill them with anger against McCord, raise in them the will and desire to kill . . . There was a way! There was a plan that he could use. Melcomb lifted the lines and, reaching for the whip, touched the backs of his walking horses. The team broke into a trot, and the buckboard rattled as it wheeled down Pinál Canyon toward Adelphi.

In Pinál Canyon the sun went down and shadows

came to choke the dying light. On the ledge above the road Sacatone Thomas shifted position and looked back toward the trees. Windy was coming across from the timber carrying Carl Yetman's old .45-.70. He stopped and, looking at Sacatone, grinned broadly.

"I'll hold it down a while now, Sac," Windy drawled. "You had all the fun this afternoon. You can go get somethin' to eat now."

Sacatone got up and stretched and yawned. "All right," he said. "I'll be back, though." He walked away and Windy, curling his long length down in the rocks, swore at their hardness. Sacatone's boots, as he scrambled up the ridge, sent rocks rattling.

Down in Pinál Canyon, their meal finished, Ed Draper and Spike Samms and the crew disposed themselves about their dying fire. Samms and Draper were quiet, each occupied with his thoughts. The men took their lead from these, their leaders. They were surly, ill-tempered, short-spoken. The murderer growled a curse at the man who had been in the asylum and received a curse in return. The blanket spread for the card game was deserted. Ed Draper, lifting himself from where he sat, walked across to his rolled bed. "I'm goin' to turn in," Draper announced.

Spike Samms began to free rope from canvas. "Me too," he growled.

Darkness came to Pinál Canyon, darkness and a little wind that blew along the creek, rustling the trees, making the pines whisper as though they carried some secret message. The fire glowed dull red, burning the big log that the cook had placed for his skillets to rest upon. Horses, tied to wagon wheels, munched hay and shifted now and then with a nervous stamp of hoofs. Under a wagon a man snored in rising crescendo. Sleepers, stirring in their beds, shifted the tarpaulins above them so that they looked like gray cocoons in which the pupae moved as life arose within them. The stars hung close, touching the tops of the pines along the north hill of the canyon; and on his ledge Windy Tillitson yawned and rubbed his eyes and changed position so that the rocks struck fresh places on his lengthy body. Away down Pinál Canyon a buckboard rolled along the road, ascending the gentle slope. Where the buckboard wheels struck the rocks of a creek crossing, tilting the vehicle, a clink sounded as of cans that touched each other.

Down in Adelphi Glen Hunter talked, low-voiced, to Bessie as they sat together on the back porch of the hotel. In the Exchange Saloon Gilberto Gil spoke to Fred Lyten.

"Good night, Fred. Guess I'll turn in. It's ten o'clock."

Otis Melcomb drove the buckboard up Pinál. A quarter of a mile below Ed Draper's camp he pulled off the road and stopped his team. Alighting, he tied his horses to a tree and then, reaching into the bed of the buckboard, lifted out two cans. Carrying them, he walked back to the road and went on, climbing up the canyon.

Below the camp, where the fire glowed dully, almost dead, he left the road and circled, moving out through the sparse growth. He moved stealthily, carefully, stop-

208

ping now and again to look toward the fire. Beyond the camp he found the road again and followed it.

The road reached the first crossing of the creek. Beyond the crossing came the last steep pull to the mesa top. Otis Melcomb did not cross the creek. Rather he diverged from the road, moving in toward a growth of timber, following along the creek bank. He paused and put his burden on the ground and then, in silent Pinál Canyon, there was the sound of brush being dragged across the ground, a snapping of dead limbs, a stealthy crackling as brush was piled.

Quiet came again. Melcomb's feet splashed as he crossed the creek. Again the sound of dragging brush, of snapping limbs, came through the quiet night. On his ledge Windy heard a noise and lifted his head. The sound did not come again and, having listened, Windy grinned a little to himself.

"Deer goin' through the brush," he murmured and relaxed once more.

Again there was a splashing in the creek. A pin point of light appeared, gleaming momentarily and then dying. A black blotch moved along the road, was lost in the pines, reappeared. In Ed Draper's camp the fire had died, hidden by the ashes. At the buckboard the horses lifted their heads and snorted nervously, then, as familiar hands untied the rope that held them, were easy once again. The buckboard rolled out upon the road, headed now toward Adelphi. The horses walked briskly, then broke to a trot. On the seat Otis Melcomb held the lines, his head turned so that he looked back up the canyon.

The buckboard cleared the canyon's mouth and rolled out upon the flat. In the canyon a dull explosion sounded, a faint "boom!" as though in a mine a shot had been fired. Melcomb turned his head and sent the horses trotting along.

Away up Pinál Canyon, by the last crossing of the creek, the night roared out of its silence. Again the blackness of the mesa flame gouted up fountainlike and, like the fountain, tumbling at its top, reaching out on either side to fall in fiery beauty. In the camp so carelessly made by the lumbermen Spike Samms sat up in his bed, his eyes round and wide. He saw the flame, the gargantuan display of fireworks and, seeing, could not believe he saw. All about him men were coming from their beds, eyes big and startled.

On the ledge above the canyon Windy Tillitson, drowsing after his long day and still determined not to sleep, heard that roar and, looking down, saw the gigantic blossom of flame. The flame dropped down and momentarily was obscured, and then the terrible red of fire spread like a tide across the canyon. Windy leaped up. The wind, blowing steadily down the canyon, sung by him. One look Windy took and then no more, but, running from the ledge, the .45-.70 tight gripped in his hands, made for the mesa top.

"Fire!" Windy yelled as he ran. "They've fired the canyon!"

Down below, Ed Draper and Spike Samms watched their men throw bedding into wagons, watched frightened horses fight against the hands that harnessed them, watched the wild spread of the fire. They stood side by side, and Ed Draper, thin-voiced and contained, spoke to his companion.

"Tried to burn us out," he snarled. "Tried to get us while we was asleep. The dirty murderer. We'll settle with McCord!"

"Get them teams hooked up!" Spike Samms bellowed. "Hurry! You want to be caught in this? Get them horses hitched!"

CHAPTER XVI
INFERNO

WINDY'S YELLS BROUGHT THE MCCORD CREW TUMBLING from their beds: Carl, Shorty, Sacatone, Bobby and Lin. The Portillos turned out en masse, and lights winked at the Patrick house as Eleanor and her father, Rufina and Sandy Donald arose hurriedly and dressed. It did not take Lin long to reach the top of the canyon. There, with Windy beside him, he stood looking down at the inferno that raged below. The country was dry. Save for one little rain there had been no moisture, and now flames stealing through tinder-dry brush, licking at the bases of pines, shot high until the pines were torches and the brush a mat of fire.

"My Lawd!" Windy ejaculated and then stood speechless. Lin said nothing. Sacatone, coming up beside the other two, spat over the first sharp drop of the road, watched for a moment and then snarled, "So they had to burn us out, did they? By God, Lin, we should have worked on 'em this afternoon!"

Slowly Lin nodded, his face adamant there in the light from the fire. There could be no other construction, no other explanation for this sudden outbreak. Ed Draper and Spike Samms, that company crew down below, had started the fire. "We should have worked on 'em," he agreed.

Eleanor and her father, arriving with Sandy Donald, came to stand beside Lin and look down into the red hell of the canyon. Already the rising heat was scorching; already Lin's face was red with something other than the reflection of the fire. Neither of the Patricks spoke for a time and then Dan Patrick, his voice calm, said: "We'll have to start now if we want to save the timber on top. We'll have to build a fire line."

"It can't come up the rim, can it, Dad?" Eleanor spoke anxiously. "Won't the rim stop it?"

Patrick shook his head. "No," he answered. "We'll have to fight this all along the rim. We'll fight it as it spreads. Right now we've got to stop its coming up the canyon. Manuel!"

Manuel Portillos appeared at Patrick's elbow. *"Si, señor,"* he answered.

"Get your boys," Patrick ordered. "There are spades in the tool shed at the mill. Bring them and axes! We'll build a fire line across here," he gestured, his hand describing an arc along the rim.

"Si, señor!" Manuel turned and hurried away.

"I've saw grass fires," Windy drawled. "I've saw some brush burn. I never seen anythin' like this. What do we do, Lin?"

Lin looked at Dan Patrick. "There's the boss," he said

shortly. "What do you want us to do, Mr. Patrick?"

Patrick looked at Lin and smiled grimly. "Work like hell," he said. "Thanks, Lin."

It was Patrick who gave the orders, who outlined the battleground. Veteran lumberman that he was, he knew what had to be done and how to do it. The forces at his command were pitifully few, but he disposed them to the best advantage, placed men with shovels digging and scraping a fire line across the top of Pinál Canyon. The fire was still below, working steadily toward the sides of the canyon, coming steadily up the canyon. Only the wind, which blew down the canyon, prevented a more rapid spread. The men toiled and labored, cutting the fire line, and Patrick, himself unable to work but using his knowledge and experience to supervise the job, came to where Lin sweated over a shovel.

"If it doesn't reach the ridges and crown on us," he said calmly, "we may hold it. But if a crown fire starts—" He stopped.

Lin straightened. "How d'you mean?" he asked.

"If the fire gets to the top of the canyon it will run through the timber," Patrick said. "It jumps from the top of one tree to the next. It goes wild, Lin."

"We got to hold it here," Lin said decisively. "There's just that one line of trees up the south ridge. There's rock on the north. Will it cross that?"

"Depends on the wind," Patrick said. "If we build a line here and backfire—"

"Why can't we build a line?" Lin snapped. "Look, there's the creek. If we could turn it across the canyon

213

it would make a fire line, wouldn't it?"

Patrick nodded.

"I'm no damned good with a shovel," Lin snapped. "Oh, Windy!"

Twenty feet away Windy stopped work and rested on his shovel.

"Come on," Lin called.

"We've got to build this line," Patrick said desperately. "We've got to . . . Lin, you wouldn't quit!"

"Hell no!" Lin was running toward the camp. "Come on, Windy!"

Windy followed Lin McCord. Patrick, watching them go, shook his head. What wild idea was this? What had Lin McCord conceived?

He had not long to wait. There was a clatter and a banging on the loose rock at the top. A yoke of oxen appeared, and behind the stolidly plodding oxen a fresno bumped and slipped along the ground. Another yoke came out of the darkness into the red light. Windy walked beside them.

"I remembered that ol' plow," he yelled to Patrick. "So did Lin. Give me somebody to shake it an' somebody to run the fresno. We're goin' to build you a lake."

Instantly Patrick caught the idea. Behind the cap rock, where the canyon bisected the steep rise of the mesa, the mesa top dipped and then rose again. Through the little ridge the creek had cut a path. A dam thrown across the creek would turn it to the depression. A ridge of earth piled across the road and the dip of the canyon would hold the water thus diverted. That water would form a barricade to the advancing fire. With it in place the immediate point of danger would be the line of trees running from the ledge where Sacatone had lain concealed to the top of the mesa.

"I can do a hell of a lot more with a yoke of oxen than I can with a shovel," Windy stated, stopping beside Patrick. "Where do you think we'd better begin?"

Here were new arms with which to fight. Patrick utilized them. "Manuel!" he called. "Manuel!"

From somewhere to the right Manuel Portillos answered and presently came running. To him Patrick spoke rapidly, his Spanish clear and fluent. Manuel Portillos nodded as he got his orders and learned the plan. He lifted his voice in a shout, calling to his sons. They came running, listened to what he told them and dispersed. Adolfo and Huberto went toward the creek where presently their axes were heard as they felled a pine to drop across the water. Windy, with another of the Portillos boys to hold the plow, started his oxen. The plow point scraped against rock and slithered through soft dirt, and a furrow grew. While Windy plowed, the tree crashed down across the creek. Men toiled to tumble rocks against its branches. Lin, his fresno loaded with the dirt that Windy's plow had loosened, reinforced the rock. Across the creek bed a dam arose.

It was not perfect; there was no need for it to be perfect. The water, diverted, rose and, trickling out of the little lake that was forming, followed a furrow toward the road and seeped into it. Above the ledge axes sounded as men strove desperately to break the line of timber that reached toward the mesa top.

"Make your bank here, Lin," Patrick ordered, selecting his battleground. "Throw the dirt up here. That will spread the water."

The oxen, stolid and slow, toiled against the yoke. Across the road the ridge grew slowly. On the ledge a tree crashed down and then another. In the canyon the fire, fighting against the wind, crept slowly, formidably, toward the top.

"We'll hold it," Patrick stated, estimating the advance of the enemy. "If the wind doesn't change, we'll hold it."

"Come morning an' the wind will change," Lin said grimly. "It blows up the canyon in the morning. Haw, Buck! Haw! Come around there."

"Eleanor!" Patrick called sharply, "you and Sandy get out in front now. Start the backfire. Watch it. Go on, girl!"

Down in the canyon, perhaps three miles below the mesa, Spike Samms stood holding a lantern. A big man, Samms, heavy-shouldered and black-bearded, unscrupulous and bad, but a lumberman.

"Pile out, you bastards!" Samms bellowed. "Here's where you work your way! Here's where we make a fight. Pile out!"

From the wagons that had stopped at his command men climbed down, big men, strong and fierce. There were axes and shovels in their hands, spades and mattocks, tools to which they were accustomed.

"We'll make a fire line across here," Samms called. "Start right here in the road an' work both ways. Dobie, you an' Tony get into that brush an' get it down. We'll hold it here!"

Samms stopped. Beside him Ed Draper stood, his hand on Samms' arm. "We're goin' to have to have some help," Draper said levelly. "I'll go to Adelphi."

"Go on, then!" Samms growled. "Turn out the town, Ed. Get 'em up here."

Draper strode away out of the lantern light and Samms, turning, called his orders again. "Scrape down to the rock. We'll start a backfire an' hold it here!"

In the little town of Adelphi Glen Hunter bade Bessie good night. It was almost midnight. He kissed the girl and patted her cheek and Bessie, opening the kitchen door, went into the hotel. Hunter stood on the porch for a moment after Bessie was gone and then walked down the steps.

A stepmother had begun Glen Hunter's lessons in humility when he was six years old. Undersized, undernourished, unwanted, Glen had learned then the bitterness of neglect, of being pushed aside so that other more fortunate mortals might have a place in the light. That was the beginning. At twelve, his father dead, he had gone to work, running errands, blacking shoes, doing what he could to keep his soul in his body; and because of his lack of physical strength he had been forced to' be cunning. Like the jackal who follows the lion, Glen Hunter learned to fawn upon the strong, to cower and so please the vanity of the bully, to run and hide, to lie and cheat in order that he might live.

Living had not been kind to Hunter, if living his existence could be called. Living is never kind to the weak and the defenseless. In his thirty-four years Hunter had learned many things, most of them unkind, and in those years he had built within himself a sort of philosophy, a method of thought that made living possible. He wore loud clothes because they gave his scant physique importance. He listened, eavesdropping, not because he wished to use the stealthily gained knowledge for his own advancement—he was too cowardly to do that—but because the very possession of that knowledge made him important to himself. At night, when no one could hear or see, he could lie awake and build grandiose dreams, dreams in which he was the powerful one and the others were weak.

Always Hunter was afraid, but now with Bessie, as with other weaklings, he boasted. He invented long stories in which he was the hero and told them to Bessie, and sometimes, in a moment of indiscretion, he told Bessie the truth in his boasting. For Bessie loved him. Bessie thought that he was grand. Bessie looked at him adoringly, and with her adoration Glen Hunter gained in mental stature. Given Bessie to love him and Glen Hunter was almost a man.

He walked now from the back of the hotel toward the front, intending to enter the front door and climb the stair to his room. When he reached the board sidewalk in front of the hotel he stopped. There was a light in the company office. After a moment's pause Hunter walked toward the light. In Adelphi that light could mean nothing bad, and to investigate it, to come upon Spike

218

Samms or Ed Draper or even Otis Melcomb, to show that he was alert and watchful, would add to his importance. He could, having investigated the light and found it to be harmless, return to the hotel and there, in bed, invent a fiction in which the light was not of harmless origin and in which he, Glen Hunter, was a hero.

When he reached the building he felt relief. There was a buckboard in front of the office, the team standing by the hitch rail, and Hunter knew that the buckboard belonged to Otis Melcomb. A strong odor of kerosene assailed his nostrils but he thought nothing of that. He pushed on the office door. It opened, and he went in.

The light came from Melcomb's office. Hunter, crossing in front of the familiar railing that barred the bookkeeper's desk and the safe from the rest of the office, made toward the light, but before he had reached Melcomb's door the light was blotted out and Melcomb stood in the opening, his clothing in disarray, his face gray.

"Anything wrong, Mr. Melcomb?" Hunter asked. "I saw the light and I came down . . ."

"What are you doing here?" Melcomb rasped hoarsely.

"Why, I saw the light," Hunter explained again virtuously. "I thought that there was something wrong so—"

"You were spying on me!" Melcomb accused. "That's what you were doing."

Hunter recoiled a step. "No," he protested, "I wasn't spying. I saw the light—"

"Spying!" Melcomb took a long step and reached out toward the smaller man.

Hunter dodged that reaching hand, retreating toward the door. "No!" he shrilled. "No, I wasn't. I—"

He dodged again, ducking under the hand that reached for him. Melcomb advanced, penning Hunter in a corner, shutting him off from the door. "I'll teach you to spy," he growled. "I'll teach you—"

Fear filled Glen Hunter. Desperately he tried to elude the bigger man, dodging, trying to reach the door. Melcomb's big hand caught his shoulder, and cloth ripped as Hunter pulled free. "No!" he screamed in his fright. "No! Don't!"

He was caught now. Melcomb had him. Melcomb's hands, terrible in their strength, had seized him. In his panic Hunter fought blindly, kicking, scratching, screaming. The walls muffled his cries, and Melcomb's hands held him helpless despite his struggles. Then, freeing a hand, the big man struck, the blow crashing home against Hunter's face.

There was insanity in Otis Melcomb, an insanity of fear. Having struck the man he held, feeling his fist crash home against flesh, he struck again and again and yet again. Even when Hunter went limp in his grasp, when Hunter's body slumped, Melcomb struck. Once more cloth ripped in his hands, and Hunter dropped to the floor. And now, in his madness, Melcomb kicked the fallen man, kicked the twitching body with his heavy boots until the twitching ceased and his boots thudded against inert flesh. Savagely, insanely, all reason gone, Otis Melcomb savaged that limp body. He did not hear a horse come pounding into the silent town. He heard nothing, realized nothing, save that here was sodden flesh that he could batter and brutalize and vent his insane rage upon; and then, striking through his rage, penetrating it, came a sound. Otis Melcomb stopped and stood listening. Above Adelphi, sending the ethos reeling in the night, a tocsin sounded. Someone had reached the tower, the tall wooden structure that stood in the center of the little town: the bell tower. Someone was ringing the fire bell, sending its warning pealing through the night, shattering slumber, spreading terror.

Otis Melcomb turned from the limp body on the floor and ran to the door. All through Adelphi lights were blossoming. All through Adelphi men, roused by the tocsin, were getting up, hastily drawing on clothing, running out to the street. Otis Melcomb pulled the door shut behind him and heard the night latch click. Then he too ran toward the bell tower.

Ed Draper was ringing the bell. Gil, mustache bristling, was already at the tower; and Draper, between pulls on the rope, was throwing words over his shoulder at the deputy, telling him of the situation in Pinál Canyon. When Melcomb arrived the deputy knew what was happening and immediately drew the big man aside.

"We'll have to get men up there right away, Melcomb," he snapped. "I'll want to get teams from the barn an' wagons an' the men from your camps."

"Of course," Melcomb agreed. "I'll go up there and take charge, Gil. We'll get a bunch of men started right away. We'll have to get tools and have some kind of organization. This won't be the first fire I've fought."

"Quit ringin' that bell!" Gil roared at Draper. "You got everybody out of bed now. No use ringin' it any more. All right, Mr. Melcomb, you take a crew up there an' I'll get things organized here. I'll send out to your camps for the men there an' bring 'em right along. You go ahead."

The deputy turned away. Draper, leaving the bell rope, reached Melcomb's side.

"Well, Ed," Melcomb asked, "What about it?"

Draper's voice was savage. "McCord started this," he snarled. "He tried to burn us while we were sleepin'. I'll settle with McCord if it's the last thing I do!"

"We're going to have to fight fire before we settle with McCord," Melcomb said. "Help me out now, Ed. I want a crew to go to the canyon right away. Come on and we'll get the men we want."

The two men strode off together while Gilberto Gil's voice, lifted in command, pierced through the voices that raised from assembling Adelphi. On the sidewalk in front of Cora Ferguson's millinery store Bessie stood peering out into the street. The man she sought was not there. Bessie turned. Cora was on the step of her store, and Bessie went to her.

In the company office Glen Hunter lifted his battered head from the floor and then let it drop back. Blood came in a tiny trickle from the corner of his mouth, and as he breathed his breath rasped in his chest. Once more he lifted his head and then, laboriously, an inch at a time, he moved his battered body, crawling feebly, stopping, crawling again, inching toward the door.

"I don't see Glen out there," Bessie told her friend. "Have you seen him, Cora?"

"No," Cora answered absently. "He's some place around, though, Bessie. Look! There goes Otis Melcomb an' Ed Draper. They're takin' a crew of men out to the fire. I wish . . ."

"What do you wish, Cora?"

"I wish I knew if that big-mouthed Windy Tillitson was all right," Cora blurted. "Come on, Bessie, let's go up the street. They're leavin' from the company barns."

Morning light, seeping down through the haze of smoke that spread across the country, found the town of Adelphi deserted except by its women. It found Bessie and Cora in the millinery shop, Cora trying to comfort her companion. Bessie was disconsolate. She had not found Glen at the hotel; none of the men at the barns had seen him. In all Adelphi there was no sign or trace of Glen Hunter.

"He's a coward," Bessie wailed. "If he wasn't a coward he'd have gone to the fire. I won't marry a coward, Cora."

"You've got no business callin' him that," Cora refuted. "Likely he's already at the fire. Just because them men at the barn said they hadn't seen him is no sign. You make me mad!"

"But where is he?" Bessie demanded. "I couldn't find him. Oh, Cora! If anything happened to Glen . . ." Cora found her arms well filled with the weeping Bessie.

Cora herself was worried, albeit not concerning

Glen Hunter. She had seen the red glare of the fire limned against the rising smoke from Pinál Canyon. She knew that somewhere Windy fought the fire. With no certainty as to Windy's safety, worried concerning Eleanor and Dan Patrick, Cora had scant sympathy for Bessie. She shook Bessie irritably. "You're actin' like a fool!" Cora snapped. "You'll get word from your precious Glen pretty soon. I'm all out of patience with you, Bessie. You go on back to the hotel an' get cleaned up an' get your clothes on. You'll hear from him."

Bessie, shaken to sanity and recalled to the knowledge that she was scantily clothed, ceased her wailing. "You'll go with me, Cora?" she asked. "You'll come to the hotel with me?"

"All right," Cora agreed, "I'll come."

The two women left the millinery shop and went out to the street. When they reached the sidewalk Bessie stopped. "Maybe Glen's at the office," she exclaimed. "I'm going down there, Cora. I want to see."

Cora heaved a resigned sigh. "All right," she said, "all right. We'll go to the office, Bessie, an' then you've got to go to the hotel an' get cleaned up an' dressed. Come on. We'll go to the office."

CHAPTER XVII
BABE IN THE WOODS

ATOP ROUGH MESA MORNING FOUND MEN WHO, IN SHORT hours, had poured out their energy to the point of exhaustion and who yet could not stop and rest. Where the road ascended the mesa top there was now a stretch of burned country reaching down into the canyon. Behind that backfire, reinforcing it, was wet soil and a dike of dirt and rock thrown up. There were breaks in this dike where water had gone across, and the creek, now in its accustomed bed, had eaten through and was running down into the canyon. On the south ridge there was a gap in the line of timber that stretched up from the ledge. Here trees had been felled and pulled back by oxen. Through this gap the black safety of the backfire stretched, and beyond it men were stationed to control the little fire that remained. The wind, coming now from the southeast, was pushing the fire up the north side of the canyon. That area was not heavily timbered, most of the covering being brush with one sharp V of aspen running down from the ridge. Lin McCord, with Dan Patrick, Donald and the men of the McCord crew, was gathered close by the road watching the fire spread to the north. They had held the battle line here, but the enemy was moving to flank them. Through the pall of smoke they could see the fire steadily working up the canyon side, attacking the brush, making headway toward the ridge.

"There's a bench beyond the timber," Dan Patrick

said slowly. "Lin, we're going to have to fight fire all along the rim to the north."

Lin nodded. With red-rimmed eyes squinted against the smoke, he watched the progress of the fire. He knew of the bench that Patrick mentioned, knew that behind the ridge on the north side of Pinál Canyon there was a wide stretch of country that reached out north until Loblolly Canyon bisected it. He knew, too, that the fire would reach that area and that to hold the fire from the mesa top a crew of men must constantly patrol the rim to the north.

"They ought to be coming out from town," Dan Patrick said. "We need help up here, Lin."

"We'll be the last ones to get help," Lin said shortly. "You don't think Melcomb would send men up here, do you? It was Melcomb's men that started this fire."

Patrick shook his head. "We can't let the mesa burn," he said wearily. "We can't do that, Lin. If only it would rain . . ."

Lin lifted his head and looked toward the sky. He could see nothing but the haze of smoke. "Rain!" he said shortly. "It hasn't rained but once since we took the lease. I don't think it'll rain now."

Over beyond Patrick, Manuel Portillos spoke deprecatingly. *"Yo pienso . . ."* Manuel said.

"What?" Lin looked at the speaker.

"Yo pienso que va llover," Manuel stated.

"You're the only one that thinks so," Lin said. "I hope you're right, Manuel. I hope it does rain."

Sacatone looked at his hands, hands that were blistered by unaccustomed toil. Lifting his eyes from his hands, he spoke wearily. "Can't we ride the rim?" he asked. "We can cover more country horseback, Lin. A little bunch of men can get over all that ground if we take horses."

Lin looked at Sacatone and grinned. He knew just how Sacatone felt. Cowmen work on horseback, and Lin and Sacatone were cowmen. "We sure aren't goin' to walk along the rim," Lin said. "You're right, Sacatone. We can cover more country on horseback."

"We cain't all of us go," Windy drawled. "Some of us have got to stay here an' watch. It might break through the fire line."

"Well"—Lin's voice was tired—"we might as well get at it. You keep what men you want, Mr. Patrick, an' I'll go run in the horses. Where's Bobby?"

All through the night small Bobby had been with the men. As well as his young body and crippled leg allowed he had worked. Bobby had carried water, he had brought hot coffee, he had done a hundred little self-appointed chores. Now he was missing.

"Bobby's gone to the house with Eleanor," Dan Patrick answered. "They're cooking something to eat. I guess you're right, Lin. You can cover more country on horseback and do a better job."

Lin brought the horses and penned them. The remuda, frightened, made spooky by the smoke, was hard to handle. Lin worked them through the corral gate, closed it and went to the Patrick house. His crew was there: Shorty, Windy, Sacatone and Carl. They were sprawled out on the porch, and there were plates and cups beside them. Eleanor, seeing Lin, went into the house and returned, bringing him food. Lin ate hastily, the girl waiting beside him. When he was finished he got up. The rest of the men also came to their feet, rested a bit, refreshed by the food.

"You'll be careful, Lin?" Eleanor asked. "You won't take any chances?"

Heedless of the men, Lin bent and kissed the girl full on the lips. "You bet I'll be careful," he promised. "Don't you worry."

Eleanor smiled at him tremulously. Returning that smile, Lin led the way toward the corral.

He had been gone perhaps ten minutes when Bobby McCord appeared at the door of the house. Bobby looked at the empty porch, at Eleanor standing on the steps looking off toward the north and then, limping hastily to the girl, asked: "Where's Uncle Lin?"

Eleanor dropped her arm over the boy's shoulder. "He's gone to watch the rim," she answered.

"I'm going too." Bobby slipped out from beneath the girl's arm.

"No, Bobby." Eleanor caught him and drew him back. "You can't go. You've got to stay here."

Bobby twisted out of her grasp. "Why have I got to stay?" he demanded. "Lin's gone. Why do I have to stay here?"

"I need you, Bobby," Eleanor answered. "You'll stay and help me, won't you?"

Bobby said, "Well . . ." dubiously and returned to stand beside the girl.

Lin and his men rode north, following along the rim

of the mesa. Besides the spades and axes they carried, Lin, Windy and Sacatone were otherwise armed. Lin had a gun belt strapped around his middle, a Colt hanging snug against his thigh. Sacatone's rifle was on his saddle, and Windy had a gun shoved down inside his trousers. None of the three was conscious of their armament. They had been armed when Windy's call brought them to fight fire; they simply had not laid aside their weapons.

Following the rim, they could see the progress of the fire. Early in the morning as it was, the wind had not yet reached any great volume. The fire was working out of Pinál Canyon toward the north, burning now in the timber that formed a line along the canyon top. The smoke rolled upward, and where the fire attacked standing timber they could see the flames beneath the billowing smoke.

As yet the fire was not spreading west to any extent. There was a slow spread from the timber toward both east and west, but for the most part the advance of the fire was toward the east. Below the riders the sheer escarpment of the mesa rim dropped away toward a bench. For perhaps fifty feet the rock wall fell steeply, a sheer descent. There was a little timber—mostly scrub cedar—and some brush below the wall, and then the mesa sloped off toward the bench. The slope was covered with scrub oak, and on the bench itself the scrub oak grew, interspersed here and there with clumps of pine and spruce.

"It can't get over the rim," Windy said, riding beside Lin. "Just can't do it."

Lin shook his head. "There's places where it could come up," he refuted. "Look there, Windy."

Following Lin's pointing finger, Windy could see where the rim was broken by a sharp cleft. Here great rocks had broken from the lava cap and gone tumbling down. Between the rocks grass grew, and here and there was a scrubby bunch of oak or a little cedar.

"It could come up them places," Windy agreed. "But they're all we got to look out for."

"You can't tell about fire," Sacatone observed sententiously. "Can't tell what it'll do. You think we ought to make a fire line around places like this, Lin?"

"I don't know," Lin said slowly. "Maybe we ought to, Sacatone."

By mutual consent the men halted at the crevasse and looked out over the bench below. The haze half hid the bench. Lin shook his head. "I wish I knew," he said. "I think . . . Look, why don't we make a fire line up on top an' then go down an' set a backfire? We can watch it an' let it burn up through the crack. Wouldn't that do it?"

Grave consultation followed. Presently Lin's scheme was decided upon. Dismounting, the men tied their horses. Where the crack in the rimrock reached the top they grubbed out brush, felled a small cedar or two, Sacatone dragging them away at the end of his saddle rope; and then Lin descended, carrying a shovel, and Windy followed him. At the bottom of the steep cleft, impassable save to a man on foot, Lin and Windy stopped and started a little fire. They followed it as it burned slowly up the cleft, now using the shovels they carried to throw on earth and control the spread of the

230

flame, now waiting for the backfire to burn through a small patch of scrubby brush. When finally they reached the top, they stood beside the others and looked back at their handiwork.

"Fire won't come up that," Lin said with satisfaction, pointing down to the smoking cleft. "There's nothing in it that will burn."

Sacatone grunted, and Windy made a suggestion. "Maybe one of us had better stay here an' watch it a while," he said. "Make sure it's out."

Lin nodded. He had not intended to ride off and leave the still-smoking brush and grass. "You stay here, Shorty," Lin directed. "When you're sure it's all out you can follow us. The rest of us will go on along the rim."

Mounting again, leaving Shorty Morgan to watch the cleft, the little party rode on.

There were not many breaks in the rim such as the one they had left; there were, however, numerous other threats to the safety of the mesa. At times the cap rock was not sheer and steep but sloped away, weathered and broken, into great heaps of rock. Between these the grass grew thick and dry, a brown menace. At another point the oak brush overran a steep slope leading to the top, and beyond that scrub cedars followed a niche, choking it with their thick greenery. It was a hopeless task, the one Lin had in hand, and as they rode he realized its hopelessness.

"We can't do it," he said at length, pulling his horse to a stop. "There's too much country to cover. We can't do it, Windy."

Windy nodded morosely. "Not much chance," he agreed. "The fire's workin' this way too, Lin. You can see it in the scrub oak on the bench."

Lin looked down. Remorselessly the fire was spreading across the wide bench that divided Loblolly Canyon from Pinál Canyon. The smoke haze hung thickly, so heavy that the bench was almost obscured. About him Lin's men were silent, waiting for him to decide upon the next move. There was no next move. Three miles of country, three miles of rim between the break into Pinál Canyon and the break into Loblolly. Lin McCord had five men to spread over that distance, and every foot of the way was a menace, a potential trail up which fire might come. It was Windy who voiced the opinion of all the rest.

"We got to have some help up here," Windy said. "We got to, Lin."

Slowly Lin nodded.

"An' we better get it pretty soon," Sacatone added. Again Lin nodded. He turned to face his men. They stood looking at him. Lin was the boss; upon him was the responsibility.

"I'll ride down Loblolly," Lin announced. "They'll be fightin' the fire down below. I'll get some help."

Sacatone shifted in his saddle, reaching into his pocket for his chewing tobacco. "I'll go with you," he stated in a tone that brooked no argument.

Lin looked at Sacatone and then at Windy. "We'll hurry," he said. "We'll get back as soon as we can. You watch it up here. Maybe the wind'll change and it won't hit us." His shoulders slumped wearily. There was no hope that the wind would change. For days on end the wind had blown across the mesa from the southeast.

"Sure," Windy said with false heartiness, "maybe it won't hit us. You go ahead, Lin. If Loblolly gets on fire before you come back, you can make it up Cedar Canyon sure. You'd better hurry, though."

The sharp note of anxiety in Windy's voice spurred Lin. When Windy was uneasy there was something to be frightened about.

"Let's go, Sacatone," he said sharply and started his horse ahead, Sacatone following. When they were gone Windy looked at Carl Yetman.

"I hope he makes it," Windy said. "I sure hope he does, Carl. If he don't there's goin' to be a lot of barbecued steers on Rough Mesa. Let's go back an' see how Shorty's comin'."

Back at the Patrick house Eleanor Patrick and her father stood, side by side, looking over the expanse of smoke that hung like a pall in the sky. Dan Patrick had come up from the canyon utterly worn out. What hidden reservoir of strength had kept him going neither he nor his daughter knew. His face was gray with his fatigue, and he rested his weight on the arm he had placed across his daughter's shoulders.

"Do you think Lin's all right, Father?" the girl asked. "Do you think he's safe?"

"I think he's safe enough," Dan Patrick answered slowly, "but I'm afraid the mesa's going, Eleanor. The fire is working north, and we haven't enough men to hold it below the rim. I'm sorry that I let Lin go. I should have kept him here. If the fire crowns out along the rim—" Patrick stopped.

"Lin's cattle!" Eleanor exclaimed breathlessly. "The steers!"

Patrick shook his head. "We needn't worry about them," he said. "If the fire reaches the mesa they'll run. There's only the fence on the west to hold them, and they can go through that. No, girl, that's not the danger. But if the fire reaches the top it will run through the timber. We may be lucky if we get out with our lives. I wish that I had kept Lin here."

Sandy Donald, coming up from the barn, stopped when he saw Patrick and his daughter. Donald's face was worried. "Have you seen Bobby?" he asked. "I went down to the barn a minute ago to get same sacks. We're goin' to wet 'em and put 'em around our feet. All the horses are in the corral but Chub. I didn't see him an' I didn't see Bobby's saddle in the barn."

Stark consternation flooded Eleanor's face. "He wanted to go with Lin," she exclaimed. "You don't suppose . . ." Breaking off, she ran toward the barn. Dan Patrick, his fatigue forgotten, and Sandy Donald followed her.

Chub was gone from the corral. Bobby's saddle was not on the long pole in the barn. There was no sign of the boy. Eleanor, running from the barn, stopped when she reached Donald and her father.

"He's gone!" she cried despairingly. "He's gone to find Lin. I've got to find him!" Turning, she ran back toward the barn, Donald following her.

"I'll go," Donald called. "I'll go. You can't—"

Eleanor came from the barn, dragging her saddle, and her bridle tossed over her shoulder. "Help me catch a horse," she stormed. "You'll have to stay with Father, Sandy. They need you here. I'll find Bobby."

Donald ran to the corral and pulled the gate open. The girl dropped her saddle and went into the pen. Inside, the horses, already alarmed, stampeded to the far side. The girl, holding her bridle, advanced toward them. "Help me!" she commanded.

It was Redskin that they caught, Redskin, more gentle than all the others now that Chub was gone, that finally stood and allowed Eleanor to wrap a rein about his neck. The girl bridled swiftly and led the horse out. Donald was holding her saddle and tossed it up on Redskin's back, catching the cinch and pulling through the latigo. He had hardly finished before the girl was in the saddle and Redskin was pounding off toward the north. Donald dropped his empty hands and turned toward Dan Patrick. Patrick's eyes were closed and he was swaying on his feet. Donald ran to catch the man before he fell.

Eleanor Patrick rode straight north from the corral. She missed the big curve in the mesa where Windy and Carl Yetman and Shorty Morgan waited and watched together. Along a trail through the timber Redskin pounded and then, swinging to the east, came into a clearing. At the edge of the clearing a clump of trees marked the entrance to Loblolly Canyon. The girl made toward them and reined Redskin in beside the trees. She could see now, a hundred yards below her, the little park that had served for a picnic ground. The park was deserted. The fence that barred off Loblolly Canyon from the mesa top was just in front of her, and in the fence the gate gaped, dropped to the ground. Someone had gone through the gate. The girl sent Redskin along until the gate was reached and the horse turned through it. Redskin's head was up and his ears pricked sharply forward. The girl started him down, and the horse picked his way cautiously along the trail, turning and angling back and forth in that first steep descent.

When the park was reached Eleanor stopped the horse again. She was in the open and could see more clearly. Away down below her, in the depth of Loblolly Canyon, there was motion; impossible to see clearly through the haze of smoke and yet, motion, she was sure. A puff of wind whipped the smoke away and she saw below her a horse come into a clearing and then disappear again.

"Bobby!" Eleanor called despairingly and sent Redskin down the slope. Rocks rolled and clattered; Redskin slipped and almost fell and then, heedless of consequences, conscious only of flaying reins and heels that dug into his sides, Redskin ran. Full out, disregarding rocks and brush, Redskin came headlong down the trail like any mountain goat, and on his back, clinging to the saddle, hair flying and her mouth opened as she screamed Bobby's name, Eleanor Patrick came with the horse.

In Loblolly Canyon, following along the trail, Bobby McCord, frightened but determined to find Lin, rode Chub. Chub, gentle as he was, was as frightened as the boy. Chub minced along the trail, head up, ears cocked, nostrils wide.

"We got to find him, Chub," Bobby told the horse. "We got to find Lin. The gate was open. He come down here."

Chub turned an ear back at the sound of Bobby's voice and then pricked it sharply forward again.

"We got to, Chub," Bobby said desperately. "Whwhoa, Chub! Whoa! . . . You . . ."

Chub shied violently. Something, perhaps a rabbit scuttling out across the trail, perhaps a rock squirrel running across his path, had frightened Chub. He shied and left the trail, running, spooked by whatever he had seen. Gentle as he was, Chub momentarily lost his head. Under a pine he went, and Bobby, caught by a limb, was swept from the saddle. Bobby fell, and Chub, more frightened now than ever, ran down the trail, stirrups thumping his sides, urging him to greater effort, reins flying. He stepped upon a rein and it snapped; Chub went on, and Bobby, struggling to his feet, hurt by his fall and thoroughly frightened now, ran limping after him.

A few steps Bobby took, then stumbled and went down, only to struggle to his feet again. Chub had disappeared. On down the trail Bobby ran, breathless, panic-stricken, frightened out of his small-boy wits. "Chub!" he called vainly. "Chub!"

He could run no further. Bobby sank wearily to the ground. From his right came a murmur, a menacing, muttering roar that whispered in the air. Bobby looked up. Smoke obscured the sky, smoke that lay like a blanket and yet, unlike a blanket, stirred with life.

"Lin!" Bobby called. "Uncle Lin . . . Where are you, Uncle Lin?" Round face hidden in his hands, Bobby McCord crouched there in the trail, shaken with frightened sobs.

CHAPTER XVIII
DEATH TAKES A CHANCE

ALL THE MEN WERE GONE FROM ADELPHI THE MORNING of the fire—all the men save four—and some of the women also. Pop Vicars remained at the depot, pacing restlessly back and forth across his office, listening for the click of his telegraph sounder. At the livery barn the barn boss and a hostler remained; and in Bessie's room in the hotel two anxious women bent over a man that lay swathed in bandages upon Bessie's bed. From time to time Bessie lifted the man's head and Cora, wiping away a tiny trickle of blood from his lips, placed a glass of water to his mouth. Sometimes Glen Hunter sipped a bit of the water, his eyes open and looking up at Bessie. Sometimes he did not drink at all, nor open his eyes, and an occasional moan escaped his lips.

In the depot the sounder began its clattering, and Vicars went to the desk. He broke his key, tapped "i i" and closed the key again. The staccato of the sounder resumed. Pop Vicars wrote upon a yellow message blank and, the message finished, acknowledged it; then, leaving the sounder still clattering letters that formed questioning words, he took the message he had copied and ran down the street to the company barn.

"They're comin'," he shrilled at the barn boss. "Engine an' three cars out of Junction. They're sendin' men. The sheriff's with 'em an' a doctor. Be here in about two hours."

The barn boss shrugged. "Got plenty of time," he drawled. "Two hours. You sure don't run any expresses on your railroad, Pop."

"Ain't the railroad's fault," Vicars stated hotly. "I never got that message till just before Gil left. You ask me, they're doin' pretty good."

Once more the barn boss shrugged. "We'll be ready for 'em when they get here," he stated. "We'll send 'em right out to the fire."

Vicars wheeled and, clutching the message blank, started back toward the depot. He had answered some of the questions the clicking sounder asked, when he was called from his key. Cora Ferguson, face white with strain, was at the window.

"I want to send a message to the sheriff," she stated, answering Pop's inquiry as to what she wanted. "I want to send it right way, Pop."

"Can't get the sheriff," Pop announced importantly. "He's on his way up here. They're runnin' a special train out of Junction, sendin' men to fight the fire. The sheriff an' a doctor's with 'em."

Relief showed on Cora's face. "When will he get here?" she demanded.

" 'Bout an hour an' a half," Pop answered, looking at the big clock on the wall. "That special's makin' good time. What's the matter, Cora? What do you want the sheriff for?"

"I just want him," Cora answered noncommittally and turned away from the window to stave off further questioning.

"Now what's the matter with her?" Pop asked himself and, getting no answer, went out of the office and to the station door. Looking to the west, he could see the smoke rising skyward from the fire. Pop shook his head. "Sure looks bad," he commented. "It sure does."

It was bad. The fire had driven Samms and his men back down the canyon almost to its mouth. Here the reinforcements had arrived and here the battle still raged. The fighters now were helped by the wind which, blowing from the southeast, held the fire back. A fire line had been built across the mouth of the canyon and a backfire started, but that backfire, whipped now by the wind, was running up the canyon slope toward the north and bade fair to get out of control.

Melcomb experienced a growing fright at the thing he had done. He had seen forest fires, small affairs that were easily controlled and stamped out in timber that was not too dry. But here he had unleashed a monster that laughed roaringly at the efforts to control it, a Frankenstein that lapped and devoured timber, that ran resistlessly across all efforts to check it. Melcomb had assumed charge when he reached the fire, had distributed his crew, had sent help to Samms; had, to all appearances, been the bully boy with the crockery eye. Now, as his plans failed, as the fire overran his battle lines, he wanted and needed help.

Gilberto Gil sensed Melcomb's fright and insecurity. So did Ed Draper and Spike Samms, both of whom acted as Melcomb's lieutenants in the battle. Gil could see where and how Melcomb's ideas and plans had failed. He could not offer any constructive advice as to how they could be improved. Samms, a giant for work, his strength apparently undiminished by his ceaseless efforts, spoke to Melcomb with frank contempt, challenging the decisions the big man made. Draper said nothing but watched Melcomb with sullen, baleful eyes. It was not until Dave Sawyer, the tobacco-chewing boss from Camp Two arrived upon the scene, that order began to come from chaos.

Sawyer was not a big man but he was a hard one. He chewed tobacco the while his shrewd eyes sized up the situation. Then, turning to Melcomb, accepting him as the leader, Sawyer made suggestions.

"Got to hold it against the mesa an' let it burn out," Sawyer stated and spat a brown stream over his shoulder. "Got to send a crew up on top an' hold it on the benches. Right now it's workin' north. There's a bench up there. We ought to build a fire line on the bench an' backfire from it. No sense of spoilin' a lot of good timber. Got to back off from it here some; we can't never hold it in that timber. If we clean off some of this slash with teams an' build a backfire an' watch it, we can keep it in. Ain't no sense of workin' on the south side. That's bare rock over there, an' the wind's against the fire."

"That's what I think," Melcomb agreed. "I didn't see

241

any reason for building a fire line across the canyon mouth. The timber there is gone anyhow."

"You get the men started, Sawyer," Gil directed. "You take hold of it. There's some more men comin' up from Junction. I telegraphed for help. They'll be here any time now. You go ahead, Sawyer."

Sawyer looked questioningly at Melcomb. Melcomb nodded. "Go ahead, Dave," he confirmed. "Take right ahold. I'll be here if you need me."

Draper and Samms had drawn aside and were talking, low-voiced. Sawyer spat, the spittle making a dark stain on the rock, hitched his trousers as might a man who tackles a job and moved forward. "You take about twenty men an' go up on the mesa, Mister Gil," Sawyer directed. "You'd better go up through Cedar Canyon. I ain't so sure Loblolly's goin' to be open very long. The fire's makin' over toward the mouth. You'd better get up there right away. With this wind them boys are bein' pushed up on top."

Gil said something quickly and hurried off toward the fire line at the canyon mouth. Sawyer had stopped a little bunch of men and was talking to them, waving his arms and gesticulating toward the long dark slope that ran down from the bench between Loblolly and Pinál.

"How about it, Mr. Melcomb?" one of the men called.

"You boys do what Sawyer says," Melcomb called in answer.

The men moved off, Melcomb watching them go. Ed Draper and Spike Samms came up and stood on either side of the big man. Draper spoke softly. "We're goin' up on top, Spike an' me are."

Melcomb looked quickly at Draper. "You're going up on top?" he said.

"An' you're comin' with us." There was menace in Draper's voice. "We're goin' up an' settle with McCord."

"But . . ." Melcomb began.

"There's a road up Loblolly, part way," Draper said. "We're going in your buckboard. Nobody's goin' to ask you where *you're* goin', Mr. Melcomb. You're supposed to be the boss!"

Melcomb's eyes glinted. It was working out, the plan that he had conceived; the plan, the fruits of which now blazed skyward, was succeeding! "All right," he said. "I'll take you as far as the road goes, anyhow."

"An' you'll go the rest of the way," Draper stated with finality. "McCord tried to burn us out last night, damn him! We'll settle with him for that, but this is one time you're goin' to be along when the settlement's made."

Melcomb looked at the men on either side of him. There was determination on Draper's face, sullen hatred shown on Spike Samms' countenance.

"An' don't try to get out of it," Draper snarled. "We're goin' now, an' you're comin' along. We're goin' to get there before Gil an' them others do. We got to go by Loblolly. They'll go around by Cedar Canyon, an' that'll take time."

Melcomb felt himself being pushed forward. Samms had a grip on his arm. Draper was beside him. Dave Sawyer, coming back from where he had been placing men, called to Melcomb.

"I'm goin' to send a crew into Loblolly now."

"We're goin' up there ahead of the crew," Draper shouted his answer.

Sawyer stopped and then called: "Show the men where to start, will you?"

"Sure," Spike Samms shouted back. "We'll show 'em."

"Come on," Draper growled in Melcomb's ear. "Come on."

They moved on. Before they reached Melcomb's buckboard Samms let go his grip and trotted over to a wagon that stood deserted, the team unhitched and pulling at slash and down timber, dragging it back from the fire line Sawyer was building. Samms came back carrying a long-barreled rifle and took his grip on Melcomb's arm again. They reached the buckboard and stopped.

"I'd better stay here," Melcomb said nervously. "They'll think it's funny if I—"

"Climb in!" Draper rasped. "Start drivin'. This is once you don't crawl out of it. Climb in, Melcomb!"

Otis Melcomb climbed up to the buckboard seat.

Draper got up beside Melcomb, and Spike Samms, clambering over the endgate, settled himself in the bed of the buckboard. Draper reached out and took the lines from where they were wrapped on the whipstock. "You're goin' to see just how it's done, Melcomb," he rasped. "This is once you're goin' to be in at the finish. Yesterday you said Spike an' me was yellow. Now we're gain' to see just how brave you are."

Melcomb seemed to shrink on the seat. All the iron was gone from the man. The team started, Draper guiding the horses toward the north and west.

"You don't want to do this, Ed," Melcomb pleaded. "You don't want to drag me into this. Go ahead if you want to, but leave me here. I can protect you if things go wrong. I can—"

"You can shut up an' come along," Draper snarled. "You try to get out an' Spike 'll slap you down. This time you're goin', an' there'll be no backing out."

Again Melcomb wet his lips with the tip of his tongue and glanced sharply at the man beside him. Draper's face was hard, implacable, and his jaw was set stubbornly. On the seat of the buckboard Melcomb seemed to shrink further into his clothing. Back in the bed of the buckboard Spike Samms sat holding his rifle upright beside him. "Somethin' smells funny back here," Samms commented. "Smells like coal oil."

Draper did not heed Samms' statement. He sent the horses along at a trot now, for they had reached the road that led to Loblolly Canyon.

Back at the fire line Dave Sawyer spoke to a party of men who were climbing into a wagon. "Mr. Melcomb's goin' up there," Sawyer said. "He'll look it over an' show you where to run your line. There'll be another bunch along as soon as I can get 'em together. All right, go ahead!"

The driver lifted his lines and clucked to his team. The heavy lumber wagon rumbled ahead, moving toward Loblolly. Dave Sawyer stood and watched it go and then, turning, hurried toward the fire line once more.

The smoke was thick when the buckboard entered

Loblolly Canyon. Frightened, the horses tried to turn, and Draper used the whip to urge them forward. Samms, peering to the left through the smoke, spoke to the driver, concern in his voice. "Maybe we'd better not try it, Ed. That fire's comin' this way mighty fast."

Draper, the lines held tight, did not turn his head. "We're goin' if all hell's loose," he snarled back over his shoulder. "I told you I'd settle with McCord, an' Melcomb too. I'm goin' to do it."

"Fire's mighty close, Ed," Samms warned. "Wind's comin' up too. If you ask me—"

"I didn't ask you," Draper replied tersely. "You damned sons"—this to the horses—"you get along or I'll—" The whip whistled viciously and came down across a sorrel back. The horse that was struck lunged ahead. Again the whip descended. Both horses were running now. The smoke hung like a shroud over the land. Draper tried vainly to pull the horses down, but the animals, mad with fright, were beyond control. Spike Samms clung to the side of the buckboard with both hands, his rifle, forgotten, bumping across his legs. Otis Melcomb rose from the seat of the buckboard, his voice rising in a shriek. "You'll kill us! This is suicide. You—"

He tried to jump. Samms' big hand, detached from its grip on the sides, shot up and pulled the man down to the seat. The buckboard lurched and careened along the road. Draper was cursing the horses, trying to control them.

Loblolly Canyon was short and rough. Barely four miles long, the road ran but half the length of the canyon. Horses at a plunging run, wheels rattling and bouncing over rocks, narrowly avoiding disaster where the road turned sharply, the buckboard careened up that road. Draper, feet braced against the dash, hauling back on the reins, by some miracle kept the team to the road. Samms clung grimly to the side of the buckboard with one hand; the other was wrapped tightly in the skirts of Melcomb's coat, and Otis Melcomb, too frightened now to scream, too frightened to do anything but cling to the iron rod that formed a side for the low seat, kept his eyes tight shut in his ashy gray face and somehow kept his place.

The road played out. Where some ancient timber hauler had swung out from the main canyon toward the bench on the left the team failed to make the turn. There was a crash and a splintering of spokes and rim as a wheel struck a rock, the buckboard lurched and went down, bounced once upon the denuded hub and then turned on its side, and the tongue, broken short where the kingbolt went through, snapped like a dry match.

When the buckboard went over, the men were thrown clear. For an instant Draper clung to the lines, then, as the team lunged ahead, he let them go. With the broken tongue banging between them, the double-trees dragging at their heels, the horses went mad. They kicked and ran, disappearing in the smoke toward the right. Beside the bed of the buckboard Spike Samms sat up slowly, lifting his hand to his head. Melcomb lay dazed where he had been thrown, and Ed Draper was stretched out full length where the team had dragged him. After a time Draper stirred and then crawled to his feet. He looked at Samms and at the prone Melcomb. Then he walked slowly back to the buckboard.

"Are you all right, Spike?" he asked.

Spike Samms shook himself. He looked at the buckboard and at Melcomb but did not get up. "Now we got to go on," Samms said. "There ain't no goin' back now, Ed."

Draper knelt beside Melcomb. Melcomb put his arms protectively over his head. Draper pushed the arms roughly aside. "Get up!" he ordered scornfully. "Get on your feet. Get up, Melcomb!"

Samms, still sitting by the buckboard, was looking back down the canyon. Below them, perhaps three hundred yards, pines grew down the side of the canyon like the V of hair on the nape of a woman's neck. As Samms stared, fire burst in the pines, ran through their tops and then, a red bomb in the air, leaped roaring across the canyon and attacked the timber on the other side. The fire had crowned, was running mad through the timber!

"Look!" Samms shrieked.

Ed Draper raised his head, then once more he prodded Melcomb. "Now will you get up?" he rasped. "The fire's across the canyon. We got to go on!"

Not half a mile from the overturned buckboard Lin McCord and Sacatone were out of their saddles and standing beside Bobby and Eleanor. Chub, coming down the canyon, had run by the two men and Lin, spurring Jug, had gone after the horse. When he caught

Chub he knew that Bobby was somewhere behind him. Chub was Bobby's horse and Bobby's saddle was on Chub. Lin led the horse back to Sacatone, shouting that they must go back, that Bobby was behind them, and the two men turned to retrace their way up Loblolly Canyon.

In the meantime Eleanor, coming down the trail on Redskin, had reached the boy. Dismounting, keeping a tight grip on the reins, she stooped over Bobby and gathered him up in her arms. Bobby, sooty face tear stained, buried his head against Eleanor, and the girl's arms, strong about his shoulders, comforted him. When Lin and Sacatone arrived Bobby had stopped crying, but as he talked he took long shuddering breaths that spoke of his terror and the tears that were so close to the surface.

"I wanted to find Uncle Lin," Bobby gasped. "He was down here. I wanted to find him. I came through the gate an' a limb knocked me off Chub an' Chub ran away."

Eleanor did not reproach the boy. She held him close, and when she saw Lin and Sacatone coming through the smoke her heart sang a paeon of thanksgiving.

The two men dismounted and Lin, his hands rough in their tenderness, took Bobby from Eleanor's arms. Bobby was scratched and bruised but not badly hurt. Lin finished his examination swiftly, then looked at the girl. "We'll go back," he announced. "Right away. You get on your horse, Sacatone, and I'll hand Bobby up to you. I'll lead Chub. Are you all right, Eleanor?"

Relief from her tension had weakened the girl, but

she smiled wanly and nodded.

"Then we'll go," Lin said. "Right now, too."

Down below, the fire raging across the canyon sent the roaring echoes of its progress up the narrow gorge. Both men listened and Sacatone nodded. "Fire's gone across," he snapped. "Let's pull out of here." With that he mounted, and Lin handed Bobby up to him. Eleanor got on Redskin and Lin was mounting Jug when the sorrel team, free from Melcomb's buckboard, the broken tongue, singletrees and doubletree gone but the horses still held together by the neckyoke, came charging past. The running animals frightened the others. Chub broke free from Lin and went up the canyon after the team. Eleanor managed to control Redskin, and Sacatone held his grulla horse down and under control. Mounting Jug, Lin hopped on one foot as Jug circled, managed to get his leg over the saddle and dropped into it. He had seen that the running team was harnessed and knew that somewhere down the canyon there had been an accident.

"You take 'em out, Sacatone!" Lin ordered. "There's somebody in trouble down below. I'll go see!"

"Don't be a fool!" Sacatone rasped. "Let 'em look after their own trouble. Come on, Lin."

Lin had already started the nervous Jug down the trail. "Go on," he threw back over his shoulder. "I'll catch you. Pick up Chub if you can. Go on, Sacatone!"

Sacatone had Bobby in his arms. His hands were full with the boy and his fretting, frightened horse. Redskin, paying no attention to Eleanor who tried to hold him, was already heading back up the canyon. Redskin had his own ideas and he believed he knew where safety lay. Eleanor tugged and tried to pull the horse around, but Redskin had the bit in his teeth and, although he did not run, he kept going up the canyon. With a curse Sacatone followed the girl. It was the only thing he could do. Lin had disappeared in the smoke.

By the time the three, Sacatone, Bobby and Eleanor, reached the end of the canyon where the trail sloped up steeply to the little park, the girl had control of Redskin. She stopped just before that sheer rise, and Sacatone stopped beside her. Just below them the fire was burning in the scrub oak at the canyon top. Sacatone looked at the girl, at the fire and then pulled Grulla close to Redskin. "Can you take Bobby on up?" he rasped.

"Of course," Eleanor replied. "I—"

"Then take him!" Sacatone leaned toward the girl, shifting Bobby to her saddle. "I'm goin' back for Lin!"

Eleanor's arms closed on Bobby and drew him to her. Redskin tossed his head and started up the trail, picking his way with swift caution. Sacatone, on Grulla, turned that smoke-colored horse and went back down the canyon, Grulla fighting his head but obedient to the man on his back.

Down in the canyon, beside the buckboard, Ed Draper tried to pull Samms to his feet. Samms got up, groaning, tried to stand and then collapsed, and Draper eased him back to the ground. "Ankle," Samms muttered through clenched teeth. "It's broke."

Draper's face was white. He took a swift step and kicked at Melcomb. "Get up, damn you!" he snarled.

"We got to carry Spike. We got to get out of here!"

Melcomb groaned. Draper reached for the gun at his belt, found it gone and kicked at Melcomb again. "Damn you!" he raged, "damn you for a coward. Get up! Get up!"

Melcomb lifted his head. Draper, stooping, caught the big man's collar and heaved and tugged. Melcomb raised a little, got his hands under him and pushed himself up. Down below, the fire roared frighteningly near. Melcomb hid his face in his hands and would have slumped back to the ground save that Draper held him.

Through the smoke that swirled up the canyon a man appeared, a man riding a big buckskin horse. Lin McCord! Draper saw that apparition and let go of Melcomb. The buckskin stopped.

"It looks like you're in trouble, Draper," Lin McCord said conversationally.

For a moment Draper did not answer. Lin, keeping tight hold of Jug's rein, got down and walked forward, the horse following mincingly. Not five feet from the overturned buckboard Lin stopped.

Now Draper spoke. "Spike's hurt," he said. "He can't walk."

"We'll get him on Jug," Lin said. "How about you?"

"I'm all right." Draper's voice was gruff. "What you doin' here, McCord?"

"I started for help," Lin said. "Looks like we can't get out below."

"You played hell when you started this fire," Draper rasped. "You—"

"When *I* started it? *You* started it, you mean!"

252

The men stared at each other. Suddenly Draper swore. "Hell, you didn't start it, did you?"

Lin shook his head. "It was you," he said.

It was Draper's turn to shake his head. "Not me," he denied. "I thought . . . Me an' Spike both thought it was you fellows up above. You—"

Samms, beside the buckboard, rapped two words. "Look here!"

Lin did not move. Ed Draper took two long steps and stopped. Samms, his face beneath his beard contorted with pain, was pointing to the bed of the buckboard. There on the dry wood were two dark rings. "Kerosene," Samms growled. "I said I smelt it!"

"Melcomb!" Draper accused. "It was you. You—"

Melcomb raised an arm as though to protect his face. "I didn't think!" he whined. "I didn't know it would get away, Ed. I—"

Samms reached for his rifle, thrown clear of the buckboard when it overturned. Failing to reach it, he sprawled out, his long arm extended, hand groping for the riflestock.

"You thought you'd throw me an' McCord at each other," Draper rasped. "That's why you did it, Melcomb. You thought—"

Melcomb had lowered his arm. He was watching Spike Samms, his eyes wide with fright. Samms' clutching fingers touched the rifle, pulled it toward him, only the finger tips in contact with the stock. The gun moved a little, the fingers lapped on the butt. Samms' face, his eyes terrible, was turned toward Otis Melcomb. Again the gun moved, sliding now. Samms' hand closed on the stock.

Otis Melcomb shrieked: "No! No!" his voice high and shrill. Then, head lowered, heedless of direction, he ran wildly. Lin took one step and stopped as Jug pulled back on the reins. Draper stood motionless. Samms had the rifle and was pushing himself up, twisting around. Straight down the road Melcomb went, running, arms pumping, stumbling, and, recovering before he fell, straight into the fire!

"My God!" Lin rasped. "He'll—"

Melcomb reached the line of fire and plunged into it. His shriek of agony rose, shrill and terrible. For a bare instant he was visible as he ran blindly on into that inferno, then the curtain of the fire closed down and he was gone. Lin stood, legs widespread against the nausea that suddenly filled him. Ed Draper turned slowly.

"No use tryin' to go after him," Draper rasped. "No use."

Gathering himself against his weakness, Lin agreed. "No use," he agreed. "We'd better be goin' if we want to get out. There's fire above—"

Draper yelled: "Spike!" and jumped toward the buckboard. Spike Samms had moved. Swiveling upon his buttocks, he swung the rifle toward Lin. There was murder in his movement, in his eyes, in the swing of the rifle. Lin stood rooted, unable to move. From behind him, up the canyon, a shot roared. Still holding the rifle, Samms swayed gently, then, the rifle falling, he leaned against the overturned buckboard as though, suddenly very tired, he sought support. Sacatone, his .30-.30 held in his hands, his grulla horse mincing after him, came out of the smoke.

"He was goin' to kill you, Lin," Sacatone said simply.

Ed Draper looked at his friend, leaning against the buckboard. He raised his eyes and looked first at Sacatone, then at Lin. "He was goin' to kill you," Draper confirmed. Then, after a moment, his voice grim: "He always was a dry gulcher. He killed your brother, McCord. Just that way."

Sacatone got down and, leading the grulla who hung back and snorted, approached to view his handiwork. There was a gleam in Sacatone's eyes as he raised his head and looked at Ed Draper. "You were along?" Sacatone demanded, every word a threat.

Draper shook his head. "Not when it happened," he said. "I come along later. It was me that put McCord's boot in the stirrup an' started his horse. What you goin' to do about it, Thomas?"

For answer Sacatone lifted his rifle, moving slowly as an executioner about a scaffold. "Sacatone!" Lin ordered sharply. "Stop it!"

Sacatone reluctantly lowered the gun.

"What the hell?" Ed Draper snapped. "We can't get out anyhow, McCord."

"We'll get out," Lin promised. "I'll get you out, Draper."

Draper moved swiftly. There on the ground, where he had fallen when the buckboard overturned, his pistol lay. Two swift steps; Draper stooped, came up, and the gun was in his hands. "You'll not take me out!" he rapped. "Not to be hung!"

Sacatone had half turned. The Winchester was at his hip, the muzzle centered on Ed Draper. Draper saw that menace and laughed. "Go ahead," he challenged. "I'll get McCord, anyhow." The rifle barrel lowered a trifle.

Again Draper laughed, a short, harsh bark of sound. "Dead men," he purred. "Three of us, an' we're all dead men. There's fire above an' below. We can't get out. I don't want to get out. What do you say we settle it, McCord? Here's your chance. I'll give you a break. We'll draw an' shoot it out. We'll see who's the best man. What do you say, McCord? Are you yellow?"

There was a taunt in the man's voice, an excitation, a tantalizing stimulus. Lin McCord's eyes narrowed as he watched Ed Draper.

"Don't be a fool, Lin," Sacatone rapped. "Don't—"

"I'll take you," Lin McCord said suddenly. "How do you want it, Draper?"

"I always said you wasn't afraid," Draper exulted. "You're a man, McCord, an' so am I. Let's make it who's the fastest. We'll let Thomas give the word. That suit you?"

Lin did not answer directly. "Put down the rifle, Sac," he directed calmly. "Give us time to get set, an' then count three. How about that, Draper?"

"Let's go."

Sacatone slowly lowered his rifle, placing it on the ground. There was a plea in his eyes that Lin McCord ignored. Too, he ignored Ed Draper as, reaching back, he lifted his Colt in its holster, freeing it and letting it settle once more. Draper, watching each movement, waited until Lin's gun had dropped back, until Lin's

256

hand hung loose at his side. Then Draper grinned and put his Colt upon the swivel at his belt.

"Just any time," Ed Draper said softly.

"You ready, Lin?" Sacatone's voice was harsh.

Lin nodded, keeping his eyes on Draper.

"You know I'll kill you anyhow, Draper," Sacatone rasped. "All right: one . . . two . . . three . . ."

On top of Rough Mesa Windy Tillitson, Carl Yetman and Shorty Morgan rode slowly toward the entrance of Loblolly Canyon. Below them they could see the fire spreading as the wind blew. They saw the flame crown into the trees and leap the canyon.

Windy shuddered. "I hope Lin an' Sacatone got through," he said, and his words were a prayer. "I hope they did. The canyon's blocked now."

"He's had plenty of time," Shorty stated sturdily. "Plenty. He got through all right. He . . . Look, Windy!"

From the top of Loblolly Canyon a horse emerged, a bay horse that heaved himself up the last steep slope and stopped when the top was reached. Eleanor Patrick was on the bay, and tight in her arms she held a boy.

Windy, with one high, inarticulate shout, kicked in his spurs and rode toward the girl, and behind him the others came thundering.

Windy slid his horse to a stop. "Lin?" he roared. "Where . . . ?"

"In there," Eleanor said. "In the canyon. Oh, Windy—" She broke off. Above the mutter of the fire, above its menacing sibilence, sound came, the muffled

257

boom of an explosion followed so closely by another that the two blended and were as one.

"Shots!" Windy snapped. "He needs help. Come on, Shorty!"

CHAPTER XIX
ASHES

THE MEN FROM JUNCTION, ARRIVING AS REINFORCEMENTS at the site of the fire, were distributed and placed at work by Dave Sawyer and Gilberto Gil. Some were sent up Cedar Canyon to the top of the mesa and others were dispatched to the north of Loblolly Canyon. Already word had come back to Sawyer that the fire had crowned across Loblolly, and he had to revise his plans, making allowances for the new territory that must be covered. Seventy men had come from Junction. With these and the men from the camps, from the mill and from Adelphi itself Sawyer had a force of nearly two hundred men at his disposal.

There were just three sides of the fire to fight: the mesa top, the lower line and the north end. The fire line along the lower side of the fire was nearly completed. Already from Pinál Canyon almost to Loblolly the fire line reached, the backfire beyond it presenting a broad black strip to the menace of the fire. Sawyer had sent men to the mesa and now sent more men. Having done so much, he shifted his own headquarters north toward Loblolly and concentrated his forces on the ridge beyond the canyon proper. Here there was favorable terrain and, working well back from the fire, the men built their line.

It was while Sawyer superintended this operation that Sam Rideout arrived. Rideout found Sawyer busy. His line reached now from the very bottom of the mesa's cap rock on down toward the flat. There were a hundred men at work along that line, cutting brush, felling timber, backfiring, building a strong fortification against the advance of the fire. When Rideout rode up Sawyer was giving directions to a party of men who were standing about him. Presently these went back toward the south, and Sawyer came over to the sheriff.

"How's it goin'?" Rideout inquired.

"I think we got it licked," Sawyer announced. "We got a line built from the curve of the mesa almost to here, an' we're buildin' up from the flat. I can use teams down there to haul slash back an' then we backfire. It crowned on us an' jumped Loblolly Canyon, but the wind ain't so strong now, an' we ain't got the big timber where we're workin'. It's pretty near a brush fire on this end."

"Where's Melcomb?" Rideout asked. "They told me in town he was out here."

Sawyer shrugged. "He went into Loblolly," the camp boss answered. "Him an' Draper an' Samms. I guess they went up on top. I was sendin' a crew in there after them, but the fire jumped the lower end before the crew could get in. I ain't heard from them."

"Do you think they got caught?" Rideout asked sharply.

Sawyer shook his head. "I don't think so," he said.

"They had plenty of time to get through the canyon an' out the other side. Of course I can't tell. If they did get caught it's all up with them."

Rideout debated with himself, then he looked at Sawyer again. "How many men you got on top?" he asked.

"I've sent sixty up there," Sawyer answered. "They've got a pretty good chance up there. If they hold the fire along the cap rock they can't have much trouble."

Again Rideout debated. "Do you need any more men?" he asked.

"We can use 'em if they come," Sawyer said. "We're gettin' along pretty good, though. I can't tell yet. It looks like the wind's dyin' down. We want to hold the fire against the mesa an' let it burn out. That's the way I'm tryin' to do."

"I left word in Junction to round up any more labor that they could an' send it up here," Rideout stated. "There ought to be another bunch along by tonight. I'm goin' up on top, Sawyer."

"You'll have to go by Cedar Canyon," Sawyer advised. "You can get up that way all right. If they need some more men, you send back word, will you? I ain't heard how they're comin' up there."

"I'll send back word," Rideout promised and, turning his horse, he rode away.

"Be sure to let me know," Sawyer called after him.

Rideout went down toward Pinál Canyon. As he rode he saw the teams at work, pulling back slash and down timber. Beyond the space they cleared little parties of men, two and three in a group, set backfires, watched until the backfire had burned clear of the fire line, occasionally checking the creeping fire with shovelfuls of earth and then moving on to a fresh site. Rideout passed Final Canyon, where big trees still burned and where the dull glow of coals, whipped to life by the wind, showed against the black devastation left by the fire, and rode on toward Cedar. At Cedar Canyon he received company. Cora Ferguson and the hostler from the livery barn were at the bottom of the canyon, engaged in hot debate. The hostler announced that he was going no further, that Cora had hired him to bring her to Cedar Canyon and that he had fulfilled his contract and was through. The hostler appealed to Rideout.

Cora, dressed in bib overalls pulled on over a dress, was adamant. She was going to the top of Rough Mesa. That was the contract, Cora said, sitting astride the heavy work horse she had hired in Adelphi. The top of the mesa or no pay. Rideout settled the difficulty. He would take Cora with him.

They left the hostler and went up the canyon. It was rough, and Cora's big horse was stiff-gaited, even at a walk. He climbed cumbersomely. Cora made no complaint but hung on grimly. Rideout, for his part, did no talking. He had already interviewed Cora in Adelphi, had accompanied her to Bessie's room in the hotel and there had listened to a weak-voiced man who, bandaged and stopping to cough between each labored word, had recounted a story. Halfway up Cedar Canyon Rideout spoke. "Melcomb's on top," he said conversationally.

Cora did not answer him, being engaged at the

moment in staying on her leviathan while he climbed around a big rock.

When the top was reached, the two again encountered activity. Adolfo Portillos was close by the top of Cedar Canyon, posted there as a guide. The men, Adolfo said, were strung all along the mesa from Pinál Canyon north. The fire? It had not yet come on top of the mesa. Otis Melcomb?

"Yo no sé."

"There'll be some more men comin' up," Rideout advised. "You send them along to me at Pinál Canyon."

Adolfo grinned. *"Sí. Seguro."* He would send them along.

Rideout and Cora left Adolfo and went on. When they reached Pinál Canyon they found Sandy Donald, Manuel Portillos and two more. Rideout saw the earth dyke, the soil still damp, the black devastation of the backfire. There were crews all along the rim, Donald said, looking curiously at Rideout. So far the fire had not crowned out from the benches below except in one place, just this side of Loblolly Canyon. It was being fought there. Donald's face was gray with weariness and his voice was tired.

Cora had left Rideout before Pinál was reached, branching off toward the Patrick house.

Rideout asked a question. "Is Melcomb up here?"

"They'll tell you at the house," Donald said. "They know about it there." Again he favored Rideout with a curious look. Rideout grunted and, turning from Donald, made his way to the Patricks'.

Dismounting, he tied his horse and climbed the steps.

It was nearing evening. The sun, a red ball that shone dully through the smoke, was a sullen artist painting the mesa in red. As Rideout mounted the steps Windy Tillitson came through the door and stopped.

Windy was an odd sight. He had no eyebrows at all, and that lack gave him a peculiar, hairless appearance. His whole face was smeared with white, as were his hands. There were holes burned in his shirt and one Levi leg was charred.

"Hello, Sheriff," Windy greeted. "You're a little late, ain't you?"

Rideout did not answer the question. "Where's Otis Melcomb?" he demanded. "I want him an' Draper an' Spike Samms."

Windy cocked one hairless brow. "You're goin' to have to go to hell to find 'em," he drawled. "That's where they are, I guess."

"See here, Tillitson!" Rideout began angrily. "You—"

"Come on, Sheriff," Windy interrupted. "We'll go back to the kitchen. You can talk to Sacatone."

"Where's McCord?" Rideout demanded. "Is he here?"

"In bed," Windy answered. "Sacatone brought him out of Loblolly Canyon through the fire. Lin was all right, just one leg shot from under him; but comin' out, the branch of a tree come down on his head an' laid him out. We got him in bed. He's comin' around all right but he ain't feelin' good enough to be talked to yet. You talk to Sacatone."

Rideout followed Windy through the door.

In the big living room Dan Patrick slept, sprawling in his big chair, the deep lines of his face showing his weariness. On Patrick's lap, head against Patrick's chest, was Bobby McCord. Bobby, too, was asleep, the tear stains still showing as long streaks against the soot and dirt on his face.

"We had a hell of a time," Windy commented conversationally. "The kid got lost. He started to follow Lin. Come on, Sheriff."

Rideout followed Windy to the rear of the house.

In the kitchen Sacatone, naked to the waist, bestrode a chair, his back turned toward the outer door, his face toward Rideout. Sacatone's arms were bandaged from finger tips to shoulder, and he held them, stiff and awkward, down beside him. Behind Sacatone, smearing grease upon his back, stood Cora Ferguson, still outlandishly dressed in bib overalls, her veil thrown back over her hat. As Rideout entered, Cora's veil fell and she brushed it back with a greasy, impatient hand.

"Here's the sheriff, Sacatone," Windy announced. "He wants to know what happened."

"Hold still!" Cora commanded as Sacatone started up.

Sacatone sank back into the chair. "I wish you'd get her out of here," he complained. "I got some burns on my legs. I ain't goin' to take off my pants while she's in here."

Cora's face was red as the fire itself. "Well, I should hope not!" she flared, turning to leave.

"You better get out, Cora," Windy advised. "I'll fix Sacatone's legs. Why don't you go help Eleanor?"

As Cora flounced out of the room Sacatone heaved a sigh of relief.

"I want to know what's happened up here!" Rideout snapped. "Tillitson, what did you mean about my going to hell? What's happened?"

"Tell him, Sacatone," Windy drawled. "Go on an' tell him while I get yore pants off."

Sacatone stood up. "I'll tell you," he agreed.

While Windy pulled Sacatone's trousers from his lean flanks, smeared lard on burned places and applied soda in a thick dust, Sacatone talked and Rideout listened incredulously. He heard how Sac and Lin had started for help, how Bobby had followed, the finding of Bobby and the girl together, the runaway team that told of trouble down the canyon: all those facts and events Sacatone narrated in a drawling voice. He spoke of his killing Spike Samms as casually as a man might speak of killing a sheep-killing dog; he told of Draper's taunts and challenge. All the tale came through Sacatone's thin lips, cracked and dry and burned.

"So I counted for 'em," Sacatone concluded, "an' they made their play. Lin beat him." There was utter satisfaction in the statement. "He shot a leg out from under Lin, but Lin caught him right in the heart, first shot. Then I brought Lin out." Sacatone stopped his recital. Sam Rideout, eyes wide with astonishment at the tale he had heard, stared at the narrator.

"A limb fell on Lin when we were comin' out, but lucky it just grazed his head," Sacatone completed. "We were in the fire right then an' I was leadin' both horses.

I'd had to blindfold 'em. I like to never got him out, but Windy showed up an' we made it."

"Pull up yore pants an' see where it hurts," Windy advised. "I wish we had some axle grease, Sacatone. This lard don't stick so good."

"You pull 'em up for me," Sacatone directed. "I can't take hold."

Windy stooped to obey the command. Reaching around Sacatone, he buckled the old man's belt and then, looking over Sacatone's shoulder, regarded Rideout.

"That's what happened," Sacatone concluded.

"What do you aim to do about it, Sheriff?" Windy challenged.

Rideout let go a long breath. "Nothing," he said. "I come up here to arrest Otis Melcomb an' Spike Samms an' Ed Draper for murder. You see, I knew about them killin' John McCord."

It was the sheriff's turn to talk. He did so, sitting on the edge of the kitchen table while Windy and Sacatone listened, hanging on his every word. The tale that the sheriff told was more complete than that Sacatone had recounted. Glen Hunter had all the knowledge and had told it all.

"An' that's what happened," Rideout completed. "Hunter knew all about it. Melcomb like to beat him to death, but Hunter's goin' to get well, I guess. Doc Vorfree's worked over him, an' that big girl, Bessie, is lookin' after him. Thing I'd like to know is: who started the fire?"

"Melcomb!" Sacatone and Windy spoke together.

266

Then: "Lin told me," Windy said. "Draper accused Melcomb of it an' he confessed before he run into the fire."

"So it was Melcomb?" Rideout mused. "It was Melcomb all the way through. Say"—he looked narrowly at Windy—"I thought you said McCord couldn't talk."

"I just didn't want you hornin' in on 'em," Windy answered, unabashed. "Him an' Eleanor are in there together an' they're havin' too good a time to spoil. Say, Sheriff, what you goin' to do about all this, anyhow?"

For some time Rideout sat in silence, then he looked up at Windy and Sacatone. "Who knows just what happened?" he asked.

"Me an' Lin an' Windy," Sacatone answered. "Shorty an' Carl know some, an' so does Patrick an' the girl, but they don't know it all."

Again Rideout stared at the tips of his boots. "Melcomb an' Draper an' Spike Samms were caught in Loblolly Canyon," he stated slowly. "The fire caught 'em. The business about them killin' John McCord will have to come out. The rest needn't. We'll save trouble that way."

Windy and Sacatone exchanged glances. Then, side by side, they advanced upon the sheriff. "You're all right, Rideout," Windy said. "I'd like to shake hands with you if you can stand the grease."

Sam Rideout got up, looking oddly abashed. "I can stand the grease, all right," he said. "There's no use makin' that girl feel bad, is there? Let's let it go at that." Gravely the three men shook hands.

"Now," Rideout stated, "I'm goin' along the rim. I

want to see what's happenin'.''

From the door Cora spoke in offended dignity. "Can I come in now? If you're all through . . .''

"Sure," Windy consented. "I'll go with you, Sheriff. I'll—"

Cora came in. "You'll do no such thing, Windy Tillitson!" she snapped. "You'll stay right here and be looked after. You go on about your business, Sam Rideout, whatever it is, and leave these men alone."

Sam Rideout picked up his hat. His eyes twinkled as he looked at Windy's soda-smeared face. "Yes, ma'am," said Sheriff Rideout. "I'll go right along."

Full dark had come before Sam Rideout returned to the Patrick home. He had ridden the length of the rim. All along the rim men were stationed. Where the fire had broken through and reached the top, perhaps an acre of blackened timber spoke of its fury. Down below there was still a red glare against the smoke, but the fire had not spread. There were men enough to hold it now, men enough to combat it and keep it in check, and as though that was not sufficient, Sam Rideout returned to the Patrick house through a slow drizzle, a steady fall of rain that spoke of more to come. He was wet when, dismounting, he tied his horse and climbed the steps of the Patrick house again. He did not see the two figures sitting side by side out in the yard, the slow drops of rain falling on them.

The living room of the Patrick house was cheerful. Men lounged about it, weary men who were singed and burned but happy: Shorty Morgan, Carl Yetman, Sacatone, Windy Tillitson, and beside the table Cora occupied a chair, keeping a proprietary eye upon Windy who had gone to the door to let the sheriff in. Just inside the door Rideout stopped, and Windy, playing host, spoke cheerfully.

"Just in time, Sheriff. We're havin' some coffee. Pour the sheriff a cup, Cora."

Cora reached toward the coffeepot but Rideout made a dissenting gesture. "After a while," he said. "I'd like to see McCord if I can."

"I'll find out," Windy announced and moved toward a door across the room. Opening it, he went in and his voice came clearly: "Sheriff's outside, Eleanor. He wants to see Lin."

Eleanor Patrick appeared at the door, her cheeks flushed and her eyes lighted with happiness. The door closed behind her. Inside the bedroom Windy bent down. "You tell her, Lin?"

"No," said Lin McCord.

"Don't. It's all right with the sheriff. No need to tell her."

Lin's hand shot out and gripped Windy's fiercely. The door reopened and Eleanor came through, conducting Sam Rideout. "I've told the sheriff he could stay just a minute, Lin," she announced. "He wanted to see you."

Rideout walked over to the bed and looked down. He smiled. "Thought I'd come in an' say hello," he announced. I wanted to tell you that it was all right. *It's all right, McCord.*"

Eleanor seated herself on the edge of the bed. Protectively her hand went out and clung to Lin's. "Of course it's all right, Sheriff," she said, smiling up at Sam Rideout. "The fire's under control and it's raining and Lin's not too badly hurt. We want to tell you, Sheriff: Lin and I are going to be married." Her hand closed tightly upon Lin's. "Just as soon as we can," the girl concluded.

Rideout looked at the two, a smile hovering on his lips under his mustache. "Congratulations," he said slowly. "To you both. On everything."

Out in the yard Bobby McCord moved a little closer to Dan Patrick. "Uncle Dan," Bobby said, "we're pardners, ain't we?"

"Yes, Bobby." Dan Patrick's voice was steady. Again Bobby hunched closer. "Maybe we're crippled up some, but we're pretty good men anyhow," he stated. "Yes, we are, Bobby."

There was silence for a moment. Then: "You'll teach me the lumber business, Uncle Dan?"

"Of course."

Again the silence. Dan Patrick's arm settled over the boy's shoulders, around his strong young body. It would not be long now until, the injunction dismissed, the sublease forgotten, Rough Mesa would be Dan Patrick's once more. But never again would it be his alone. There was Eleanor and there was Lin. There was Bobby McCord . . .

"I already know the cattle business," Bobby commented.

"There's room enough," Dan Patrick said, not answering Bobby but speaking his thoughts. "There's room enough for us all." The man's arm tightened about the boy.

"Sure," agreed small Bobby McCord, and his own short arm, reaching out, extended to its full length, circled about the man. "Sure there's room. All we got to do is run things right."

Neither noticed the rain that soaked their clothing.

Center Point Publishing
600 Brooks Road ● PO Box 1
Thorndike ME 04986-0001 USA

(207) 568-3717

US & Canada:
1 800 929-9108